SO. S.F. PUBLIC LIBRARY
GRAND AVENUE

SOUTH SAN FRANCISCO LIBRARY

3 9048 05370783 6

G

PAUL CHARLES
music agent, author and Beatles' fan, was born
and raised in Northern Ireland. He now lives
and works in Camden Town. *I Love the Sound
of Breaking Glass* was the first DI Christy
Kennedy mystery, and he is currently working
on the fifth, *The Hissing of the Silent Lonely
Room.*

Other titles in the series:
I Love The Sound of Breaking Glass
Last Boat to Camden Town
Fountain of Sorrow

First Published in Great Britain in 2000 by
The Do-Not Press Limited
16 The Woodlands
London SE13 6TY

Copyright © 2000 by Paul Charles
The right of Paul Charles to be identified as the Author of this
work has been asserted by him in accordance with the
Copyright, Designs & Patents Act 1988.

C-format paperback: ISBN 1 899344 57 8
Casebound edition: ISBN 1 899 344 58 6
Limited edition casebound: ISBN 1899 344 59 4

British Library Cataloguing in Publication Data. A catalogue
record for this book is available from the British Library.

All rights reserved. No part of this publication may be repro-
duced, transmitted or stored in a retrieval system, in any form
or by any means without the express permission in writing of
The Do-Not Press having first been obtained.

This book is sold on the condition that it shall not, by way of
trade or otherwise, be lent, resold or hired out or otherwise
circulated without the publisher's prior consent in any form of
binding or cover other than that in which it is published and
without a similar condition being imposed on the subsequent
purchaser.

h g f e d c b a

Printed and bound in Great Britain by
The Guernsey Press Co Ltd.

The Ballad of Sean & Wilko

The fourth Detective Inspector Christy Kennedy Mystery

Paul Charles

SO. S.F. PUBLIC LIBRARY
GRAND AVENUE

Thanks are due to Catherine, Ivan and Ciara for their invaluable work on the manuscript. Thanks to Asgard for what has turned out to be valuable years of research in the music business – long may they continue. To Edwin and Jim for boldly going …. To my ever-growing family, Andy and Cora, Matt and Lila, Gerry and Nuala, Laura, James, Eoin, Carmel, Paul, Katie, Oisin, Darragh and Maeve. But most of all, and much more than thanks on a page, to Catherine for proving that dreams really do come true.

One

'Listen to that racket, would you?' Detective Sergeant James Irvine complained to his boss, Detective Inspector Christy Kennedy.

'Well,' Kennedy replied, surveying the several hundred bobbing heads which filled Dingwalls Dancehall, Camden Lock, 'If you can't beat them…'

Irvine looked at his DI in disbelief. He couldn't believe that Kennedy was going to join the thronging masses on the floor for a bop, particularly at a time like this. Kennedy winked and finished his sentence.

'…get the DJ to turn the music off and ensure no one, but no one, leaves the club.'

Dingwalls Dancehall was by now overrun with members of the Camden Town CID. The owner, a Miss Violette Rodgers, didn't know whether she was more nervous now or when the dead body had been discovered in the basement dressing-room twenty minutes earlier.

Not that it was actually Miss Rodgers who discovered the body. She had been in the box office, rubbing her hands gleefully over the happy punters that gladly paid over their twelve pounds and fifty pence to enter her establishment on a wet Thursday night, mid-November, to bop continuously to the sounds of Circles, a blast from the past, followed by a hip DJ.

Six-hundred-and-fifty-three people playing £12.50 each; that's £7,037.50 gross door take. After expenses and the band's fee of £1,500, she would still be left with a clear profit of £3,772. Her other costs (venue upkeep, staff wages etc.) would be more than covered out of her profits from 653 thirsty people crowding the venue's long bar. It was proving to be a bit of a gold mine for Violette, this current seventies revival rage.

As the remainder of the Camden Town CID team secured the venue, Irvine led Kennedy into a small room in the basement; the one furthest from the stairwell. The wood of the door post around the lock was severely broken and splintered, and the body was lying sprawled out on a cold concrete floor.

The room and the corpse were brightly lit by three large wall lamps. As well as a dressing area, it seemed to be a storage room for soft drinks with lots of cases of Lucozade, Seven Up, and Coca-Cola stacked up against the far wall. To the right of this cylinders were scattered around the floor haphazardly with transparent plastic tubes attached to the pressurised containers and making their way up through the roof of the basement and into the bar overhead. Kennedy assumed that the dumb waiter in the corner was the lazy man's route to the bar for the soft drinks.

In the opposite corner, the dressing-room area, was a pine table with a free-standing mirror on top. Forming a semi-circle around the table were eight mismatched chairs that all looked as though they might have been purchased at an odds and sods stall in the nearby Camden Market. All eight chairs had various pieces of clothes hung about them like one might expect in a football team's changing room when the team were out at play. Except in this instance one lifeless player had remained behind, sprawled on the floor close to the soft drinks corner.

'Do we know who he is? Who found him?' Kennedy inquired, unconsciously buttoning up his Crombie. He was convinced that any room of death was at least ten degrees colder than any other part of a building.

'Aye,' Irvine began, shielded from the cold by his effective tweeds, 'He's called Wilko Robertson. His group was called Circles. They were playing here tonight.'

'Circles?'

'Aye.'

'Hang on, I remember them. Didn't they have a couple of hits during the seventies?' The DI hoped one of the titles would come to him. ann rea was great at that, she could remember everybody's hits.

'Aye,' Irvine replied unhelpful.

'Yes, I remember,' and Kennedy searched for the melody, knowing that if he caught the melody the title would follow. He also knew the more he concentrated on song titles the longer he would delay the matter of dealing with a dead body. 'Yes, I've got it, "She Loves Rain". And then there was a big one. The big summer hit of, it would have been '74 or '75, a girl's name. Kathleen, Catherine. Col…Yes that's it. Colette, "Colette Calls". Yes, that was it.'

'He was found by his roadie, a Mr Kevin Paul, known to all as KP,' Irvine added as Kennedy answered his own question.

'Roadie?'

'Sorry, Sir, Road Manager. I think he's more of a Tour Manager, actually. Circles is a seventies group. I believe groups nowadays call their roadies "Equipment Technicians". The chaps who look after the instruments and such,' Irvine explained.

'Right, right,' Kennedy cut him off. He was nervous around corpses, and Irvine was sympathetic when he and Kennedy were close to a corpse and, consequently, at the beginning of another case.

By this point, WPC Anne Coles had arrived and was in the process of showing the portly pathologist, Dr Leonard Taylor, to the crime scene. Dr Taylor had been more closely involved in Kennedy's last case than he ever intended to be and he was happy, relatively speaking, not to recognise the corpse. Not from the rear, at any rate.

Kennedy had recently found himself stealing glances at WPC Coles. Her long bottle-blonde hair was clasped up in some elaborate style which was designed more to fit in her pillbox hat than to turn heads. She had very pale skin; so pale in fact it allowed her full lips and trim dark eyebrows to be the defining features of her angular face. He wondered was his new found attraction to her based on the recent difficulties he and ann rea were experiencing or was she simply blossoming into a beautiful woman right before his very eyes?

'Goodness,' Taylor announced theatrically, 'This body is not yet cold.'

He was kneeling – his girth had long since prevented him the luxury of hunkering – over the body. He felt the victim's throat in search of a pulse.

'Dead, certainly,' Taylor announced. 'But not long since. I'd say he's been dead less than an hour.'

'Try less than forty minutes, Doctor,' Irvine said. 'He was on stage forty minutes ago.'

'Goodness,' Taylor said again.

Kennedy couldn't find much goodness around this room. The police photographer had shot the body from as many angles as possible and Irvine and Taylor were both convinced there was nothing to be gained from further examination. They turned the body over on it's back.

At least the eyes were closed, Kennedy thought. The Detective Inspector was always disturbed somewhat when the corpse's eyes were still open. It was as though they were trying to communicate something from the other side.

Wilko Robertson was dressed and groomed as though the eighties and nineties had never happened. He wore royal blue flared trousers, a green shirt with a butterfly collar and a Ferrari red V-neck tank top with a large "WR" embroidered into the front in white. Kennedy pegged Robertson as unhealthy and continuously fighting his weight. He was around five foot nine, almost six foot if you included the red platform shoes. He had long ginger hair, parted in the middle that, with his ginger face stubble, gave him the look of a fiery highland warrior. But the real shock was that, to the naked eye, there was not a mark on the body. No blows, no blood, nothing.

Taylor had sealed both of Wilko Robertson's hands in plastic bags.

'That's all I can do here, chaps and chapesses,' he said. 'When you finish your examination I'll remove the body to St Pancas All Saints' Hospital and carry out the autopsy. I'm afraid it'll have to wait until tomorrow morning, however. I couldn't possibly complete it tonight.'

'That'll be fine, Doctor. We've a lot of people upstairs and we need to take their details. They'll all be getting agitated so we'd better deal with them as soon as possible. Any sign of a cup of tea?' Kennedy asked no one in particular. PC Allaway took the hint and went off in search of the DI's favourite liquid refreshment.

Following the departure of Dr Taylor and the late Wilko Robertson, Kennedy instructed his team to take the names and addresses of everyone upstairs. He further instructed them to, 'Take a Polaroid of everyone to dissuade any fibbing. And I'd like to see the road manager chap…ah…'

'Kevin Paul,' Irvine offered helpfully.

'Yes. K.P. That's my man. Show him down here please,' Kennedy announced, more relaxed now that the corpse had been removed. The sole memory of Wilko Robertson, the gravelly voiced singer of seventies sensation Circles, was his chalk outline on the cold concrete floor.

Two

'A bit of a murder mystery vibe, man isn't it?' was Kevin Paul's opening remark.

Hardly the way to speak about your former employer, Kennedy thought. At the same time he found himself warming to this softly spoken Irishman and his tight smile.

'You don't mind if I prepare a roll up, man, do you? Bit of a pressure vibe, you know what I mean?'

Kennedy nodded, assuming Kevin meant nothing stronger than tobacco.

'Ah, Kevin…'

'Oh, call me KP, man. Everybody does, man,' the tour manager offered with a strained smile.

He was dressed from head to toe in black and of a style more nineties than his employer. Black Doc Marten boots, well-fitted black slacks, black Armani copy shirt, black linen waist coat and black three-quarter-length leather jacket. He was dangerously thin, Kennedy thought. His black wiry hair was mostly hidden under a black skullcap, a kind of baseball cap with the peak removed.

Kennedy offered the road manager a tea.

'Nah man, caffeine's bad for you, man. I've had my quota for the day. I'll have a mineral water though, no ice, if one is going,' and he stared at Allaway so directly that the constable found himself doing as KP had directed.

'You found the body?' Kennedy began.

'Yes, man.'

'Can you elaborate?'

'Well, about three quarters of the way through the set our principals, Sean and Wilko, take a break and let the band go around the houses a few times.'

'Why?' Kennedy asked.

'You know, a bit of an ego vibe, man. Sean and Wilko write and sing all the songs and consequently they get all the glory and the royalties. So the musicians, as well as getting their five hundred quid a week, once a night they get to show off their chops, sorry man, musicianship, on a ten minute improvisation jam, man. It's based on the b-side of a Circles' hit single. The B side is called "Gollyworbetson" and the A side was called "Colette..."'

'"Calls."' Kennedy interrupted.

'Cool, cool man,' KP smiled a genuine smile and Kennedy felt he would have liked to have added, "Cool fuzz vibe, man."

Kevin Paul had such a small face and such large black eyebrows that all his facial expressions were exaggerated. He had no other facial hair and although he looked like he may have been in his early forties, his boyish features appeared never to have been skimmed by a razor.

'Anyway, as well as giving the chaps their ego spot, it also allows the principals a bit of a breather. Wilko always goes down to the dressing-room to change, a bit of an over-sweating vibe, man, and Sean usually finds a quiet spot to watch the band. He generally hooks up with me to inquire if I've picked up the fee. If we're on a percentage deal – where our income is based on the number of paying Billy Bunters, punters, you know. Tonight we were on a straight fee, 1500 quid. I saw him when he came off, told him, "It's a bank vibe, man" – you know, the money is as good as in the bank, I've picked it up.

And he went off somewhere.' KP stopped as Allaway handed him a bottle of water. 'God bless you, man.'

He looked to Kennedy as though he was getting a bit exhausted by having to explain all his isms. Kennedy worried that he was making him feel like a bit of a foreigner and if an Irishman can't feel at home in Camden Town where *can* he feel at home?

'Sean and Wilko usually regroup at the side of the stage about ten minutes into the song and join the band, and the audience, in the final sing-a-long chorus. I'm there with Sean but there's no sign of Wilko and it's getting closer and closer to his on-stage time. He just doesn't show. Sean gives me one of his "where the feck is he" looks, as he goes back on stage, tambourine in hand, to lead the audience in the singing. So off I go looking for Wilko.' KP paused as he lit up the ciggy he'd been elaborately rolling for the previous few minutes.

'So I come down here and the door is locked. That's not unusual. He always locks it when he's changing. I knock on it a few times. He doesn't answer. I imagine he's having a problem hearing me because of the racket upstairs. The audience is *so* loud, man. It's the sing-a-long vibe man, and it always raises a lump in my throat. I love to hear an audience sing, it's a truly wonderful feeling. I hammer on the door. Still no response, and I'm getting desperate. Wilko sings lead on the first song after the sing-a-long, which I can hear coming to an end upstairs. I'm getting frustrated. So I kick the door in. It's like action movie vibe, man, but nowhere near as glamorous. I feck up my arm and shoulder something rotten but I get the door open and Wilko's on the floor over there.' KP nodded in the direction of the chalk marks.

'You didn't move anything, did you?'

'Hey, man, I watch Inspector Morse. I know the script vibe, man. Never touch anything at the scene of a crime.'

'Why did you think it was the scene of a crime, K.P.?'

'Lack of breathing vibe, man!'

Three

Meanwhile, Irvine had organised Camden Town CID's small but efficient team upstairs. With the help of several Polaroid cameras they took the names, addresses and the likeness of everyone on the premises. The DS also kept the deceased's band mates on the premises until his DI chose to either chat to them or let them go.

The musicians and crew gathered together in Miss Violette Rodgers' office. Whatever money and space had been saved on the basement excuse for dressing-rooms had obviously been lavished on the owner's space. It was situated to the front of the venue, just above the box office, and had a spy window, which afforded a view of the audience and stage below.

Violette Rodgers was just this side of pretty without a trace of make up. She was dressed in a dark blue suit, waisted jacket and knee length skirt. Her outfit was completed with a plain white male shirt. She anxiously hovered around the office, attempting to keep the musicians and police from uncovering her office's secrets; secrets like the four monitor screens Irvine had noticed her turning off just as he entered her office several minutes ago. She concealed them behind cupboard doors but not before Irvine had noted the cameras were catching scenes inside the box office, outside the front door, along the main bar and the finally on the stage to catch the band in action.

WPC Coles, who accompanied Irvine, inquired hopefully about obtaining the video tapes from these monitors, which could make all their work that much easier. Sadly her hopes were shot down in flames. The equipment was merely for monitoring purposes, so the owner could, literally, keep an eye on everything. Miss Rodgers apologetically informed Coles than when the equipment was being installed she had opted for the cheaper, non-recording, version.

Fair enough, Irvine thought, it's her money.

Circles were not really sure what to do with themselves, trying to strike up some kind of conversation with each other. Anything was preferable to being alone with one's own thoughts of career security now that one of the main members of the group was dead. They huddled around the owner's desk, quietly consoling themselves with a nine year old malt that was kindly volunteered by Miss Rodgers from her bottom drawer.

The band had been formed in 1969 when two people moved from their native lands in search of fame and fortune. Sean Green – real name Sean Pratley – had left his parents plush home in Dun Laoghaire just outside Dublin. He'd been playing guitar (self-taught) since he was eleven years old and had been in various beat groups since he was fourteen. Sean was soon to cross paths with another similarly motivated soul; one Wilko Robertson from Paisley. Whereas Sean had the musicianship and an ability to write songs Wilko had the voice. A voice to die for. It wasn't that Sean had a weak voice, he could hit all the notes and hold a tune but it was average, soulless and forgettable, very forgettable. A good voice for the high harmonies but a terrible voice to sell you the sentiment of a lyric.

Wilko, on the other hand, had an amazing soul voice in the tradition of Rod Stewart, Bonnie Tyler and Frankie Miller. He had a voice which made you believe the lyric, a voice which sold you the secret of the song each and every time he performed it. It was a voice tuned and tainted with whiskey, abusive father, poor childhood, having to bring up his two younger sisters and (older) brother when his mother died, losing his childhood sweetheart in the mass exodus to Australia and to some more whiskey.

They met each other at the Marquee Club in Wardour street the night Joe Cocker and the Grease Band made their London debut, Tuesday 25th June 1968. That night was a turning point in their lives and a turning point in the London music scene due to Cocker's devastating performance. Following England's finest singer's performance that night "average" was no longer going to be an acceptable word in music circles. Both Sean and Wilko were with friends and stayed behind because someone knew someone, who knew a guy who used to go to school with the sister of the guy who cleaned John Wilson's cymbals and they said it would be okay to stay behind and hang with the band.

At that point Sean had been in London six months, living just off Arlington Street where it cuts across Delancey Street and he was desperate to make a musical connection. Wilko had been London based for three years and, at twenty-two, was four years older than Sean.

Neither of them got to meet either Joe Cocker nor any of the members of the amazing Greaseband that night but they did get to meet each other as they hung around outside the dressing-room in hope. Being musicians they were like beacons for each other and arranged to meet the following Saturday morning at Sean's bedsit for a bit of a play. Wilko couldn't make it until the Saturday as he was holding down a job as a barman. Sean, on the other hand, was surviving on an allowance from his father. He claimed that to make a go at the music business, he had to devote all his time and energy to it. He persuaded his father to fund him by agreeing to return to Dun Laoghaire within twenty-four months to run the family Hardware store if he failed to make a living performing, and writing, music.

Sean knew immediately he'd found a focal part of his band.

One verse into Wilko's version of "With A Little Help From My Friends" was all it took to convince the Dubliner he was off the starting blocks.

They messed around for a couple of hours playing Beatle and Beach Boy songs, Sean on upright piano and Wilko on one of Sean's acoustic guitars. Wilko wasn't a great guitarist by any means; he knew enough chords to start off most of the songs but by the time the vocals started he would get lost in the singing and bit-by-bit his guitar playing would disappear.

With Wilko's voice Sean didn't mind. Although he'd be playing alone again he was convinced that once he found the voice for his songs, the rest of the band would be easier to find and then, as bandleader, he'd have all the time in the world to play with and off other musicians. They took a break and went up Camden to the Dublin Castle for a refresher.

They liked each other, got on well together and, by the time they returned to the bedsit, Sean had build up enough confidence to play Wilko a couple of his own compositions. And that was it. Wilko loved Sean's songs as much as Sean loved Wilko's voice. They had found in each other what was missing in themselves. Wilko had a few uncompleted bits and pieces of songs, great melodies to suit his perfect soul-steeped voice, but as a lyricist…well, generally he would start with a good idea but he'd never develop it.

They played around on the songs until well past midnight that first night and Sean developed one of Wilko's ideas into a well-polished tune. Wilko crashed at Sean's place and the following morning they were back at it, back working on songs having agreed to form a group together. They even had agreed a name for their group, Circles. Something to do with life being nothing but a series of circles we all travel around in until we make the connections we do and then drop out of interwoven circles. They tried several times to work this sentiment into a song. Thankfully, they never succeeded.

But now twenty-nine long years, and many musicians, later

only one of the duo survived and he was sitting in the office at Dingwalls Dancehall. To Irvine he didn't look particularly upset but then again, quietness and peacefulness may have been his way of dealing with the death of his long-standing musical partner.

Irvine and Coles split the band and crew, seven in total and took statements. Irvine started with Sean Green, while the beautiful WPC drew the short straw of the unattractive roadie Dan Hudson, a grunge refugee.

Sean Green, at the point Irvine interviewed him, looked his age; a reality he'd continuously avoided on stage. At forty-seven he should have been long past appearing at places like Dingwalls while contemporaries like Rod Stewart and Elton John were able to fill Wembley Stadium. But you never give up hope in the music game, there's always the possibility of another hit around the corner. However, Circles last hit had been in 1979 with an incredible version of Buddy Holly's "Together Again". That single backed on the B Side, and sharing the royalties with an original Green & Robertson composition, "Heather Honey", peaked at number nine and was their last appearance in the very exclusive Top Ten.

Irvine couldn't believe how small Sean Green was. Irvine had assumed, as did the rest of the nation from the regular television appearances, that Sean Green must have been at least six foot tall. He was thin, which helped created the taller stage and television illusion. He was obviously used to people recognising him but then doubting he was the performer due to his stature.

'Yea, I'm the same, I do the same double take ever time I see a television personality in the flesh,' Green said.

'No sorry, it's just that…'

'Oh, it's okay. We are what we are. I can deal with it,' Sean replied, his Irish accent long faded into a mid-Atlantic wash.

And he did deal with it, Irvine noticed, by wearing even taller platform shoes than Wilko. He also had an afro hairstyle, which added at least another five inched to his height, and a handlebar Zapata moustache. Irvine noticed marks on his nose and close to his ears that indicated he wore glasses, but only when out of the public spotlight. "Well preserved" were the words Irvine's mother would have used to describe him. Sean Green's stage gear, which still hung about his wiry frame, consisted of a pair of black flares, a white frilly shirt and a three quarter length, beautifully cut, black jacket.

Green relayed similar details to the ones Kevin Paul was simultaneously disclosing to Kennedy.

'Where did you go to during your break?' Irvine asked.

'Well, I usually go for a wander around the venue, keep out of the punter's way, we do the meet and greet afterwards of course, but I like to check out the sound in the house and make sure KP has not been having any problems,' Green replied.

'You never join Mr Robertson in the dressing-room for a breather?'

Green paused, then smiled.

'Oh, you mean Wilko. Mr Robertson sounds so formal. I've never known him to be called than. Some of his Paisley mates call him Robbo but never Mr. Robertson. No, not really. You see Wilko sweats a lot on stage, each and every one of his pores opens and gushes the minute the lights hit him. Every stitch is literally soaked by about half way through the set, so he loved to come off and use the "Gollyworbetson Jam" to change. He then hangs up his wet clothes, has a fag and catches his breath. To be quite honest with you there's always a bit of a pong and anyway, I like soak up the audience vibe, as KP would say. So I just hang out until it's time to go back on stage.'

'When did you realise there was a problem?'

'Well we, Wilko, KP and me, meet up at the side of the stage towards the end of the jam for the final chorus, only this time, Wilko wasn't there. I didn't think it was a big deal to be honest. I just went on by myself, and sent KP off to find him,' Green said. Irvine noted that the performer didn't seem to have any problem with eye contact.

'Had he ever missed the cue before?'

Green smiled, half to himself and then full on to the policeman. He nodded at Irvine's tweeds and two-tone brogue shoes. 'Shall we just say that some of your fellow Scots have a reputation for their love of the juice-of-the-barley. Wilko was no exception and on a few occasions when he was a bit the worse for wear, he wouldn't be able to find his way back on to the stage. It was always a bit of a farce like the scene in the movie, Spinal Tap, where the entire band get lost back stage and wander around forever along all these corridors. Well he was a bit like that. If he's had a few drinks and didn't hook up with KP he'd have trouble getting back on stage. But once on that stage, Sergeant, drink or no drink, no matter the amount, he could still sing with the best of them,' Irvine noted that the question was answered with more than a little pride.

'How did you finish the set without him?'

'Oh, I did two of the songs, two of the hits so the audience could be heard singing as much as myself and the bass player, Simon, has a passable voice, he sang Wilko's big ballad, "She Loves Rain."'

'The one from...' Irvine hesitated.

'The one from the TV Shampoo advert, Yes. Oh, we don't knock it, the money that brought us...' Green started and then stopped, his voice dropping to nearly a whisper; 'It won't do him much good now though, will it?'

Irvine decided to try to move on from this point quickly.

'Was he in good health?'

'Do you mean could he have died from natural causes?'

'Aye, that's what I mean.'

'Well, I suppose his liver had taken a bit of a hammering over the years and he never seemed to ease up, but then again he was as strong as an ox. We never missed a gig you know. Not many bands can say that. Circles never ever missed a gig. That's quite a boast for a 29 year career.'

The Whiskey had picked up the band a little bit by now, their voices were beginning to rise above a murmur, and Irvine leaned in close to Green to afford more privacy.

'Did he have any money problems?'

'Set up for life. Both of us were,' Green said quietly.

'Woman problems?'

'Show me a man who hasn't woman problems and I'll show you a liar,' Green replied, still quiet.

'Do you think he could have…' Irvine began but before he could complete his sentence Green cut in with his own.

'How did he die?'

'We don't know yet, Sir,' the DS replied honestly.

'I mean are we talking natural causes or unnatural causes?'

'Well we won't really know until after the autopsy,' Irvine replied.

'Which will be carried out when?'

'Tomorrow morning I believe' Irvine answered, visibly frustrated at not being able to get in his own questions. 'Do you think there could be a reason which would have meant him taking his life?'

'Now there's a question, Sergeant. You'd have to ask someone who was closer to him than I was.'

Coles, at the other end of the office, was still questioning the grunge-influenced roadie. Today, all things considered, was an easy gig and they arrived at noon to be met by the local stage crew who helped them to unload the equipment. The various crew members depending upon their expertise, and loyalties, would go off and set up their part of the equipment. Drums, keyboards, bass guitar-stack, lead guitar-stack, on-stage microphones, sound and monitor- system and off-stage house sound.

They would break for lunch around two-thirty and hope to have everything set up by the time the musicians arrived at five o'clock for their soundcheck. The soundcheck was for fine-tuning all the instruments and equipment, setting their individual sound levels for the musicians on stage – through the monitor system – and, for the audience – through the house system. Then they'd play several songs together to make sure the individual sound levels fitted into the overall sound balance. Once the sound balance was perfected they may use any remaining time to run through a any of the songs requiring additional work.

This sound check would finish at seven o'clock, it had to finish at seven o'clock because that was the time the doors of the venue were opened to the public. Road crew and band members would then dine, at the expense of the promoter, and some who didn't like to perform on a full stomach, would either take a day room in a local hotel or go home. Circles never used a support act so they been on stage since ten past eight until Sean and Wilko took the breather from which Wilko failed to return.

The remaining members of the Circles entourage seemed unable to throw any additional light on the mysterious death of one of their principals. Coles and Irvine did learn that amongst the musicians, Pat Bell, drums, Simon Rutland, bass guitar, Mark Giles, keyboards, that David Cooper the guitarist was the longest serving and, after Sean and Wilko, most important member of the band and Dan Hudson was hired not because of his ability but because he also worked for a supposedly cool indie band which accounted for his lack of dress sense. So said the other member of the Circles' road – crew Mick, 'Litch' Litchfield.

Kennedy returned from the basement with KP and on checking with his DS that all statements had been taken he decided to leave further questioning until such time as he had the trusted Dr Taylor's report advising him of exactly what had happened to Wilko Robertson.

The death could still quite possibly be accidental or natural, in which case questioning all these musicians, interesting thought it may be, could prove to be a total waste of time. In the meantime Kevin 'KP' Paul had given the DI more than enough information to be going on with.

There were major sighs of relief all around as the musicians were allowed to go home. Not without a few gripes though, because the police were unable to allow them to return to the dressing-room to change into their street clothes. As they all headed off out into the cold night Kennedy thought that they more closely resembled participants in a fancy dress party than members of the once phenomenally successful Circles.

But then wasn't that always the way with circles, Kennedy mused, they had a habit of returning to from whence they started.

Four

Detective Inspector Christy Kennedy decided to walk the short distance from Dingwalls Dancehall to his home in Primrose Hill. It was a cold night but his favourite black Crombie sheltered him from the brisk night air as he made his way along the Regents Canal and crossed into Primrose Hill itself. About a third the way across the greenland he turned left and instead of going to the comfort and warmth of his house he headed to the crown of the hill.

It was a clear night with the full moon two days old. He had the hill and the amazing view of London to himself. Many a night he and ann rea had stood on this very summit in each other's arms, drinking this breathtaking view. Sometimes not being satisfied with the view alone they would seek full satisfaction under the cloak of darkness and bushes.

Kennedy was fine. He kept telling himself he was fine, so it must be true. Yes, his romantic life was a mess, an absolute mess; but he was fine. There was just a little niggling feeling that every time he tried to convince himself that he was fine, it usually meant that he wasn't.

He always had believed that with girls you bought into the whole package, like he did with ann rea. She looked great – stunning, drop dead gorgeous more like. But it was her eyes that incessantly got under his skin. The first time Kennedy saw her eyes, brown with a hint of an oriental shape, he was scared that she would catch him looking at her. That first time, at Heathrow, she looked so stunning – not a hair out of place, curved eyebrows, full figure – she made Kennedy feel he had such a thirst to quench that water alone would never satisfy him again. Otis Redding had captured the feeling perfectly in the Smokey Robinson song, *My Girl*.

They'd sat, as it happened, side-by-side on a flight to Dublin that day. Kennedy awkwardly started up a conversation and discovered she wrote for the local paper, the *Camden News Journal*. He learned that she always spelt her name in lower case just like k. d. lang, had a passion for music, would have liked to have been a carpenter, and drove a maroon Ford Popular which she suspected was drinking Poteen. After they had accidentally met up a few times around Primrose Hill Kennedy, eventually, invited her out to dinner. Things had developed from there but she still took his breath away each and every time he saw her.

She dressed as cool as anyone who knew how to dress avoiding designer labels. She had a figure the memory of which still sent Kennedy to sleep with more than a grin on his face. She was intelligent; she was excellent company, so great Kennedy still couldn't work out where the hours went, where in fact their fifteen months together had gone. But everything was, as he thought, part of the complete package. So from the outside and practically from the inside too, come to that, ann rea seemed to be the perfect partner. Especially for an unconfirmed bachelor settling in to his early forties.

ann rea seemed like the perfect deal. However, she had one main character flaw; a flaw which Kennedy had discovered to his cost. The flaw? ann rea wasn't in love with him. Her exact words had been, "I don't think I'm in love with you." She found it impossible, when she started this relationship, to accept it as natural genuine love. She seemed incapable of dealing with and accepting the real thing. She forever doubted her feelings for

Kennedy and because of this…this…flaw she found it impossible to commit to a relationship.

So, in Kennedy's book, why prolong the pain of splitting up? Why not just fecking get on with it and part company? Why not indeed? It wasn't as though Kennedy was anxious to seek out other female company, sadly he preferred his own, it was just, well that he'd been hurt twice before in life and he knew it would never ever be quite so painful again. He knew he could deal with it, so, he was prepared for the pain and preferred to get on with it, the splitting up that was.That in itself, in Kennedy's case, wasn't the major problem. No, the major problem was that Kennedy's future ex-girlfriend, the very same ann rea, experienced great difficulty in letting Kennedy go. And, truth be told, he had the same difficulty losing her.

However his romantic woes were going to have to take a back seat for a time now. He was about to embark on a case which he was sure would take him across ann rea's path. He was convinced he would see her several times in the coming days because, as well as being his beautiful future ex, not to mention current heart breaker, ann rea was a local journalist with a goldmine of information in the wheelings and dealings and comings and goings in the music business.

The view from the top of Primrose Hill cleared his head and set his resolve. He turned toward home.

Five

The last Friday in November brought rain, half the month's total rainfall in one day, in fact. This made Kennedy's morning walk to North Bridge House, the home of Camden CID, invigorating and as breathtaking as any of his favourite walks along the coast at Portrush where he was brought up and both his parents still lived. London had enjoyed a wet summer and a dry winter. The greenness and freshness of Primrose Hill and neighbouring Regents Park was as spiritual as any countryside. Kennedy was surprised, but not disappointed, that more Londoners chose not to sample these life-enriching sights.

Such a soulful experience would set up even the most sceptical of persons for the trials and tribulations of their imminent day in the office or their job of work, whatever it may be. Even on the wettest of winter mornings two magpies had elected to greet him. He pulled up the collar of his Crombie, drank in a mouthful of damp air, and put an inch to his step. His day was going to start, he hoped, with the autopsy results on the corpse of Wilko Robertson. Dr Taylor was an early bird and no doubt was already at work.

It was eight o'clock when he reached North Bridge House. Desk Sergeant Tim Flynn's weather-beaten Irish smile greeted him.

'Top of the morning to you, Sir.' Flynn had been using the greeting for so long that no one took offence at it.

'Aye, Timothy, great day – if you are a duck, that is,' Kennedy offered in good humour as he unbuttoned his coat. Underneath he wore a dark blue three-piece suit, brown leather shoes, white shirt and yellow tie. Kennedy loosened the tie a little and undid the top button of his shirt. Once inside North Bridge House the only time his tie and top button were done up was when he went into Superintendent Castle's office for a briefing.

'You've had two calls this morning already, Sir. One from ann rea.' Flynn passed down the two green telephone message slips to Kennedy with a smile, 'How come we see so little of that beautiful woman these days?'

'Ah, now there's a story, I'm sure. And if I ever find out I'll let you know,' Kennedy replied as he disappeared behind the swinging door, which separated the public lobby of the station with the police's private quarters. The swinging doors were still swinging by the time Kennedy had climbed one flight of stairs and entered his wood-panelled office. He sat down at his desk and turned in his swivel chair to see his Guinness green felted notice board was empty. His last case, The Roseland Romeo, was now but a memory contained in the numerous five by three index cards and several photographs that once covered his board. The case was now successfully solved and cards and photos meticulously filed by the Detective Inspector.

Kennedy dialled the number of the person on Flynn's second green slip.

'ann rea speaking.'

'Hi, how are you doing?' Kennedy replied, his accent making the "are" all but disappear. The sound of her voice still left him gasping for air. She had a very sensual voice; no noticeable accent and he loved to hear her speak. Everything about her was still a turn on. That was the problem. Kennedy thought if only he could find one fault with her he'd be out of troubled waters. He couldn't allow himself to accept it as her fault that she wasn't in love with him.

'Kennedy! Hey there, had a haircut yet?' ann rea inquired.

'No, not yet, but it's getting there.'

'Ah, leave it Kennedy, trust me it'll look great.' She was forever encouraging him to let his jet-black hair grow just a fraction beyond respectable. Tempted as he was, however, he wasn't sure how the Super would react to a longhaired forty-four year old Detective Inspector wandering around the halls of North Bridge House.

'I'll take it under consideration.'

'Listen, Kennedy, you're in big trouble.'

'Really?'

'Yes. I thought we were mates,' ann rea continued.

'We were,' Kennedy replied defensively. 'We are.'

'Yes, well then how comes you didn't tell me that Wilko from the Circles was murdered last evening at Dingwalls?'

'Aha. Well, we're not entirely sure he was, at this point.'

'Okay then. Even telling me that he was found dead would have been okay for starters.'

'Well, it all happened so late…'

'Late, Kennedy? Late? I remember you ringing me at three o'clock in the morning. Shit…' ann rea continued in a whisper, 'I remember waking up one morning with an Ulsterman in my arms who wasn't there the night before.'

'Ah, so it's true about you and the Rev. Ian Paisley.'

'Very funny, Kennedy. Don't forget *I* was the one who rang *you* to tell you that Pauley Valentini had hijacked GLR. Hey, remember that?'

'Yes, I do as a matter of fact. Whatever happened to him?'

'The police let him off with a suspended sentence. It was the worst thing they could do to him,' ann rea advised her former lover. 'The minute he was released all the fuss, not to mention his record sales, died down. The record company dropped him and he's now a painter and decorator over Harlsden way. You see, there you go again.'

'What?'

'You have a way of getting out of trouble by the questions you ask. Here I am trying to be mad at you and you turn all this back on me with your continued questions, all the time avoiding talking about Wilko.'

'ann, there's really nothing to tell. Off the record?'

'Off the record? You tell me there is nothing to tell, "really", and then you hit me with an "off the record?"' ann sighed over the phone. 'Go then, I'll bite. Off the record, naturally, of course.'

'They, Circles, were playing a gig last night at Dingwalls. Towards the end of the set, Wilko Robertson and his partner Sean Green went off and let the band do a song by themselves. Wilko goes off and locks himself in the dressing-room to change…'

'And drop a tab or two of something no doubt. Sorry, continue.'

'…And he doesn't make it back to the stage. His tour manager, KP, breaks the door of the dressing-room down and finds one Wilko Robertson sprawled dead across the floor.'

'Are there any windows in the dressing-room?'

'No,' Kennedy replied quickly and then added by way of explanation. 'It's in the basement.'

'And the tour manager fellow is convinced the door was locked from the inside, not just stiff or something.'

'Yes, he was convinced it was locked. He further claims that he has done his shoulder and arm in breaking down the door.'

'Wimp, where's Arnie when you need him?'

'Well he *is* somewhat feeble, but a nice man all the same. A bit of a hippie vibe, if you know what I mean, man,' Kennedy replied tongue firmly in cheek, thinking maybe you had to be there.

'So there couldn't be any suspicious circumstances then, could there?'

'Why not?'

'Well, I may not be a detective, *detective*, but surely if the door was locked from the inside then no one could have got out again without unlocking the door. Unless they had Scottie beam them up, of course.'

'Well, our particular Scottie was dead,' Kennedy reminded ann rea. 'But seriously, there could be several explanations.'

'For instance?'

'Okay, your drugs scenario. Wilko goes into the dressing-room and locks the door behind him. From all accounts he sweats a lot on stage and he always uses this point to change his clothes. He changes his clothes. Sits down for a breather, does whatever it is that gets him off. Either his heart gives out with one blast too many, or the drug was spiked with something which killed him or he OD'd.'

'For and against?' ann rea quizzed.

'For. Mainly the fact that the door was locked from the inside. So whatever damage was done we would expect to be self-inflicted. Against, I've seen a few OD's and Wilko didn't look like one. He looked peaceful. A bit flushed about the cheeks but that could be excused with all the sweating on stage. I have to say he didn't look like he died a terrible death. On top of which we found no evidence of drugs in the room at all.'

'And so your scenario would be, Detective?'

'Well, let's examine the facts. Who found the body?' the DI quizzed his friend.

'This Tour Manager person.'

'Yes, KP, short for Kevin Paul. And he was alone at the time. We have to take his word that he knocked the door down and found the singer inside. What if he tapped on the door, the singer opened it. KP went inside and murdered him, then went back outside the dressing-room, locked the door behind him – from the *outside* – then kicked the door in? All he has to do then is replace the key in the inside in the Chubb lock, and *presto*.'

'Well done, Kennedy. Another case wrapped up successfully. KP's your man.'

'I'm not so sure. For starters we still don't know if Wilko Robertson died from natural or unnatural causes. On top of that, I'm not sure this KP chap has what it takes to murder someone. I took to him immediately. He and I got on well. So, a solution perhaps but instinctively I doubt it,' Kennedy said. 'Well, I better head and get stuck into this.'

'Hey, hang on a bit, Kennedy. Remember *you're* returning *my* call, that means *I* rang *you*, which means I had a point.'

'Sorry, I thought it was about Wilko,' Kennedy offered as a genuine apology.

'Well that was the excuse under which I rang you.'

'Really? And the real reason?'

'Gosh, Kennedy, what does a girl have to do around here to get invited out to dinner?'

'How about tonight in the Queens?' Kennedy replied, just a fraction too quickly.

'Perfect. See you there at eight, Kennedy. Bye.'

With that ann rea was gone, leaving Kennedy with the phone still at his ear and the second bit of green paper in his hand.

LESLIE RUSSELL RANG AT SEVEN FORTY-FIVE, PLEASE RING BACK

Six

Leslie Russell was the most dapper solicitor in Camden Town, and an acquaintance of Kennedy's. He was also, Kennedy discovered, the legal representative for the group Circles. Russell suggested a chat, "to put you in the picture." Kennedy suggested they meet at eleven at the Delancey Street café. Both arrived early. Formalities over and refreshments ordered, the men got down to the business at hand.

'How was he murdered, Christy?' Leslie Russell spoke as he looked, the perfect English gentleman. The solicitor had the voice, diction and phrasing that defied you to not to listen to him. He dressed as his father – the senior partner in the firm Russell, Phillips and Partners – had dressed; in expensive, well lived-in suits. To the manner born, thought Kennedy.

'Very deviously, Leslie, I can tell you. Taylor had nearly missed it. Wilko Robertson was stabbed straight into the heart by something "thinner than an ice pick but stronger than a knitting needle." He was stabbed through the chest and there was only one little speck of blood. Death was immediate, the heart stopped and no blood was spilt. Taylor reckoned the blood was dropped as the murderer removed the weapon. When Taylor spotted the speck of blood he found the wound.'

'So Wilko saw his murderer?' the solicitor inquired.

'Not necessarily,' Kennedy continued, 'We think the

assailant crept up behind Wilko, grabbed him around the neck with one arm while he stabbed him with the other hand. At any rate, all of it went on behind a locked door, which remained locked, from the inside.'

'How so?'

'Ask me one on cricket,' Kennedy replied. He had given as much information as he was going to give. 'How long have you worked with the group?'

'Personally eight years, although the firm, through my father, has represented Circles for the last nineteen,' Russell replied.

'A long time.'

'Absolutely, old chap. Although we are finding that, with all the changes these musicians make in their career – record companies, publishers, agents, managers, and so on – they do like to keep one pillar of stability in their organisation. Generally their lawyer or their accountant,' Russell explained.

'I can see the logic in a solicitor, but I thought an accountant just looked after…' Kennedy began.

'The accounts, yes I know,' Russell cut in. 'But these days accountants *and* solicitors are becoming, much more, confidants and advisors.'

'Even above the managers?'

'Oh, absolutely above the managers. In terms of the big deal, you see, the manager is almost always going to vote in favour of his own best interests. In the long term, this can work out to the artist's disadvantage. Not always, of course. But these older clients, who have perhaps gone through a few managers, tend to run ideas past their solicitor or accountant or even both, depending on the relationship. Both bill their clients by the hour and so our advice is less biased, or so we'd like to think.'

'So, the early managers wield more power than the later ones?' Kennedy suggested.

'Absolutely. The first manager is really more of a boss, in fact. The eager musician will happily do as told; so desperate are they for success. The balance of power begins to shift in direct proportion to the amount of success the artist achieves.'

'So how hard have The Circles been on managers?'

'Well, for a thirty year career, not too. Three managers in total. The first one, Kevin Paul…'

'KP?' Kennedy cut in.

'Yes, KP.' Russell smiled indulgently. 'Kevin was their first manager and a very good one at that, but after five or six years he grew bored with it and dropped out. They then hired Frazer Williams, less flamboyant than Kevin but very stable. He was the manager when my father became their solicitor.'

'What happened to Frazer?'

'It's sad. Circles were past their peak when he took over their management, and as the eighties progressed, the less successful they became. Someone had to be blamed.'

'Frazer?'

'The very same. He was fired. Then they managed themselves for a time. That would have been in the late eighties, when I came aboard. But it was mostly housekeeping at that point as Sean Green made all the decisions, and some good ones at that. A few of his deals, completed during the manager-less period, set the band up for life. Wilko had left the band at this stage. Although Sean formed the band, business-wise Circles had always been a partnership between Wilko and himself. Unless they were both keen on something it wouldn't be done. When Wilko left the group, Sean was able to tie up a lot of loose ends, which had been hanging around for ages. He was able to move the band forward. The current manager…'

'Hang on a wee minute, here, would you?' Kennedy interrupted, 'Before we get on to the current manager tell me about Wilko leaving the group.'

'Well, he was drinking a lot,' Russell began to explain. 'The band was no longer successful, except in Germany. He and Sean were arguing constantly. One night, after one more dismal performance, they were fighting in their typical fashion. Sean was spouting away, trying to come up with original ideas to help the band become successful again. Wilko grandstanded. "If you're so sure what to do with the band," he said, "buy me out and you can do whatever you want." The next day, Sean did exactly that. He paid Wilko one hundred thousand pounds and that was be the end of Wilko's involvement in Circles.'

'He bought him out entirely?'

'Well, no. Not entirely. The deal they struck was that everything the band had released, to that date, would still be subject to their original royalties deal. Wilko would still get record and publishing royalties at the same rate. However, on everything released *after* that date, all royalties would go to Sean alone.'

'So Wilko cut himself a good deal,' the detective assessed.

'Well...' Russell hesitated.

'The band was finished, you said. They'd passed their peak. A hundred grand in pocket would be about three hundred now. That's a lot of money for quitting a washed up band,' Kennedy offered.

'Perhaps. But Wilko had been a wee bit too keen to snatch the money, I think. A bit of the penny rich and pound foolish.'

'How so?'

'The minute the contract was signed and the money paid over to Wilko, Sean started putting the band's business in order. For years their record company had been pestering them to put out a Greatest Hits package. Wilko had always refused. But now, Sean had a free hand. He went to the record company. Not only would he give them their Greatest Hits package but he would help them put it together. He would even give them two new songs to put on it. Very clever.'

'How so?' Kennedy inquired.

'With a Greatest Hits package their record company was going to pull out all the stops with promotion. Television, radio, press. They were going to fly-post the streets of England and Europe. High profile promotion, which Circles had not been enjoying for years. Sean was able to use this launch as a platform for his new material and new lead singer. The first single was to be one of the new songs.'

'He must've made a lot of money for the new deal?' Kennedy guessed.

'He took not a penny in advance. What he wanted, in exchange for this Greatest Hits package, were the rights back for all of the Circles' master recordings. He would then lease back to the company all the albums, including the new Greatest Hits package and two albums of brand new material, for ten years. He also wanted the band's royalty rate increased from eleven percent to twenty percent, which would have put him on par with Rod Stewart. He also negotiated a royalty escalation that would earn him maximum of twenty four percent on everything if the Greatest Hits package sold three million copies. This took him up to the rarefied air enjoyed by the likes of Paul McCartney.'

'And the record company told him to sod off?'

'No. As a matter of a fact they didn't. From their point of view, the Circles catalogue was dead in the water. They were selling about ten thousand copies across their entire catalogue worldwide per year. The record company had already made their money, so what did they have to lose? They were getting their Greatest Hits package on top of which they got keep everything for ten years, and it didn't cost them a penny. Of course they went for it, they nearly bit his hand off.'

'Clever cookie, our Sean.'

'There's more. In the middle of all of this he went to the song publishers and told them he was considering the record company's request for the Greatest Hits package. This was manna from heaven for them, because apart from the Buddy Holly cover "Together Again", it was *all* Green-Robertson material. He said he would agree to the record company deal if they, the publishers, would give him back the copyrights to all of Circles' back catalogue of songs. If they did he would do a collection deal with them to cover that material and all new material for the following ten years. It was like money in the bank for them.'

'Wow!' was all the detective could say.

'THE FIRST EVOLUTION: THE GREATEST HITS OF CIRCLES has sold, to date, nearly five million copies worldwide. The Greatest Hits also drew attention to Circles' other seven albums, which have since sold an additional eight hundred and fifty thousand copies. Sean pocketed the majority of that. He assigned all the publishing rights to his own publishing company, Goode Olde Songs. Sean employs a chap called James Mac Donald to run the publishing company. Jones' job it to get covers, chase the main publishers on the collection of the monies and deal with day-to-day enquiries. James is on a small percentage of the company, you know, to encourage him to work harder at it. Sean still pays,' Russell paused for a second. 'Or I should say he still *paid* Wilko his original royalty rate.'

'If anything, Leslie, what you have told me should have resulted in Sean Green being found dead on the floor in Dingwalls,' Kennedy considered. He then sat up in his seat and continued. 'Which brings us neatly to the third manager?'

'Yes, Nick Edwards.'

'And his story?'

'Well, let me give you a hypothetical situation. You have a group, who don't have a manager and are not very current, but they sell major amounts of records worldwide and extraordinary amounts of tickets in Germany. Then you have this manager of cool acts, none of whom can sell enough records or tickets to cover their nightly bar bills at the Jazz Cafe. So the manager does just enough to keep in with the un-hip band, in the hopes of a large commission cheque. That is a certain type of manager.'

'Nick Edwards?'

'What? Sorry. No, no I was giving you a hypothetical

situation, don't you see,' Russell replied, the master of discretion.

'Any other skeletons in the Circles cupboard, hypothetically speaking of course?' Kennedy smiled.

'Come on, Kennedy. You've got a band who've been on the road for nearly thirty years now, quite a few of them with their guitarist David Cooper in tow. They're bound to pick up a few enemies along the way. Being in a band is a lot like being a member of a family. The main difference, though, is that with a family you can just say "Sod off." However, with this band, sorry with any band the financial ramifications of taking off can be far reaching. So, band members tend to stick with it and so consequently the bickering becomes a lot more bitchy and, potentially, violent than family bickering.'

'Violent enough that it would end up with murder?' Kennedy pushed. He was getting impatient. Russell was a discreet solicitor and to gain more information Kennedy needed to know the correct questions to ask because he knew that although Russell would never willing offer information which could be potentially damaging to one of his clients equally he would never lie on their behalf.

'Well somebody did, Christy.'

Seven

'Okay,' Kennedy began back in North Bridge House, 'DS Irvine, could you go and interview Nick Edwards, Circles' current manager, here're his details. WPC Coles, these are the details of guitarist David Cooper. Outside of Sean and Wilko he's the longest serving member of the band and I'd like you to go and interview him. We've got 29 years of information to dig up. After you finish with him, please meet me back here. We're interviewing Sean Green, at his house, at three p.m. Oh, and Irvine, you take PC Allaway with you and Coles, take PC Lundy,' Kennedy said, leaving them both sitting in his office and more than slightly bewildered.

The Detective Inspector was about to depart North Bridge House when Desk Sergeant Flynn caught him.

'Not so fast DI Kennedy, the Super wants to see you.'

'Okay. I'll see him when I come back.'

'He said it was urgent,' Flynn persisted, just as Superintendent Thomas Castle himself came bustling through the swinging doors, more Doc Watson than Dr Watson.

'Ah, Kennedy the very man.'

'Yes, Sir. I was about to come and see you,' Kennedy lied. Flynn rolled his eyes skywards.

'Fine, fine, walk with me to my car, why don't you?' Castle was, as ever, immaculately turned out. The buttons of his uniform were shone so well you could see all the Gloucester Avenue autumn foliage in them. 'I wanted to talk to you, Christy. Someone at the Met has brought to my attention that you've never applied for promotion.'

'Ah, no, Sir.'

'Well, there are a few people up there who are mighty impressed with your success rate.'

'Oh no, Sir,' Kennedy interrupted. '*Our* success rate. We're all part of a team, after all, and I couldn't do what I do if you weren't doing what you do, Sir. And that goes for Dr Taylor, Irvine, Coles and the rest of the squad as well.'

'My goodness,' Castle stopped in his tracks. 'Well, that's very kind of you, Christy. We like to think that in our own small way, what we do is important. But...'

'Yes, and I've been meaning to talk to you about WPC Coles. I think she's ready to move over to the detective side, permanently,' Kennedy continued, adding an inch to his step. Where's the Super's car when you need it, he wondered.

'Yes, yes, of course we can discuss Coles later. But this is about you. They'd like to see you take your Chief Detective Inspector exams. They, sorry, *we* would like a man of your calibre amongst our ranks.'

'You see that's the problem, Sir.'

'What problem, Kennedy? There are no problems.'

'No, Sir, no real problems. But, as you know, I love the art of detection, solving the puzzle. I enjoy it immensely. But I couldn't for the life of me ever do what you do, Sir. You know, keep this organisation running like clockwork. Our little team works well. You keep the organisation together and you obviously love doing it. As I said, the Met are happy with us because our figures are good. Why upset that?'

Castle muttered a few things as they reached the Super's car. He opened his door and stared at Kennedy.

'Look, all I'm saying, Kennedy, is that you'd better think about it. It's not up to me, you understand. It'll soon be out of

my hands and all your flannelling won't be able to save you.'
With that, Castle offered his most successful detective a warm
smile and a wink of the left eye. Odd, thought Kennedy. Most
people use the right eye. Kennedy walked across the road, and
in the general direction of KP's residence.

Eight

'Hey, it's the Philip Marlow vibe, man. God Bless you.'

A sleepy Kevin stood inside his small house, just the wrong side of Chalk Farm Road to be Primrose Hill.

'Still in bed at twelve-thirty?' Kennedy joked, as KP led the detective to his living quarters at the rear of the house.

'It's just with all those years on the road, man, I've found I've become half man half mattress. Hey, fancy a brew up?'

'That would be excellent,' Kennedy replied, thinking to himself, "This should be interesting." KP disappeared into the kitchen, leaving Kennedy in the living room alone. He could hear water running. To a casual eye, the house looked a bit hippie but closer inspection revealed KP's care and attention to detail. KP had simple functional furniture, but the walls and shelves were covered with trophies from the tour manager's incessant touring. Surprisingly enough, although there was lots or rock-n-roll memorabilia around, none of it belonged to Circles. He had a beautiful, framed Van Morrison 'It's Too Late To Stop Now' album poster. The walls were decorated with lots of Roundhouse posters and leaflets, all identically framed, announcing shows by the likes of The Doors, Fruupp, Thin Lizzy, Pink Floyd and the Undertones. There was an equal amount of wall space afforded to the posters of Bill Graham's Fillmore West shows featuring The Grateful Dead, The Buffalo

Springfield Band, The Faces, and the Jimi Hendrix Experience. The little space left on the walls was covered with black and white photographs of The Beatles, John Lee Hooker, Muddy Waters, The Rolling Stones and Bob Dylan. KP's house was crammed to the roof with bric-a-brac, but spotlessly clean. In fact, KP would certainly lead the short list for "Camden Town's most house-proud hippie."

KP returned with a pot of tea and two large mugs.

'So, you didn't tell me you started out as the group's manager,' Kennedy opened, sitting down.

'Yea, well someone had to do it, didn't they?' KP replied. Though just out of bed, KP was dressed immaculately, his trade mark skull cap adorning his crown.

'How did you meet them?'

'Sean Green. I knew Sean Green,' KP began, 'I knew Sean Green when he was Sean Pratley.'

'Sorry?'

'That's his really name, man,' KP replied. 'I kid you not. Green is a bit of a stage name vibe, man. Actually it was my idea, the Green bit. I'd known Sean in Ireland. I'm from Naas in Co. Kildare and it's a small town vibe, man. There wasn't much happening there in the late sixties. Showbands ruled in the country and you had to go to Dublin to see the beat groups. Most of the good ones were from the North, people like The Interns and the Gentry. But they'd come down and play in Dublin in places like the Stella Ballroom. I used to hang out at the Stella all the time and eventually the ballroom owner let me book in three groups every Monday night. It was a dead night for him anyway, and within a month we were regularly pulling in 400 heads, man. It was far out. I got to know the regulars. I even had a weekly pop column in one of the rags. Sean Pratley was one of our regulars and he stood out immediately because he was so tiny. Always very polite but he did love his music and we'd hook up at some point every Monday and have a chin wag over a pint or a brew up. You have to realise that this was way before there was a music business in Ireland. We were making it up as we went along. Eventually the Showband vibe became so frustrating that I had to move to England. All I knew was that I wanted to do something connected to music, and I couldn't do it in Ireland. I knew in my gut that if I had a chance that chance must lie in London. Shit man, the Beatles were in London. So off I went, man. Ended up, not a million miles from here in fact, in a squat in Arlington Road. I was working in a record shop during the day and helping out in a cafe four evenings a week to make ends meet. I was still writing my weekly column for the Irish rag and so I'd go and hang out in the Marquee Club in Wardour Street on nights I wasn't working in the Cafe. Guess who'd be there? Yep, Sean Pratley from The Stella Ballroom. We became good mates and he'd hang around the record shop a good few hours every week, checking out all the new releases, and then he'd be hanging out at the cafe I worked in, down on Parkway, a very buzzy vibe in those days man.'

'Sounds like heady times, all right,' Kennedy agreed.

'Oh, yes man. They were. So, Sean's been writing these songs and supposedly putting this group together. I'd always say, "Yea, yea great man, let me hear it." I figure, little guy, big talker. Good luck to him, mate, each to their own. Then one day he comes in the record shop all excited and blurts out that he's found the voice for his songs, the singer for his group. "Yea, yea. Great man, let me hear it." "Sure, no problem," he says. "Come around to my flat this evening." I do and he introduces me to this Scottish geezer, Wilko Robertson. We have a beer just to relax and then they start into the songs. Well, man, I don't know if I was more excited about the songs or the singer. They were both brilliant. Sean had had the goods up his sleeve all along. Over the next few months they put together the rest of the band. Writing for the Irish papers, I got to know some of the club owners around London and I got them a few support gigs, as you do. It wasn't that I wanted to be manager. I didn't even know what a manager did. I was just helping out my mates. But Sean would ask me about *everything*. I'd go to all of the gigs. By default, I was becoming part of their entourage.'

If Kennedy had been taken aback somewhat by the smell of KP's strange tea he found the taste to be totally satisfying, not to mention invigorating. "Purely Herbal" KP had offered to Kennedy's quizzical look. On draining the tea Kennedy was pleasantly surprised not to see the trade mark hippie three month tea stain on the inside of the mug. He replaced the mug on the table, clasped his hands on his knee and sunk back into his seat as KP continued his narrative.

'So one day we're at a gig, the Toby Jug at Tolworth, and this geezer comes across to me and says, "You the manager of this lot then?" and I say no, I'm just their friend "Well," he says "the little fella says you're his manager." Oh," I say, "Well, it must be true then because it's his band." I must admit I was feeling quite proud at being called The Manager. He wants to know, "Do you have a demo?" I told him that as a matter of a fact we had. He gives me his business card, he was from RCA, or something. And that, I suppose, was that. I became their manager, by default. It was never really discussed or anything. I had my solicitor draw up a letter of agreement and they both signed it immediately,' KP recalled with pride. 'I was about to go and see this geezer and a few other labels that I'd gotten to know, blagging for records and all that. Sean used to always mark up the boxes containing his demo tapes. "Songs by Sean" or "By Sean and Wilko Robertson." I knew he was embarrassed about the name Pratley so I says, "Look, you're Irish, so you should have an Irish name." He went through all the O'This and O'That, all of which was a bit Diddley-Eye for me, and then I remembered this song from Sesame Street called, "It's Not Easy Being Green." Like, it's not east being Irish. And I can tell you man, in those days it wasn't easy being Irish in London, but you'd know that, man, wouldn't you? You're from the North, aren't you?'

Kennedy nodded that he was from the North. He also

recalled that, even he, who'd been a policeman all the years he'd been in London, hadn't found it easy in the early days.

'Yea, man I bet you remember that vibe. Anyway, "Sean Green," I say. "That's your name. Arise, Sean Green." He loved it, we all loved it and we went off and got a record deal. They thought I got them the record deal. But the truth was, three record companies were fighting over them. Wilko had a great voice, the songs were brilliant. They were a great group in those days.'

'KP, who'd want to murder Wilko?' Kennedy asked, point blank.

'God, man, I've been racking my brain since yesterday evening to come up with a list of suspects for you, but in the music business there are so many. Those you shaft on the way up are still waiting for you as you slide back down that greasy pole of success.' Kevin Paul suddenly looked tired and weary and all of his fifty-one years. 'Could have been any of us then, really. It was always a one for all and all for one vibe, man. Really.'

'Why did you give it up?' Kennedy changed tact.

'What, managing the band? Mmmm. Good question. I suppose I was bored with it all. First time around the houses it was brilliant, exciting. You know, getting mentioned for the first time in the Melody Maker, playing Friars Aylesbury for the first time, getting in the charts, getting your first gold disc, selling out Hammersmith Odeon for the first time, paying off all the band's debts for the first time, going to Europe for the first time, going to Japan for the first time, going to America for the first time. All the firsts were great. But when we didn't break America we started to mark time over here. Plus I'd loads of dosh saved. I'd a very soft mattress, if you know what I mean. In the early days…well let's just say there was the potential to do deals in cash. So I was okay. I'd enough money. More, I figured, than I'd ever spend. So what was the point? I didn't need to do it. I wasn't enjoying it. And the relief I felt when I jumped from the treadmill, I couldn't believe it. It was like getting my life back again – a part I never thought I'd see again. It dawned on me that life doesn't depend on whether or not you are mentioned by some little spotty herbits in the New Musical Express or the Melody Maker. You stopped listening to every new band as if they were the competition. Hell man, when I split, I even started to listen to music again. I bought my house and took my time doing it up. I put my feet up and watched the world go by. Spent some time in America. I watched the four seasons come and go while travelling around Ireland. That was great. I got to meet up with real people again.'

'Then you came back. After what you've said I'm surprised you bothered,' Kennedy responded.

'Well, I know. And I know what you're thinking, but I didn't need the money. Sean contacted me when Wilko left and he was putting together the Greatest Hits package. He wanted my help. It was fun, it gave me something enjoyable to do the fill the days. Sean made sure the Record Company paid me well and he gave me a royalty on the record, which he didn't need to do. He wanted someone he could trust to help him in the studio. I thought I was co-producing but the credit, when it came out, was "Produced by Sean Green." I got a credit for "co-ordination and compilation," which was fine. It's only words, man. We got on great again. When we'd finished the album he and Leslie Russell took me out to dinner at Odette's in Primrose Hill, so I figured it must be important.' KP broke off to chuckle at his own joke, sliding his black and brown skullcap slightly to scratch his forehead.

KP cleared his throat and continued, 'And Sean invited me to manage the band again. I told him I was flattered but I just wasn't up to it, I preferred being his mate. I suggested that they hire someone else to be the manager, but I said I'd help out with TV and touring on a freelance basis. It's changed a lot since my time; tour managers used to do all the work. Now they do none – they hire in a team of assistants to do their job for them. Wilko rejoined. We were building up to an important tour next year and someone goes and tops him. That's a heavy vibe, man isn't it?'

A few minutes later, he bid the detective farewell with his traditional, 'God bless you, man.'

Nine

DS Irvine and Constable Allaway found Circles' management, "Nick Edwards and Associates", situated in a refurbished warehouse overlooking Camden Lock and, remarkably, just in front of Dingwalls dance hall. Nick Edwards, Irvine noticed wryly, had no associates. The surprising thing about Edwards' top floor suite of offices was that although the walls were adorned with posters, press cuttings, photographs and album artwork, mentioning several varied artists, there was not one mention of Circles.

A plump, smiling fellow-Scot called Jill greeted them and took a shine to Irvine's accent. Although the feeling was not reciprocated, Irvine was charming as ever, exchanging pleasantries for several minutes until the great associateless man deemed it appropriate to see them.

'Come on in, won't you?' Edwards' began, his Brum accent making a mockery at his attempt to smile. For one who had just lost a major client, Edwards was working under the "Business as Usual" banner when DS James Irvine and Constable Allaway came calling. He wore a telephone headset, earphones and microphone, leaving his hands free to compulsively tidy his already tidy desk.

'It's a shame all this. Wilko was a wonderful warm human and will be sorely missed by all his colleagues, family and friends. He, along with Sean of course, leaves behind as a lasting legacy, a body of work as strong as any other seventies groups,' the manager began.

'I couldn't help but notice that Circles are conspicuous by their absence from your walls,' Irvine offered in reply.

'Well, of course you have to realise that we specialise in a much younger, more cutting-edge type of band…'

'But you *are* the management for Circles?' Irvine asked.

'Were.'

'Sorry?'

'Were. We *were* their management company. They don't exist any more, you see.'

'But surely with all the albums, the lasting legacy as you say, there's a lot of work to be done – particularly now?' Irvine puzzled, thinking of artists careers that had snowballed even after death.

'Not exactly. We were retained to do a job by Mr Green and his solicitor, Mr Leslie Russell, on the *future* career of Circles. As of last night they have no future. I am not involved in any of their earlier product.'

'Oh, I see,' Irvine sympathised. For the first time since he'd arrived he felt sorry for the man. People rarely felt sorry for the manager, Irvine imagined. 'So you're not involved in any of their records?'

'No, they'd just started up again and, well, Sean didn't like to rush things. He wanted to get a set of material which matched up, in his eyes, to the earlier hits. It's all extremely difficult you know. They say you have a lifetime to write your first album, but after that, well…In the early days you write songs because you have to get them out of your system, as it were. Then you have a few hits, a couple of million selling albums and the perspective changes, doesn't it? This time you sit down to write hits. And, Officers, I'm here to tell you that people don't write hits. They write songs and some of those songs are, hopefully and magically, hits.' Irvine noticed Edwards was tidying his desk for the third time. Pencils were moved and then carefully replaced by the side of his note pad, as he droned on.

'Sean was having problems. He had already done it once. He'd proven it to himself, and his peers, that he had the talent to write and record successfully. He wasn't going to do anything new, was he? He was just going to repeat himself. He wasn't hungry, financially *or* artistically. Maybe he still wanted to prove that he could do it in America, I don't know. At any rate, he set a goal for himself. Twenty new songs. And he'd just about completed them. We were looking around for a deal. The next stage would have been to record the album and then take to the road, around the time of the album release next year.'

'Was a deal imminent?' Allaway asked.

'Well it wasn't easy, I can tell you. Sean controls the *entire* back catalogue, including the Greatest Hits, and that still has life in it. If I'd been able to offer one of the majors the back catalogue as part of the deal, they would have jumped at it. We could have named our price, literally. But no, Mr Green was adamant. Only future work, no back catalogue. So at this point there were no takers amongst the major record companies. The smaller ones couldn't afford us. A few people were sniffing around – the heads of Sony/Germany flew in to see last night's show and have a chat...'

'Were you at the show last night?' Irvine asked, just a fraction ahead of Allaway.

'Actually, no. Not during the actual performance. I've seen the set several times, you understand, and I was working here until quite late. It had been my intention to go across to Dingwalls at the end of the evening to meet up with the record executives and introduce them to Sean and Wilko. But I found that by the time I got there the boys in blu...I found several police officers blocking my entrance, claiming that they couldn't let me in. I advised them that I represented the band and demanded to be let in. I was still refused admission so I came away and tracked down Mr Green on his mobile, who advised me about all that had happened.'

'How well did you know the deceased?' Irvine asked.

'Well, personally not very well,' Edwards continued in his Midland's drawl, 'I was taken on to look after the business side of things. Of course I knew him. But I'd never go out drinking with him or anything like that. Most of my Circles dealings were either with Mr Green or with Leslie Russell.'

'Did he have any enemies?' Allaway inquired.

'I wouldn't have a clue, to be perfectly honest,' the manager replied. 'I didn't really know a lot about him, save that he liked to drink, he'd been out of the band for a time, and that he came from Scotland.'

Allaway returned to an earlier point.

'You said earlier that some of the major record companies would have jumped at signing the group if the back catalogue had been part of the deal?'

'Yes.'

'Exactly how much would they have offered?'

'Well, it's confidential information.'

'Yes, and this is a murder investigation,' Irvine prompted.

'I suppose it's a matter of record, and you could have received the same information from the major record company involved. Circles could have received 1.2 million pounds for the back catalogue, with a further half a million pounds for the new album and, of course, recording costs up to three hundred thousand pounds.'

It was funny, thought Irvine, how Edwards could make such a fabulous offer sound mundane. Funnier still that the manager failed to mention exactly what his share would have been. Irvine looked around the less than ideal suite of offices. He really did feel sorry for the man who just lost his meal ticket.

'Was there anyone with you in the offices last evening, Sir, while Circles were performing across the road?'

'Actually no. I was here by myself all the time. Jill, the girl you met on the way in, went home at seven.'

Ten

David Cooper answered the door in his relaxed casual, flopping about the house, mode. Flip flop shoes, loose green slacks, a loose-fitting Spanish-style shirt, with several of the top decorative buttons opened to reveal a V-neck vest. He answered the door with an authoritative rasp.

"Come in. Come on in."

As he led WPC Anne Coles and Constable Lundy through his house, it was easy to tell that David Cooper was a dedicated guitarist. If he had lived in American he would have had a guitar-shaped swimming pool. He occupied a converted warehouse space around the corner, literally, from KP in Chalk Farm and close to the Roundhouse. His large living space was set up with a display of about twelve guitars. The rarest, he boasted, was a Gibson Country Gentleman currently worth about two thousand pounds.

He had been playing an acoustic guitar when the police came calling. When he lead them through to his living room he returned it to its place, on a guitar stand, where it stood proudly on parade with the remainder of the highly strung soldiers.

Lundy considered himself a bit of a guitarist and immediately went into raptures over the Country Gentleman. WPC Coles considered herself a bit of a detective though and so she started the questions.

'How long had you known Wilko?'

'A good few years, I can tell you.' The guitarist leaned back into the fullness of his sofa. 'I've spent all night trying to come to terms with it, you know? We are on this Earth for but a short time and we have to enjoy each other's company while we're here. We have to make the best of it. There's no time for all this squabbling and fighting and if we think we're going to get a chance to make amends in the next life, then we should think on, for no such life exists. Wilko was, like the rest of us, human. Yes he had his faults…he had his…'

'And what would his faults have been, Sir?' Coles interrupted polite as, and as cold as, snow.

'Oh,' Cooper started to reply, shocked to have been cut off mid-flow. So shocked he didn't consider before he spoke. 'Well, he drank too much, he did too many drugs, he slept around, he cared not enough for his fellow men, he didn't fully appreciate exactly how generous Sean was to him. But you know, on the positive side he absolutely drank up his life by the gallon. It's just that he was positively speeding out of control and he must have known that his brakes would let him down at some point.'

'Tell me about the sleeping around?' she inquired, sweetly this time.

Cooper laughed.

'You're a lot like the media, you know. Here I am willing to tell you about the man's spiritual side, help you see what plane he was on, but all you want is the sex and scandal.'

'Well, Sir,' Lundy began, 'We're sure he wasn't murdered due to his floating around spiritual planes but he may have been murdered for floating amongst the sheets.'

'Yes, possibly, but I doubt it. Don't you see it was all for show. He was showing the rest of us that he was still a lad, could still be out there pulling with the best of them. Believe me, it was positively all for show. No, I don't think you'll find any jealous husbands or boyfriends waiting in the wings.'

'How did he and Sean Green get on?' Coles asked, shifting restlessly in her armchair.

'Well, they'd been together a long time, been through the wars together, so they gave each other a lot of space.'

'What, you mean they fought a lot?' Lundy asked.

'In the early days they did have a habit of getting up each other's noses. But now they were like an old married couple. They accepted that they were going to be together forever. They didn't exactly forgive each other their faults, they just made sure they weren't around each other much. In a way it was like a marriage of convenience.'

'Did they really need each other?'

'Good question, Constable. I suppose they needed each other in different ways. Wilko needed the money. He wasn't going to get another solo record deal. He wasn't going to get a job with another group, he didn't have what it took to put his own band together and he couldn't go out there and work in the real world, in civvy street. He's too young to die and too old to change. Well, until last night I suppose that could have been our Wilko. And Sean. Well, yes, I suppose in a different way he needed Wilko. He is very wealthy, but in a way, he was also trapped in the same snare as Wilko. He'd had the record sales, he'd heard the applause of the crowds and he still craved it, still needed it. In a way it was very undignified, Circles playing at bleedin' Dingwalls Dancehall last night. Did you know we used to be able to sell out Wembley? We once did three nights there, thirty thousand tickets. Last night we played to six hundred people. Hardly a fitting end to a great band.'

'If you were so against it why did you do it?' Coles asked politely.

'It's my gig, man,' Cooper replied. 'I am, or was, the guitarist with Circles. All those guitar intros you hear on the records, all those solos? That's me, every single time. No session guitarists for Circles. Even the Beatles got Eric Clapton in the play on 'While my Guitar Gently Weeps'. But no, not us.

And Sean didn't compose what *I* play. Oh no, I made all that up myself. All boasting aside, one DJ went as far as saying on air that my "plaintive guitar intro, solo and outro are what made 'Together Again' the classic it's become." That's right. That's the song that put us back on the map. And what do I get? What I've always got, a session fee. A session fee. Mind you, I can't complain too much, can I? Sean has looked after us all, particularly me, because I've been there the longest along with Wilko. There's always a bonus cheque at Christmas, a bonus at the end of each tour, and when the Greatest Hits package came out he did me right proud I can tell you. So I'm not going to complain too much, am I?'

'What can you tell us about some of the people in the camp?' Coles asked, fishing for general information at this point. The interview seemed to be reaching a natural but premature conclusion and she didn't feel that she amassed enough information.

'Who for instance?'

'Nick Edwards, say?'

'Waste of space. He sees Circles as his meal ticket.'

'Kevin Paul?' Coles hoped if she threw the names at the guitarist quickly enough he might let something slip.

'KP,' Cooper smiled. 'All round good egg, good geezer. Worth his weight in gold. Good planner, good thinker. If he'd stayed with the band the whole way through we'd be as big as Elton, or Rod or the Stones. I believe that, sincerely. He cares about people, looks after us well.'

'Simon Rutland?'

'Newest member, only plays bass 'cause he can't hack it as a guitarist, but he desperately wants to be in a band. He'll soon get over that, if he didn't last night. Many are called, but few are chosen.'

'Mark Giles?'

'Great musician and he's mastered all this computer shit. Very quiet, keeps to himself. Very much in love with his girlfriend and doesn't really have time for anything outside of her and his music. He doesn't really like the road. Ideally he'd love to be doing music in his home for adverts, TV and movies. Soundtracks, that's where he'll end up, I bet you.'

'Dan Hudson, the roadie?'

'Don't really know him. Not great at his job, but he looks cool and that's what he was hired for.'

'Mick Litchfield, the other roadie?'

'The *only* roadie. A genius, especially for me. He loves guitars and what he doesn't know about them is not worth knowing. He's a lovely guy.'

'James MacDonald?' The WPC was checking her notes.

'Could well do with going to work for a real publishing company for a few years to learn what real old fashioned publishers are meant to do. They're not meant to be *bankers*.'

Coles had only one other name.

'Leslie Russell?'

'I don't really have much to do with him, but he's a lovely fellow. A bit of the old school of true British, sort of chap. Sean swears by him, depends on him a lot. I suppose the three of them, Sean, KP and Leslie run the band.'

'Wilko wasn't part of the decision making team?' Lundy inquired.

'Oh, no. Not at all. Since he came back he was more like the rest of us, like a hired musician. Perhaps he wanted it that way. Perhaps he wanted a guaranteed wage without the worry about where the next cheque was coming from.'

'Will you continue as a group now, do you think?'

'I don't know, I doubt it. We'll see what Sean says, but I doubt it.'

Eleven

The rain over Camden Town had stopped falling by the time
Kennedy returned to North Bridge House. He was early for his
rendezvous with WPC Anne Coles but he wanted to stop off on
the way to Sean Green's house. He had Flynn radio the WPC,
who was returning from her interview with Circle guitarist,
David Cooper, to pick Kennedy up at the Bridge by Camden
Lock at 2:50 p.m.

This would give him about half an hour to spend at
Dingwalls Dancehall.

On reaching Dingwalls front entrance, he found WPC West
and PC Gaul on duty. The forensic team had concluded their
work and when Kennedy entered the club it was empty and
dark. Kennedy marvelled at the thousands of pounds worth of
Circles' equipment, still set up on the stage. The venue
appeared to slope down towards the stage, probably so that
those seated and drinking by the long bar could see the stage
over the heads of those on the dance floor. The overall look of
the place was of an American-style bar room. It smelled of stale
beer, strong but not altogether unpleasant. Kennedy walked
around the perimeter of the venue from side stage to side stage,
not really knowing what he was looking for. Something.

Who would be directly affected by the murder of Wilko
Robertson? His wife Susan, obviously. Leslie Russell had

already taken the trouble to advise and console her. He'd told Kennedy that she had appeared to take it well and had phoned her sister to come and comfort her. Kennedy would visit her tomorrow he decided, leaving a little time to deal with it.

Wilko and Susan Robertson had no children and both Wilko's parents were several years' dead. Susan and a brother, fifty-five years old and still living in Paisley. That was it for immediate family. Sean Green would be affected by the death, of course, as would the rest of the members of the Circles. The road crew, Edwards the manager, KP, MacDonald the publisher, the record company and Leslie Russell.

Kennedy considered the ever-growing inverted pyramid of people with Wilko at the top. Who in the pyramid though, Kennedy thought, would have benefited from the singer's death?

A locked-door murder wasn't a crime of passion. It had been planned. Kennedy was dealing with a specific kind of murderer. Cold and brazen as well, to carry out such a crime in the presence of six hundred people.

Kennedy took the small pokey staircase into the basement and walked back along the length of the venue, with the dance floor overhead, to the storeroom/dressing-room. The musician's street clothes still hung over the chairs as they were left the previous evening. Kennedy, pulling on a pair of rubber gloves, checked Sean Green's space first. His was easiest to recognize due to the size of the trousers. Denim shirt, denim trousers, Black leather jacket, and platform white trainers. His hold-all contained a second pair of shoes, The Independent, Music Week, Q Magazine and, at the very bottom and under a spare white soiled T-shirt, a couple of pens, a harmonica, and three condoms.

Wilko had two grey suit-bags, with red trim, hanging on the wall side-by-side. One was empty, because he had changed into his second set of stage clothes before he'd been murdered, but the other felt full. Kennedy unzipped the bag down the centre of its full length and immediately wished he hadn't. The stench of the sweat-soaked clothes, left overnight, brought tears to his eyes.

Kennedy gingerly pulled out a crumpled yellow shirt, a monogrammed tank top similar to the one the singer had been found in, and a rolled up pair of green loon pants, flared. The shape of the bag indicated several objects, one quite weighty, were still resting on the bottom.

The detective placed the foul smelling clothes, one by one, on the chair underneath the suit bags. Then he put his hand in and searched around to find three items, a sealed twenty pack of Silk Cut, a disposable cigarette lighter and a ten inch long, stainless steel spike with a wooden handle affixed to one end. The murder weapon? Perhaps, but it contained no traces of blood, at least none visible to the naked eye. It seemed too careless to hide the murder weapon in the deceased's suit-bag. It was the last thing Kennedy had expected to find and it spooked him so much so he nearly dropped it. The spike was filed incredibly thin, into a point so fine it could have injected an ant. He'd never seen anything like it, and it certainly fit Dr Taylor's description of the murder weapon. He felt a shiver run up his spine.

'Hello? Hello?

'Coles?'

'Constable West told me you'd come in here.'

'Look what I've found,' Kennedy said as Coles entered the storeroom. He held up the spike in front of her.

'The murder weapon?'

'It seems too simple, but it fits the description,' Kennedy offered as he placed the spike in a plastic bag and sealed it.

'What on earth is that smell?' Coles asked, gasping for air.

'I'm afraid that's the hiding place. I'm done with the dressing-room for now, let's get out of here immediately.'

Twelve

Ironic, Kennedy thought, that one so Irish he'd change his name to Green would live in England's Lane. The pop star's home was a rambling house set back from the main thoroughfare and partly hidden behind a grove of fine chestnut trees. Slightly suburban, very tranquil, and extremely expensive.

Coles parked the blue Ford Sierra just off England's Lane in Chalcot Gardens and they made the last 20 yards by foot. Green's maid, Gerty, ushered Coles and Kennedy upstairs, where her employer was awaiting them in his study.

Sean Green's study took up the entire second floor of the five-story house. It was a large, book-laden room, something like a loft-space. This room was lit by two floor-to-ceiling windows and contained a music centre, a large Sony Television, a video and a cabinet to one side of it containing thousands of CD's and hundreds of videocassettes. The floor was polished pine and there was a large leather sofa with two matching chairs. In the corner furthermost away from the television was the real study; Sean's work space. Set up on a L-shaped contraption was a Packard Bell computer, a synthesizer keyboard, a telephone, loads of paper scattered around a Sony DAT recording machine and rows of DAT tapes, all with unreadable hand writing on the spine. The red brick walls were covered with Gold Discs, Platinum Discs, a couple of framed Circles' posters, framed PRS certificates, framed Ivor Novello Awards, a framed copy of the original artwork for Circles' first album, "GOING AROUND WITH …" showing a fresh-faced bunch of chaps on a fairground roundabout, a framed Sgt. Peppers signed poster. There were numerous framed photographs of Sean with Elton, Sean with Rod, Sean with a couple of the old school comedians. Sean with Leslie Russell and Leslie's father, Sean with KP.

Not one single photograph of Sean and Wilko Robertson, not unless you counted Wilko's appearance on the album sleeve artwork.

'Quite a collection of books here,' the Camden Town detective admired exquisite editions of Crime and Punishment, The Odyssey, Moby Dick, The Collected Poems of WB Yeats, The Forgotten London by Jim Driver and Mark Twain's Adventures of Huck Finn.

'Mostly they are from the Franklin Classics Library. It's all done by mail order. The rest I picked up here and there over the years on my travels,' Sean replied nonchalantly. Kennedy was quite surprised at the musician's apparent "around the house casual dress". He was dressed in a suit, in his own house in the afternoon. A bleeding Armani suit if Kennedy wasn't mistaken. ann rea would have known immediately, she was great at things like that. A very sharp black suit and a grey satin shirt, top button done up. He even had the jacket on and buttoned up. His lack of casualness emphasised by black shinny leather slip-ons – black leather platform slip-ons.

'I see you've nearly all of the Agatha Christie series here?' Coles announced following her browse.

'Yes, Franklin is working its way through those at the minute.'

'You like detective stories then?' Kennedy felt compelled to ask.

'Not particularly,' Green replied, as he removed a book from the shelves. It was a Beatles-related book, George Martin's edition of "The Summer of Love", 'I personally go for books like this one, which take you behind the scenes of some of the famous moments which changed our lives.'

'What about John Dickson Carr?' Kennedy inquired casually.

'Who? Has he done a book on the Beatles as well?' came the reply.

'Ah, no. Not exactly.'

'In a few moments my wife, Colette, will bring us up some tea and coffee and then we can have our chat. Will that be okay?' Sean inquired, as he returned George Martin's book to its place on the shelves. Not, however, before giving it a quick wipe on the back of his sleeve.

'That would be perfect,' Kennedy replied, and then as an afterthought, '*The* Colette? From "Colette Calls"?'

'The very same,' Sean answered proudly and then, right on cue, a stunning, blonde-haired woman emerged from the stairwell, dressed in a black dress; both hair and dress were long and free-flowing. She was in her bare feet. A concession to Sean's height perhaps?

'Well, Colette,' Sean began as he introduced everyone, 'It would seem you have a fan in the Camden Police force.'

Colette tried a bashful, lopsided look, which didn't quite come off. She'd obviously heard variations on this line so many times before she could no longer feign modesty with any degree of success. When she spoke Kennedy and Coles were shocked to discover a thick Scottish accent.

'This is William,' she said introducing the twelve-year-old boy who was carrying one of the three trays. The first, Colette's, contained a teapot, a coffee pot, a hot water pot, milk jug and a sugar bowl. The second, William's, bore three cups, three saucers and three serving plates, all crockery was in beautiful white china. The tray was set off with three spoons and three white Irish Linen napkins plus a larger plate packed with an assortment of biscuits. Bringing up the rear, the only person in the room shorter than Sean Green, was the nine-year-old daughter Tressa, whose matching silverware tray bore finger sandwiches, 'There's egg, and ham and cheese,' Tressa announced proudly with as big a smile as her small face would allow.

The children deposited their trays on the large coffee table, said "Cheerio", and left. Colette remained behind but didn't join her husband on the sofa. Kennedy and Coles had taken one of the chairs each. Kennedy realized she had stayed behind to pour the tea and coffee because she sat on the floor by the coffee table and went around them each in turn adding milk, sugar, coffee or tea as requested. She composed her husband's mixture without direction and said, 'It's really terribly sad about Wilkeson, isn't it?'

Kennedy slowly equated Wilkeson to Wilko.

'Yes, it is,' he replied. As he did so he realized that Colette Green had been the first person so far to express sorrow at the demise of Wilko Robertson.

'Mr. Green, Sir, you and Mr. Robertson were colleagues for a long time?' Coles asked.

'Yes.' Green smiled. 'A very long time.'

'Had you made any enemies during your time together?' Coles pushed.

'Well, *he* apparently did,' Green replied. 'Look, sorry for being facetious. It's just, after yesterday evening, well it's all been such a strain. I mean in this business, of course you make enemies. We all hated the music papers for not writing about us any more or when they would write about us they were always being nasty, just to get cheap laughs. Colette keeps telling me that I should stop reading them. But I like the new groups, you know. I like them a lot. I listen to Radio One, but as far as Circles are concerned, well we're just another bunch of bankers who don't work with money, if you know what I mean. But I listen to Oasis and Manic Street Preachers and The Verve and

Ocean Colour Scene. I listen to Radio One all the time. That's where you find out all about those bands, the NME and Radio One, so I'm not going to ignore them just because they don't like my music. Yes, in one way we did hate them and they definitely hated us. When we were selling millions of records it was fine. We had a direct connection with our fans. The media would leave us alone. They had to, they'd have been laughed out of business if they were found having a go a someone as successful as us.'

Kennedy asked the next question.

'Had you hoped your upcoming work was going to wipe the smirks from their faces?'

'In reality? I'm not sure if Circles came up with an album as innovative and as brilliant and as beautiful as Sgt. Peppers it would have received anything but the usual jeers and sneers from those sitting in judgement. Sadly, we'd become a bit of a joke. We were a victim of our own success. We'd done what we'd done and that, as far as the committee concerned, was that. We had our five minutes of glory. It was a case of, "Okay. Circles. Yes we know them. They're over, done, finished with. Next please!" And in a way that's fine. We'd had a good innings and we couldn't possibly sustain our earlier success the way Paul Simon, Bob Dylan, Ray Davies and Van Morrison have done because we didn't have the American success. That's a big thing in all of this. That's when you start to lose your fans. There's a bit of a snobbish thing going on with the fans as well, you know. Initially they're part of an exclusive club. They want to be the first on the block to discover a great new band and then they take pride in turning all their mates on to it. Then they wear your success like a badge upon their chest. That's what the whole T-shirt, sweat-shirt, baseball-cap and badge thing is all about.'

Kennedy had to admit, he'd never seen anyone wear a piece of Circles merchandising, shirt, hat nor badge.

'So,' Green continued. 'You become the biggest most

successful band in a club and they are right there with you, cheering you on, one and all. Then you become the biggest in an area and then the biggest in London, and they are right there with you, cheering you on. The bigger you become, the louder they cheer. It's country by country throughout Europe and they're still with you and then you go to America and you fail. Well, when your return home you notice immediately some of the audience aren't there anymore. If you're not good enough for the Yanks, you're not good enough for them. "Oh, and by the way have you heard this new band down the Mean Fiddler, they're from Scotland. The guitarist is only seventeen and he's the best since Clapton and the girl singer, well she's just so hot. It's too early to realise it but right then you've already started on the slippery slope.'

'But,' Kennedy began. 'I'm a bit confused here. You've just been giving us an insight into the wheeling and dealings of the music business, and very informative you've been too. But, if you felt this way...if you felt that Circles could produce the next Sgt. Peppers and they'd still get laughed at. Well, then why on earth did you want to bother? Why put yourself through all of it again? You live in a wonderful house, you have a beautiful wife and children, you don't exactly need the money do you?'

'Well,' Sean smiled, 'This *is* what I do.'

Neither Kennedy nor Coles spoke.

'This is all I can do. My life is not over. I'm not going to sit around for the rest of my life waiting to die. I'm not going to just give in. There are a lot of people around who'd be happy if Circles just went away. I'm sorry, quite simply I'm not going to oblige them. Hell, I'm *not* sorry.'

'Does that mean you're going to continue even without Wilko?' Coles asked.

'Oh, most certainly.'

'Really?' Kennedy was surprised.

'Yes, of course,' Green said. 'We're not going to throw away all the new material, I think it's the best stuff we've done. Besides which, we owe it to Wilko's memory to continue.'

'So will you replace Wilko, or play on without him?' the WPC asked.

'You know Wilko was out of the group for several years, don't you?'

'Yes, KP and Leslie Russell gave us all of the background.' Kennedy confirmed.

'Well, I think that we could get his replacement back again – a very fine singer called Robert Clarke,' Green paused. 'I should say here that I'm being perfectly candid with you but I would hope that you could keep all this information confidential for the moment. I haven't discussed it with anyone yet, apart from Leslie Russell. Obviously it would be highly inappropriate if this information came out right now.'

Kennedy nodded agreement, and continued.

'Did Wilko gamble, do you know?' Kennedy asked.

'Well, as far as I was aware he'd take a flutter now and again on the horses but he wouldn't run up either massive wins or losses.'

'Was he depressed?' Kennedy again.

'He was dark sometimes, yes, but that's more a question for his mates,' Green replied.

'Who were?' Coles this time.

'Oh, you'd best ask KP that, I'm sure he knows them all.'

'Some of the boys say Wilko was sleeping around. Were there any jealous lovers? Or jealous boyfriends or husbands?'

'I didn't really socialise with him much, you see. Again, KP would be the person to ask.'

'Leslie Russell, is he the band's solicitor or *your* solicitor?' Kennedy asked.

'Both,' Green replied. 'He's my solicitor, consequently he's Circles' solicitor.'

'So Wilko had a separate solicitor?'

'Look, I think I should explain,' Green cleared his throat. 'I own the band outright. It's been my band since Wilko left some years back. Up to that point, Leslie Russell and his father before him, acted for Wilko and myself, because it was our band. The other musicians are employed by me, none are official partners in the band. In the early days, Wilko and myself took all the responsibility for the band. When he left, I bought him out. I paid one hundred thousand pounds for his share. Obviously he was to continue to get his share of the royalties as per his original deal, but it was my band. When Wilko rejoined the band, he worked for me. I felt it would be appropriate that he should have his own legal representative, to avoid any possible conflicts of interest.'

'Is that usual?' Coles asked.

'Well, you can check with Leslie Russell, but you'll find there is nothing illegal and certainly nothing unethical about such an arrangement. He quit the band. I bought him out with my own money. When he left the band I undertook sole responsibility for the band. Wilko, who in all honesty thought the band was all washed up, couldn't wait to get his money when we signed the agreement in case I had second thoughts. So, with Wilko out of the band, I was able to move at my own speed; I didn't need to go to him for approval. With the help of Leslie Russell, I did a new deal with the record company, which included the Greatest Hits package. Again with the help of Russell, I did a new publishing deal and I jumped at the chance of using, "She Loves Rain" for the shampoo TV advert. The song had been a top-five hit for us and the record company re-released it around the time of the shampoo advert. The single made the top-twenty, and it got tonnes of airplay though on Radio Two and sold another six hundred thousand copies of the Greatest Hits package. So, I guess you could say I turned the band's career around without Wilko's help. Believe me, though, even with his smaller share of the royalties he still did incredibly well.'

'So, he was on a wage like the rest of the band?'

'Well, he was on a retainer; more than a wage. He needed some cash. I think all his money was tied up in something. His solicitor, a chap called Richard Scott, would know best about all of that. We were advancing him each week, in cash I believe. Obviously for the tour I wanted to give him more than just a wage. He still was a draw, you know. Having him back would sell tickets. Up until yesterday we – Wilko, Scott, Russell and myself – were working out a percentage of the concert profit for him.'

'I think we've enough to be going on with for now, Sean. One little thing though. Yesterday evening, when you were walking around during the jam, when Wilko was in the dressing-room by himself, did you see anyone? More to the point, did anyone see you?' Kennedy prepared to put away his note book and rise from the chair.

'Do I have an alibi?' Green laughed. 'Well, no, unfortunately not. I hardly want to get spotted by the fans, so over the years, I found ways of disappearing into the woodwork for those ten minutes every night.'

'And no one saw you that evening during the band break?'

'As I said,' Green replied, standing up, drawing the interview to a close, 'I have found a way of being there without anyone knowing it. It gives me the freedom to check out the sound in the house and how well the band is doing. However, in this instance, it also means I don't have an alibi.'

Thirteen

'So, what do we have?'

It was time to regroup in Kennedy's office and review the information they had amassed so far. Not a lot, Kennedy imagined. It was coming up to twenty-four hours since the murder and it wasn't that they hadn't made much progress, no Kennedy mused, it was more a case that they hadn't even left the starting blocks.

Kennedy's team sat in his rectangular office – Irvine, Coles, Allaway and Lundy. There were already a few photographs on the notice board, showing the body from various angles in the dressing-room at Dingwalls Dance Hall. The name "Wilko Robertson" was hand written underneath. Kennedy had also put up the publicity handout photograph of Circles. The space on the felt board, usually reserved for suspects, was as green and uncluttered as an Ulster pasture. For a few moments no one spoke. Finally, Irvine stood up, walked over to the tea area, helped himself to a fresh cup, and began the conversation.

'It would seem to me that, if the roles had been reversed and Sean Green had been found dead, our prime suspect would be Wilko Robertson.'

'True, true. Does this tell us anything?' Kennedy asked, he was all for looking at things upside down, but he wasn't sure Irvine had a direction with his thinking.

'Well, if our murderer was aware of this perhaps they thought it might have thrown some dust over their own tracks,' Irvine struggled on.

'What's with all that locked door stuff?' Coles threw into the conversation.

'Yes, indeed. What good could it possibly do to lock the door from the inside?' Kennedy mused.

'A smoke screen, perhaps?' Irvine offered.

'But,' Coles cut in, 'What advantage would that give the murderer?'

'I suppose the main advantage has to be that we are being encouraged to consider more how the murder was committed, rather than who may have committed it,' Kennedy replied. 'Oh, Lundy, do us a favour. Why don't you do the honours for the rest of us with the tea, you know how everybody likes it by now.'

Lundy looked like he was about to offer some protest but chose instead to sullenly go about his new duties.

'So you're suggesting we forget about how it was done and concentrate on who did it?' Irvine asked.

'Not entirely, no,' Kennedy began. 'Just don't get so lost in the method that we lose sight of everything else. OK, let's look at what we have. One possibility is that Kevin 'KP' Paul did it. He simply staged the locked door after breaking in and murdering Wilko. Now, I could be wrong, of course, but I don't feel that KP is our man. No more than a feeling at this stage and they've been wrong before. He's an okay guy, maybe even a good guy.'

'But are you saying that just because someone is a good guy he can't commit a murder?' Coles inquired.

They all considered this point for a time before Coles continued, 'What do we know about Wilko...? He was in a very successful group, sold lots of records, toured the world, sold out concerts, liked to drink, enjoyed the company of women, spent a lot of money, gambled a bit, did some drugs...'

'Where did it all go wrong?' Irvine said, part in jest, part in regret.

'Okay,' Kennedy interrupted. 'We need to find out about his missing years. We need to find out why he left the group and why he returned. We need to speak to his wife. At this stage he's just a dead, washed-up rock star. Even his partner Sean seems to have concluded his mourning. Let's find out from his solicitor exactly what shape his finances are in. Let's find out if he owed any money and, if so, how much and to whom. Let's find his mates and see what kind of a chap he was. Let's put some flesh on his bones. See if he owed someone a lot of money, either for gambling or for drugs – both can be dangerous to your health. Find Wilko's wife. All we know is that she went to her sister's house when she heard the news. We need to find this woman. Let's check in again and follow up all leads. Can I leave you two…' Kennedy looked at Lundy and Allaway, 'to track her down this evening?'

'But I've got a…' Lundy began, but thought better of it. 'Yes, that's fine.'

'You and I will see her first thing in the morning,' Kennedy continued, addressing Coles. 'I feel we're getting behind on this one already.'

Fourteen

The Queens bar and restaurant was packed to overflowing on that cold Friday evening. As late as September, the Queens, at it's busiest, was never packed because all the clientele would spill out onto the street where Primrose Hill Road cuts into Regent's Park Road. In the summer months the first floor restaurant opens out onto a balcony affording a wonderful view of Primrose Hill itself.

Kennedy and ann rea had spent many a moonlit-night on the very same balcony watching the world go by. Those were the best times for Kennedy. Until he found Primrose Hill, he never thought he would find anywhere in London that enjoyed a small-village type of street life. Equally, he never thought he would find someone as perfect for him as ann rea. Primrose Hill he could enjoy forever and it would ask for nothing in return. ann rea, on the other hand, was a different matter altogether. She hadn't disappeared from his life completely – sometimes Kennedy felt it would be better for him if she would – but nonetheless he'd lost her. It had all started off so well. He felt immediately, from the first sighting at Heathrow, that ann rea was his soul-mate for life. The minute he looked into her impish brown eyes he knew she was the one. This certainty proved to be his undoing, because it was this confidence that gave rise to ann rea's worries. It was his sureness that drove her away.

Funny how your strength sometimes works to your own disadvantage. Tonight, together again in the Queens, there was no friction between them at all. Had Kennedy already given up, he wondered? Had ann rea? It had always been more than sex for Kennedy. It had always been love. He looked at her now across the table, smiling, relaxed, comfortable, glass of white wine in her hand and no apparent problems. She was smiling that smile that could, and did, turn heads at every table in the Queens. She was dressed in black slacks, a white silk blouse, and a black Matador waist length jacket that Kennedy had never seen before. She was stunning, simply stunning. She could have done him a favour, Kennedy thought. She could have looked haggard, in ill-fitting clothes and maybe toned down the smile just a bit. It seemed that being single suited ann rea. Kennedy would have preferred not to admit this to himself but it was so blatantly true.

'You're looking great, Kennedy. The single life seems to agree with you,' ann rea remarked jovially, after they'd chosen their meal. Cumberland sausage and mash, without the onions and gravy for Kennedy, with onions and gravy for ann rea.

'Funny you should say that. You're no tramp yourself.'

She laughed, took a sip of wine and continued. 'Hey, Kennedy, what can I tell you? I'm happy. I'm so happy I didn't even read my horoscope this morning and I've been looking forward to this meal all day.'

'Ah, but there's something more,' Kennedy continued, as he topped up their glasses with a cheap, cheerful and crisp Bregerac.

'Well it's odd. But recently as I've been pottering around in my own doom, gloom and darkness I saw an interview Francis Ford Coppola did quite a time ago. They were talking about the badness in people and what it does to them and Coppola said "If, in life, you put yourself in harmony with things you will get much better results than if you go against them." So, that's what I've been trying to do. Put myself in harmony with things. I've been going against the grain for too long and it's been getting me nowhere fast. So, here's to harmony,' ann rea said, as she raised her glass.

'To harmony,' Kennedy toasted.

The conversation inevitably worked its way around to the murder of Wilko Robertson.

'Have you any ideas why Wilko left Circles in the first place?' Kennedy asked once they got into it.

'Oh, absolutely. He thought the band was finished, which they were. He didn't want to go down with them. But it's funny, when partnerships like that split up, you get to see who was responsible for what. And it would appear that Sean was the one in the driving seat. Sure, as lead singer, Wilko got all the glory and all the credit. But when Wilko left, he figured that the band would split, and from their ashes he could start his own career. But Sean merely replaced him and moved into another gear. From what I hear that's when the real money was made.'

'Yeah, Leslie Russell has given me a bit of a background on all the deals. But Wilko did okay out of all the deals as well though, didn't he?'

'Well, he didn't do great compared to Sean. However, I understand he didn't leave penniless. The truth is, if Wilko hadn't left, they'd probably still be just another band plodding around on that chicken-and-chips-in-a-basket circuit, hoping for a comeback along with another hundred or so refugee bands from the seventies. And the nicest thing we can say about Circles is that they wouldn't have been near the top of list of groups in line for a break.'

'Who'd have been the top of the list, Elvis?'

'Presley? He's never been out of favour to be honest. All his early stuff is so brilliant and didn't he just look so beautiful in the early days?'

'Well he certainly could sing, but no I meant the other one,' Kennedy replied, he found it difficult to refer to men as beautiful.

'The other one? Nah, no chance. He lost his attraction when the band left and he got to be just a wee bit too desperate if you ask me.'

'Not as desperate as Pauley Valentini though?' Kennedy said smiling at the memory.

'I don't know about that. Anyway, as it happened, Wilko went off into obscurity. I think he'd a few false starts and nothing really got off the ground for him.'

'How long was he out of the group?'

'Must be about six years,' ann rea guessed.

'Long time to go without an income. Could he have been rich enough?'

'Probably not, although I believe he made a few bob out of the Greatest Hits Package. You see, there's another thing. That was so successful, it moved the band into another league. Set them aside from all the rest. And the new singer, Wilko's replacement, was good.'

'I must admit, I was surprised at how a band who'd being going for so long could just change singers and carry on like nothing happened,' Kennedy asked, as he ordered another bottle of wine. 'Why did it work for them?'

'Well, you couldn't really see the join. Close your eyes, listen to the vocals, there's not much difference. Same voice, different face.'

'Why then did Wilko go back to Circles?' Kennedy pushed.

'I hear he needed the money. His attempt at a solo career had fallen flat on its face and he needed to do something fast. He wasn't going to get many more chances outside of Circles.'

'Okay here's another one for you. Why did Sean Green take Wilko back into the band?'

'That's a much more interesting question altogether. I wondered about that too. There doesn't seem to be an upside to it. He had it all going his own way. He controlled the band. They were on a financial high. Sean must have been smart enough to realise that Circles were never ever going to have a creative comeback. Maybe he's just a good guy and he was repaying an earlier debt to the singer who was now down on his luck. Maybe he's a control freak, the temptation of having Wilko back in as a humble wage earner in what was now Sean's band was just too great a chance to pass up. Maybe one of the other band members, or KP, or Leslie Russell campaigned to get him back in the band. But believe me Kennedy, that is the most interesting question in all of this. If you can find out the answer to that, I think you will be on your way. To where, I'm not sure,' ann rea added with a smile.

'Speaking of Leslie Russell…'

'Yeah?' ann rea replied.

'Remember when you and I first met him. I think it was about a couple of weeks after our first date. I was talking to him about the school teacher case?'

'The Cumberland Basin drowning. Yes?'

'Well do you remember after one of our joint dinners he rang you up and invited you out?'

'Yes?' ann rea replied. Kennedy was getting the suspicion that she knew where he was going with this.

'Well, did he by any chance…' Kennedy paused to find the words.

'Did he ring me up again and invite me out, now that you and I are no longer seeing each other?' ann rea cut to the quick.

'Well, yes actually.'

'Ah, Kennedy, you're so predictable.'

'And?'

'Well, he did and he didn't.'

'Interesting.'

'Russell has far too much class to be rejected again. So, he rang me up on the pretence of something or other and then got to the subject of you, then of you and I, in a round-about way. He asked how you were doing. He said he'd heard we were no longer stepping out. Asked me if I was seeing anyone else.'

'And?' Kennedy prodded hopefully.

'I told him I wasn't and I hadn't planned on starting again.'

'But that's absurd.' Kennedy was thrilled.

'How so?'

'Well, at some point you are going to meet someone else and it's going to happen. There's no point in trying to ignore that.'

'Why do all men feel that a woman is always waiting around for the right man to come along, Kennedy?'

'That's not what I meant and you know that.'

'I'm not so sure, Kennedy. In any case, I'm here to tell you that it's not true. If I'm destined to be by myself that's fine, I enjoy my own company. I'm now starting to enjoy my life. And here's the important bit Kennedy. A woman does not need to have a man in her life to be fulfilled and enjoy herself. I have a great life, a great job which I thoroughly enjoy,' ann rea paused, drained the remainder of her glass of wine and added an, 'Although…'

'Although?'

'You did have your uses.' ann rea smiled coyly as she watched the waiter refill her empty wine glass.

'Did?' Kennedy asked.

'Do,' ann rea said with a smile.

'Dessert?' the waiter inquired.

'No,' ann rea said. 'No, thank you. We're going to enjoy our wine for a bit, and then have dessert at his place…'

Twenty-five minutes later, in the warmth and comfort of Kennedy's bed, the detective and the journalist satisfied another hunger; repeatedly.

'You know, Christy,' ann rea began, just as both were about to drift into sleep, 'I'm not looking for anyone else. I've met the best there is. If it isn't going to work with you it isn't going to work with anyone. So don't ever worry about there being someone else.'

Kennedy didn't hear the end of her sweet whisperings; he was too busy sleeping happily in her arms.

Fifteen

At eight o'clock the following morning, Kennedy quietly crept out of bed, showered and, tip-toeing around his room, dressed. ann rea had quite a bit to drink the previous evening so he decided to let her sleep on. He watched her sleep. He could lie next to her for hours, watching her as she slept.

She could let herself out when she woke; she still had her own set of the keys to his house. When they split up, Kennedy had never thought of asking her to return the keys and she'd never offered them. He left a little note saying merely, "Talk to you later? Cheers, Christy." He kissed her on the forehead, ruffled her hair and quietly left his house.

Shortly thereafter, he was out enjoying the peace and tranquillity of Primrose Hill. At eight-thirty on a Saturday morning, the hill is nearly always deserted, except for the Magpies. Kennedy spotted three. "One for sorrow, two for joy, three for a girl…" Mmm, Kennedy thought, was that girl ann rea? What had she been saying to him late last night? He racked his brain but all he could remember was, "at this point in her life she had to…" something or another. Did that mean that perhaps later? He recalled their conversation about Wilko and he remembered, clearly, ann rea advising him that he should try and find out why Sean Green had brought Wilko Robertson back into the band.

They'd made love. My God! He thought. Was ann rea being very clever? Could the thing she'd missed the most, from being separated, be making love to him? Perhaps that was it. So, by sleeping with him last night she was, in a way, helping herself to deal with not having him around. Clever. Typical of ann rea, the detective thought fondly.

He'd reached the borders of Primrose Hill. The closer he got to North Bridge House, the more he thought of his current case and the less he thought of ann rea. Perhaps that was the trick; like a magnet, her power weakened the further he was away from her.

At his desk, he found what he'd hoped would be awaiting him, the current whereabouts of Susan Robertson. He figured it would be about an hour or so before it would be a socially acceptable time of the day to go visiting the widow. Time to settle down again and work his way gradually into the day. The thought-process, he believed, only worked effectively when it was not being pushed or forced into an unnatural overload.

He made notes to himself on whom he felt he needed to interview that day. For some reason, he couldn't figure out why he kept getting flashes of Sean Green's subservient wife, Colette. He reasoned that the flashes must come from the incessant chorus of "Colette Calls" which had been battering his head since the beginning of this case. He'd kept meaning to buy a Circles' CD. He was trying to remember some of the lyrics of "Colette Calls". He was sure he had got one of the verses right:

Pictures with words
In deep shades of Blue
I once loved a stranger
I'm told she was you.

Well, yes, pretty obscure. What on earth were they about? Were there any clues out there waiting for him in Circles' lyrics? He hoped not. When Sean Green wrote *I once loved a stranger/I'm told she was you*, had he just thrown in the *you* in to rhyme with *blue*? And who was the *you*? A few questions there for KP. He'd been around when the lyrics were being written; perhaps he would have a clue what they were all about. And beside, those lyrics were written nearly thirty years ago. What could they possibly have to do with this particular murder?

Kennedy found himself, as he brewed up the first cup of tea of the morning, thinking about KP. Now there was a character. Could he possibly have murdered Wilko and then kicked the door in just to give the pretence that when he arrived at the dressing-room, the deed already done?

The telephone rang on his desk. It had been ringing for some time, he realized. He'd been so lost in his thoughts it took him some time to tune into the high tech purring. God, how he hated all this modern equipment.

'Hi, Kennedy here.'

'Oh, hello yourself, Christy. It's Rose here, Rose Butler.' She sounded almost apologetic.

'Hi, Rose. Good to hear from you. How are you doing?'

The detective heard a sigh on the other end of the phone.

'Oh, not too bad. Sorry. Listen, I'm sorry to be bothering you on a Saturday morning, but there's something I need to talk to you about,' Staff Nurse Rose Butler continued in her soft County Kildare tones. 'I mean, it's probably nothing but I need to get it off my chest.'

She and DS James Irvine had dated for quite some time but it hadn't worked out. Kennedy had been a bit sad about that, he'd felt they were well suited.

'Fine. As I'm passing the hospital this afternoon, do you want me to drop in for a chat?'

'Ah. No. I'm not ringing you from the hospital. I'd prefer to meet with you somewhere outside.'

'Is this urgent, Rose?'

'Well, I don't know, It might be.'

Kennedy began sensing that it was.

'Look I'm off to interview somebody in about twenty minutes. So, why don't we meet up at, say, noon in Camden Town?'

'Great. That sounds fine,' the nurse answered. Kennedy was sure he could hear the relief in her voice.

'Cafe Delancey or the Golden Grill?'

'Oh, the Golden Grill every time Christy and we won't need a reservation. See you there at twelve. Cheers.'

'Cheers,' Kennedy agreed and wondered what could be upsetting Rose so. If he knew her just even a little, then he knew she wouldn't be bothering him about nothing.

Sixteen

WPC Anne Coles and DI Christy Kennedy left the bustle of Camden Town behind them as Coles cut across the High Street in an unmarked Ford Sierra. They turned into College Street, into Pancras Road and came to a stop in front of the once elegant terrace of Goldington Cresent. The middle house was the home of Wilko Robertson and his wife, Susan. Susan had spent the night at her sister's in Wimbledon, but decided she'd prefer to be interviewed by the police in her own home.

It was the sister, Tracey, who answered the door. She showed them into the front room where they found a surprisingly sprightly Susan waiting for them. The widow had done herself up for the police visit. While she wasn't exactly plump, her dark trouser-suit was at least a couple of sizes too small. Her hair was tied back into a thick, unglamorous ponytail. She rose from her sofa to meet them.

Tracey offered them tea or coffee. Coles went for coffee and Kennedy opted for a cup of tea. In the sister's absence, the police offered Susan their condolences for her loss. Coles could see Kennedy was trying to ascertain how able for questioning the widow was. She seemed, on the surface, to be remarkably together.

Kennedy paced the room, taking in the details. The good room, Coles guessed, used for special occasions. It looked like a show room in a department store catalogue. Blue curtains, three piece suite and large rug just in front of the fireplace. A teak coffee table and wall unit, but no television or stereo. Most unusual for a musician's house, the WPC thought.

'Susan, are you and your sister close?' Kennedy asked, as he sat.

'Well, yes. We are really,' Susan answered, as if considering this for the first time. 'Wilko was always on tour somewhere and so, over the years, I'd become a bit of a rock widow. When Tracey moved to London she would come stay with me when he was away. She's always lived in South London. I always thought she should just move in with us. We've always had lots of room. Wilko was fine with it but Tracey would say she'd be too embarrassed to bring someone back to her sister's house. But we *are* close and I cannot remember a time in my life when we weren't. We've always been close.'

Susan stopped talking and looked at Kennedy, staring directly into his green eyes. Coles thought she appeared to be assessing her senior before imparting some information.

'This may sound weird to you, I hope it doesn't. But having Tracey…let's just say I'll get over losing Wilko more quickly because Tracey is around. Are you married?'

'No,' Kennedy answered.

'Yes, well, that's the thing you see. When you're a wee girl you dream of getting married and living happily ever after. I know everyone in the world today knows that's not reality. But I didn't. I thought Wilko was the reason I'd been born and when I met him my life was complete. To cut a very long story short, it wasn't, we weren't. Although we didn't split-up, we drifted apart, physically and spiritually. I found other things to filling up my life again. To compensate, you know? The reason I'm telling you all of this is because I realise I'm not exactly playing the part of a grieving widow and I just wanted you all to know why.'

'We all grieve in our own way,' Kennedy replied with a gentle smile.

'Refreshments!' Tracey called as she entered the room, pushing a tea-trolley in front of her. The WPC took the time to examine the widow's sister, and she was sure Kennedy was doing the same. Tracey wore no make up, had short, cropped hair and quite a sharp-featured face. She wore loose-fitting jeans and a blue k.d. lang sweat shirt. She was at least five years younger than her sister.

'Could we talk a bit about why Wilko left Circles?' Kennedy started once they'd started into the tea.

'Aye, not exactly the master of perfect timing, was our Wilko.' Susan smiled at her sister and they both had a laugh. 'He felt it was all over to be honest. He thought the band was finished. He'd all these people telling him he was the star and Circles needed him more that he needed them and that if he wasn't careful his career would go down the drain with the band. These people convinced him that he should split and go solo, before it was too late. He listened to them, he went solo and, as they say, the rest is history.'

'Who are these people?' Coles asked.

'Oh, people Sean would have kept Circles away from, but who saw a meal ticket with Wilko. There was a tour manager, he came in after KP left…'

'Simon…' her sister cut in.

'Aye, that's him. Simple Simon Peddington. He was the worst thing that ever happened to the band. He couldn't manage a piss up in a brewery. Anyway, Sean fired him for fiddling the float or something. He'd become a great drinking buddy of Wilko's and after he was fired he just kept on at Wilko about going solo, until eventually Wilko agreed. He hooked Wilko up with a solicitor, who has since done time for running off with some other client's money. Get the picture?'

Both Kennedy and Coles nodded.

'What was the name of that particular solicitor?' Kennedy inquired.

'Oh, that's an easy one, I'll never forget his name. Slime-bag. Richard "call me Richie" Slatterly.'

'So, nothing happened with the solo career then?' Coles asked.

'Oh, at first it was brilliant,' Susan replied. 'He was keen as mustard. He'd lots of energy for it. He even put a bit of energy back into our marriage. I suppose in a way, with him and Sean splitting up, it was all very traumatic for Wilkensen. They'd been together longer than Wilko and I had and with all the touring and studio work and rehearsals, they'd certainly spent a lot more time together. So with Wilko leaving Circles, and breaking away from Sean Green, he needed me. But then the breaks didn't come his way. That was the thing about Sean Green. He knew how to put together a good team of people and took his time to get it right. You would have thought that Wilko would have learnt something being around him all those years. But, no…'

'But he was the lead singer of a successful group, wouldn't he automatically have an audience?' Coles cut in.

'Well, you have to remember that Circles were on their last legs. It was all but over. Don't forget, this was before Sean Green pulled it all around. Some even said Wilko had been holding him back. When Wilko started to make his record he was making music by committee. The manager wanted one thing, the producer wanted something else. Then the A & R men would show up and they'd want something else. He'd come back here each night and he'd be at his wit's end. "Make it longer; shorter; more verses; less verses; get to the hook quicker; get to the hook later; make it faster; make it slower; get a guitar to do what the saxophone is doing; have a saxophone do what the guitar is doing." You know, things like that and on and on and on and I'd have to listen to it all at three o'clock in the morning. And that was just the A & R people. Then the next night it would be the radio promotion people, and they'd have a totally different set of opinions to express and just as forcefully, mind you. Then the press people, then the sales manager, then the marketing guy…'

'But you said Wilko didn't have any hits,' Coles said, as she considered how comfortably Susan talked about all of this.

'Yea, if it's a hit, it's because of the record company's executive input. If it flops, it's because the artist buggered it up. After it had all gone pear-shaped the record company didn't even want to put out the record.' Susan stopped speaking and broke into a smile, directed mostly at her sister. 'You can tell how I'm a rock wid…'

Mrs. Robertson stopped mid-sentence.

'God I've just realised, I've calling myself a rock widow all these years and now I really am!'

Coles thought that Susan was going to lose it and the interview would be over. But she smiled at her sister.

'At least you won't turn out like Yoko,' Tracey said.

'What, with all the fans hating her?' Coles felt compelled to ask.

'No, stinking rich,' Tracey laughed. 'With all that money who gives a shit if they hate you or not?'

'Colette, now she'll be the Yoko,' Susan added.

'Was Wilko well off?' Kennedy's turn for a question.

'Well, he once had a lot of money. I know that. But he's also spent a lot of it. To be honest, I couldn't tell you exactly how we stand financially. At the time he left Circles I know we were very flush. We had some money stashed away. Sean gave Wilko a very generous golden handshake when he left the group. He also changed the publishing deal around, I don't really know how. Wilko tried to explain it to me, but I couldn't get a grasp of it. I just know he got another cheque and was grinning from ear to ear for at least a week. In a way I felt sorry for Sean around that time. You know, Wilko had left the group and it was looking like Sean's career was over, but there he was making sure Wilko got his share. Wilko was thinking that Circles were history, they were finished, they were nothing without him. He was grabbing the money out of Sean's hands as fast as he could.'

'Was Wilko bitter when Sean took Circles on to greater success?' Kennedy again.

'I don't know if bitter would be the correct word. More hurt, you know? His career was being shot down in very expensive flames and Sean comes out smelling of roses. I think for Wilko it was more, "How can he do this so easily without me?" He began to feel bad about himself, I think. The record company had turned him down. He even tried to buy back the unreleased album. They wouldn't sell it to him. Then, believe it or not, his accountant Slatterly rings Wilko up and advises him that he had been able to buy the album back.' The wife's disbelief was still evident in her voice, all these years later.

'What? He bought it back for Wilko?' Coles asked.

'No. The bastard had only gone and bought it back for himself and then he'd the cheek to sell it to Wilko at a profit. Wilko bought it from Slatterly, spent some more money on it and his manager, Peddington, still couldn't get a deal for him. Throughout all of this Wilko was still playing the rock star-bit, you know, limos everywhere, dining at the Ivy every week, and generally wasting a lot of money. He was also spending quite a bit on the horses at this time.'

'A lot?' Kennedy asked.

'I really don't know,' Susan replied. 'I mean, look. Wilko and me, we had our differences and we lost whatever it is you are meant to have, years ago. Actually, more like a lifetime ago. But he did provide for me. A bit of the Scottish work ethic, you know. He was the man of the house; the breadwinner and he *always* provided. No matter what shit he was going through financially, emotionally, romantically, or chemically, it didn't matter, he always gave me the housekeeping money. He did have his good points too, you know.'

'Aye,' Tracey agreed.

'You know, I feel really sad now…' Susan continued.

'We understand,' Kennedy said softly.

'No, no, not like that,' Susan began. 'I'm sad that I don't feel like grieving. It's like I've already been through this, ages ago. I've spent so many nights grieving. He's been gone from my life for a long, long time. If Tracey hadn't been around, goodness, I don't know what I would have done. But the thing is, I can't cry over him. I just can't cry. It might have been different if we had any children. I might feel differently then, you know, knowing that they'd lost their dad. But it's weird. It's like being released from a long sentence. I suppose I shouldn't have told you that, I suppose it could be construed as a reason to murder him.'

'But it's okay, pet, you couldn't have. Remember you were with me Thursday night while they played Dingwalls,' Tracey reminded her sister.

'Did Wilko talk to you about rejoining Circles?' Kennedy asked, finishing off his cup of tea.

'Yes, he did actually. Quite a bit.'

'Why did he want to return, after all that had happened?'

'Well, Sean had these plans to put out a new album, to tour. The seventies were becoming fashionable again, and Sean wanted to keep Circles on top of it. He'd done very well without Wilko but I still think he wanted another crack at America and I think he felt the original band would be more viable than one with a replacement singer. He'd mentioned the idea to Wilko ages ago and Wilko used the opportunity to start up a dialogue with Sean again. They had been good mates and Wilko had met only bastards since going solo. Added to which, Sean was still Wilko's publisher, and Wilko wanted to write songs again and look for new songs for himself. So, they hung out again for a time. It was like the old days, the three of them, Sean, Wilko and KP. They were meeting up more and more and Wilko was becoming happier again.

'Sean promised Wilko he'd help him sort out his problems with the managers and lawyers, and convinced Wilko that the Circles revival wasn't going to be a long-term thing. He just wanted to have a profile for the band so that the catalogue would sell. He felt the more current they were the easier it would be. He also said there would be lots of time for Wilko's solo career and that he would help Wilko make a record after they'd done the Circles album. He even told Wilko that, if he wanted, he would set the whole thing up for him. And that's one thing about Sean; he'd a great organiser. He thinks about absolutely everything. Wilko was still existing from the money he received for the Circles stuff, so he thought if the deal was okay there couldn't possibly be a down side.'

'Was the deal okay?' Coles ventured.

'I believe they were still working on it,' was the widow's reply.

Minutes later Kennedy and Coles were in their unmarked car on the way back to Camden Town.

'So, I suppose we've added another name to our list of suspects?' Coles guessed, as she negotiated the heavy traffic on Delancey Street.

'More like three, I'd say,' Kennedy mused. 'Who were *you* thinking of?'

'Robert Clarke, Wilko's replacement. He stood to lose a lot by Wilko rejoining the band. He was my choice. So are you also considering Wilko's manager, Simple Simon?'

'Yep.'

'And…' Coles faltered. 'Not Susan, you don't think…'

'No, but perhaps her sister.'

'But they were together on the night of the murder.'

'So *she* says. And she offered the information up very quickly. But you can see she's very protective of her sister. She'd given up her entire life for her. Perhaps she felt that it was time Susan escaped from Wilko. Maybe she'd found something of her own and wanted to move on. I don't know, there's something there, I'm just not sure what. Long shots, all of them, I know, but they are the only shots we have at this stage.' Kennedy noticed they were just about to pass Arlington Road.

'Ah, good,' he said. 'Just drop me on the corner here, I've got to see a nurse.'

Seventeen

The Golden Grill was very quiet. Rose Butler had not yet arrived, so Kennedy ordered a cup of tea from Vange, the waiter, and intended to review his interview with Susan Robertson and her sister Tracey. But he found himself thinking about Rose.

Kennedy liked Rose. She'd long black hair, which she wore up in some contraption that looked like a large muffin, while on-duty at St. Pancras. Off-duty was another matter entirely. James Irvine, who had dated Rose for a few months, described her as, "A woman who believes in true love, Christian values, a little cannabis and a lot of sex."

As Vange brought the tea Rose Butler entered the cafe. She nervously looked around the small cafe, spied Kennedy in his usual corner up by the counter, and made her way to his table.

'Coffee, large and black,' Rose whispered.

'Goodness Rose,' Kennedy said. 'You're trembling. What on earth's the matter?'

Rose didn't reply. Kennedy noticed tears starting to form in her clear blue eyes. She was about to speak, when Vange returned with the coffee. Rose immediately wrapped her hands around the mug for the comfort from the heat.

'God, Christy,' Rose whispered, 'I don't know where to start.'

Kennedy reached across the table and patted her arm, offering her comfort without the words.

'Oh, Christy, we've had a non-accidental death on the wards...Ranjesus was having an affair...oh God, poor Sinead...it shouldn't have gone this far...everyone knew he was cheating...but none of us ever dreamt this...that prize "A" shit...and now he's going to get away with it' Rose spluttered in free-flow.

Kennedy knew how close she was to tears and felt a strong whiskey would have been better for her than a cup of coffee. He freed his hand and tore open three sachets of sugar, which he poured into her coffee.

'Here,' he began gently, 'Drink this down, it will make you feel better.'

'Feel better, Christy. It's worse I want to feel. This shouldn't be allowed to happen to these young Irish nurses. Shouldn't be allowed to happen to any nurse for that matter. But all these Doctors, they all think they're god's gift to women, and they're attracted to the Irish ones like bees to the Honey. The only doctors they're safe from these days are the gay ones. Thankfully their numbers are growing.'

OK, non-accidental death, smarmy Doctors, Irish girls. They were getting somewhere slowly, Kennedy thought.

'So, Sinead and Dr Ranjesus, they were operating on someone and something happened?'

'No.' A brief flicker of a smile quickly brushed Rose's ghost white cheeks. 'Sorry. He's Dr Ranjee Shareef. We call him Ranjesus because he thinks he's god gift. No, that wasn't what happened. God forgive me, but I wish it were as you describe it. No, it's Sinead, Sinead Sullivan. She's dead. God, Christy she's really dead and it's Shareef's fault.'

'He killed her, Rose?'

'I believe he did. But we'll never be able to prove it, he's going to get away with it, he's going to get off scot-free and the slimy sod planned it all, I think. Devious isn't the word for him.

If he gets away with it…I'll swing for him, Christy. I swear I'll swing for him.' Rose had her fists clenched on the table.

'Let's see if we can get Vange to do you one of his special Irish coffees, for medicinal purposes, and you can tell me the complete story right from the beginning,' Kennedy offered and made his way over to the service counter.

'Ah, I thought there was meant to be some coffee in an Irish coffee,' Rose said a minute later, following her first generous gulp. 'Sure he's barely coloured the whiskey with the coffee.'

'Irvine swears by them.' The words were out of Kennedy's lips before he 'd realised, and regretted, what he'd said. Rose and James Irvine's parting had not been an easy one and now probably wasn't the best time to be reminding her about it.

'Aye, well, he should know,' she said, taking another sip. 'So, Christy. Sinead Sullivan came over here from Youghal in County Cork about four years ago. She was a great student nurse. The patients loved her, she was always very caring and compassionate with them. The Irish nurses always seem to get on better with the patients. I don't know what it is, maybe it's just they miss their families so much that they pour their love out to the patients.

'It isn't easy for them, Christy. For a lot of them it's usually their first time away from home and the money isn't great, but they're dedicated. So, Sinead comes over here. She was getting on great. After four years she qualified as a staff nurse and met Dr. Ranjee Shareef. You see Christy, one problem with these young girls is that they're totally in awe of the Doctors. The young nurses think the Doctors are incapable of human weakness. But I can tell you these young girls were in nothing but danger in the hands of this shit. He'd a reputation for the young nurses. And sure he's married with two children and lives down on Ulster Terrace, you know the big white Nash houses over looking Regent's Park. Did that ever stop him? Did it feck.'

The staff nurse sighed and Kennedy considered he and all of mankind had been well and truly told off.

'Sinead and myself became quite close. I warned her off Ranjesus but she wouldn't listen and after a few expensive dinners he charmed her into bed. A suite in the White House hotel, if you don't mind. He kept saying, she told me, that she was his "First Lady." Poor Sinead was in love with him. She'd never been with another man. He'd let her down all the time; call off dates at the last moment. She was the "other woman" and she probably received enough flowers to redo the rose gardens in Regents Park. He was always claiming he was going to leave his wife and children for her. They just had to pick the right moment, "It wasn't fair that the children, who are innocent in all of this, should suffer." That old chestnut. But we all believe it, Christy,' Rose confessed, perhaps giving away more than she had planned. She took another swig at her 80% proof coffee.

'Anyway, Sinead felt Ranjee was cooling down their relationship. This would have been around springtime and she was beside herself with anxiety. Sinead only saw him when that old lust bug bit. He would come calling and she'd always have him back. When I spoke with her about it once in September, she had a bit of a twinkle in her eye. It was all sorted, she said. I was afraid she was pregnant. I asked her about it but she'd just smile and wouldn't say one way or another. But I knew she was and I knew her game. Catch the seed, catch the man. Old as the hills. She never came right out and admitted it, but if a nurse can't tell, who can? She said she was being looked after; I assumed she meant your man, you know, Ranjee. He was a paediatrician after all. And if he did what I think he did he's a disgrace to the name. I'm not kidding, hanging's too good for him. He's in cahoots with the devil.'

The whiskey had done the trick, and Kennedy was wondering exactly what this doctor could have done. The detective leaned in closer over the table.

'Yesterday morning, while working on the antenatal ward, Sinead Sullivan collapsed. She was bleeding profusely and died before they had a chance to operate on her.'

'God, Rose. I'm sorry,' were the only words of comfort Kennedy could find.

'I've been thinking about this a lot and I think she died due to a massive haemorrhage, which could have been the result of an undetected Placenta Praevia,' Rose continued. 'Say someone becomes pregnant. The first thing they do is go to their General Practitioner. The GP will then refer them to us, to a hospital. We will, amongst other things, give her an ultrasound scan to ascertain the condition of the baby. We can see, in advance, any possible complications and treat them accordingly. The Ultrasound scan would show up a Placenta Praevia.'

Kennedy shook his head in confusion.

'No, it's simple Christy. It comes from the Latin root, "To come before". That's all it means. The baby comes too soon. If Ranjesus was looking after Sinead and he was scanning her he would have seen, at about twenty weeks into her pregnancy, that she was suffering from this. Now normally, if this condition was detected, we would advise the mother of the possibility of a massive haemorrhage. We would have admitted her to hospital early and, if there was no massive bleeding, maintain the pregnancy until about thirty-seven week's gestation. Then the baby could be delivered by Caesarean Section. Still with me?'

'Just about, Rose.'

'I'm saying that Ranjesus noticed Placenta Praevia when he scanned her, and chose not to treat it, knowing that eventually Sinead would suffer a massive haemorrhage and mother and child would both die. He got rid of two problems at once and no one was any the wiser,' Rose sighed.

'Hang on here a minute Rose, are we not putting two and two together and getting seven?' Kennedy started. 'What brings on Placenta Praa…'

'Praevia. Placenta Praevia, Christy.'

'Yes, what brings on Placenta Praevia? Could it be brought on medically? How would he have known she was going to be suffering from it?'

'OK, one at a time. The clinical situations associated with Placenta Praevia include increasing maternal age.'

'But Sinead was very young, you said,' Kennedy cut in.

'Yes, Christy, twenty-two. I'm giving you the full list,' Rose chastised.

'Sorry,' Kennedy said and meant it.

'Increasing parity, again probably not relevant. Previous abortions. Impossible, I'd have known about it. Caesarian sections or any other uterine incisions wouldn't apply. Anemia, perhaps a possibility. Closely spaced pregnancies also ruled out. Tumours distorting the contours of the uterus, a possibility. And finally Uterine infections, again a possibility and could have been induced by a knowledgeable doctor. That, by the way, answers your second question.' Rose drained the remainder of her Irish coffee before continuing. 'Unless he induced it, he wouldn't have known about it. I just think that when he was monitoring Sinead, he became aware of her condition and took full advantage of it. He saw a way out of all his troubles by merely doing nothing to help her.'

'A sin of omission,' Kennedy said.

'Sorry?'

'A sin of omission. That's what our American friends call it when a death occurs due to someone failing to help the victim,' Kennedy replied.

'Can you get him for it, Christy?'

'Well, we have to prove it first. That's the hard part. But let's take it one step at a time. There'll have to be an autopsy, I'll make sure Dr Taylor performs it and not any of Ranjesus's cronies and then I'll interview Dr Shareef. In the meantime, if you could draw me up a list of Sinead's friends; all of them. She must have confided in someone about her affair and the pregnancy.'

'Okay,' Rose replied.

'I'm sorry about all of this, Rose. I really am,' Kennedy offered. 'Is there anyone…?'

'No, no. I'll be fine, Christy. I feel better now that you're looking into it. I'll be okay, truly,' Rose answered as she got up to leave.

Kennedy wished he could believe her. He'd never seen her so utterly defeated before. He resolved to put his all into helping prove, or disprove, Rose's theory. Rose Butler didn't deserve to carry the pain of Sinead Sullivan's death on her shoulders alone.

Eighteen

As Kennedy walked along Parkway towards North Bridge House, he reflected on how different a place the district was on the weekends. Parkway was the link between the pastoral and peaceful Regents Park and the vibrant Camden Town with its colourful shops and bizarre emporia. Even Dickens would have had trouble coming up with a cast of characters like the citizens of Camden Town. He thought of KP. Now would be as good a time as any for a chat with another of Camden's colourful characters.

Kennedy added an inch to his step, leaving behind the dark clouds of Parkway. On entering North Bridge House the Detective rang Dr Taylor. He advised his friend about the Rose Butler conversation. Meeting with Rose had left Kennedy a bit morose. He was usually able to not get drawn into his cases personally. However, when a friend of his was so upset, he tended to ignore his rules of self-protection. Taylor confirmed that he would get on it immediately and they would compare notes towards the end of the day. Kennedy was particularly interested in any additional information Taylor could come up with on Dr Ranjee Shareef.

'It's a street vibe man. I'm on the street.' Kennedy tracked down the Circles' Tour Manager on his mobile phone. 'I'm in the market, it's truly wondrous, man. All the people, all the colours, all the wares…'

'Good. Look, I'd like to have another chat. Would that be convenient?' Kennedy inquired.

'Cool, totally cool. Why don't we meet in the market, at the Stables just by the main entrance. I can see you there in about fifteen minutes?'

'Perfect. See you then,' Kennedy confirmed and set the phone back in its rest. No sooner had he done so, than it rang again.

'Hello, Kennedy here.'

'Hello to you, too. ann rea here.'

'Hi,' Kennedy replied.

'You left quietly and quickly this morning.'

'Well, you looked so peaceful I didn't want to disturb you.'

'I suppose it would've depended on what kind of disturbing you did,' ann rea replied coyly.

'Well, maybe I was a tad hasty,' he admitted.

'That's better. I was beginning to think you regretted…'

'Look, ann, about last night,' he cut in, only to be cut short himself.

'Christy why don't we meet later, I don't like talking about this on the phone. Have you anything planned for this evening?'

'No.'

'Well?'

'Sorry, yes, yes, of course. Brilliant, more like,' Kennedy struggled for words.

'You get the food, I'll bring the wine and…possibly the dessert. See you eight-ish?'

'Mmm, yes, of course,' Kennedy replied, and before he'd a chance to wish her goodbye the phone went dead.

Here was the love of his life that he'd lost, *thought* he'd lost, appearing to come back into his life. Had he missed something? It was a bit like someone had skipped past a couple of chapters in a book. Last night was one thing. Pleasant evening, good food, some wine and then some more wine and one thing lead to another and they'd ended up in bed; totally against the form. What was a poor Ulster boy to make of all of this?

The coldness of November did little to lessen the weekend crowds in Camden Market. KP was standing, at the agreed meeting point, hopping from foot to foot and blowing into his cupped hands. His clothes seemed altogether too light for a temperature fast approaching zero.

'God bless you, man,' KP offered as he recognised the approaching detective, 'Bit of a brass monkey vibe.'

'Yeah, you're not kidding,' Kennedy replied, eyeballing KP's black oriental outfit, as flimsy as a pair of pyjamas.

'I know exactly what you're thinking. It's just that I still have to do some shopping for winter-wear. I keep thinking that I won't need it if I'm going to go back to the States. The only problem is that I've been having the same thought for the past five years, yet I'm still here.'

'Are you planning to return to America then? Kennedy inquired, steering KP in the direction of a tea and hot-dog stall.

'Everyone in the music business who has ever been to America is always fixing to go back. It's a wonderful place. It's just well, man I don't think I could ever adopt that phoney Brit accent all who move there seem to acquire.' KP walked on the balls of his feet so it always appeared that he was creeping up on some unsuspecting person. He was obviously a popular market character and was continuously nodding to people, shouting to others and, at the same time, working his charm on the females. All these ladies, Kennedy noted, were beautiful new-age hippies, all in their early twenties and all enticed by KP.

Kennedy ordered a couple of teas and a veggie burger each. Generous dabs of sauce applied, they made their way across the market in the direction of the Roundhouse.

'Why do you think Wilko returned to Circles?' Kennedy inquired directly.

'A difficult question, man,' KP replied and paused for a swig of the steaming hot tea. 'Very difficult indeed. Way up there. In fact, I'm still doing a bit of a Marlowe vibe on that one myself. From Wilko's perspective, it's an easy call. His career was growing like a cow's tail. With Sean, well that's another matter altogether. He *claims* it was because he wanted the band to have another go in America and felt he'd have a better chance with Wilko. But at the same time the band was doing perfectly well with Robert Clarke, Wilko's replacement.'

'Yeah,' Kennedy acknowledged the name and then thought for a few seconds. 'Could he have just brought him back for sentimental reasons?'

'A bit of the old hippie vibe, you mean?'

'Possibly,' Kennedy said.

'Nah. There was something in it for Sean. I just can't really figure out what it was.'

'You say it's easier to see why Wilko would have wanted to be back in the band. But is that true? Wouldn't it have been humiliating for him to come back like that, with his tail between his legs?' Kennedy was now stabbing around in the dark.

'Well, in Wilko's eyes he would have been taking a step back up. The band he was rejoining was a lot bigger than the one he left. He was probably, in all honestly, missing the smell of the greasepaint and the roar of the crowd. Whichever way Sean and Leslie Russell worked it out, Wilko seemed comfortable with it. I imagine Russell must have been working miracles in the background.'

By this point they'd reached the Roundhouse. KP looked up at the venue with awe in his eyes. He led Kennedy up the couple of dozen steps to the front door.

'Great venue, absolutely a great venue. Love it to death. Loads of history in this venue. Paul McCartney used to come down here every weekend to the Implosion gigs and have the DJs play some of the Fabs' works-in-progress. Most of the audience was too stoned to realise how privileged they were.

Remember when the Beatles did that gig on the roof top of the Apple building in Baker street?' KP asked, as they continued their climb.

'Yeah, I'd love to have been there for that one. Mind you, knowing my luck, I'd probably have been the poor unfortunate copper who had to tell them to stop making the music,' Kennedy replied.

'Well,' KP began. 'McCartney had wanted them to do that particular show at the Roundhouse. The original idea was for the Beatles to rehearse an album's worth of new material and then come here to the Roundhouse and play what would have been their comeback concert. I saw the Doors in here. Jim Morrison, now there was a great performer. I saw The Undertones do one of the all-time great concerts in there. Otis Reading played on the Roundhouse stage as well. Pink Floyd, Hendrix. This is where Circles should have been playing. Much more appropriate than Dingwalls. I mean Dingwalls Dancehall is a nice venue but we should have played here, we were *the* Camden band. Come on through,' KP said, as he nodded to the security man on the door.

'Kevin, my old son how's it's hanging?' the uniformed Londoner inquired, in a gruff voice as tough as his face.

'Still on the left, Smiley, still a left vibe, man,' KP replied, 'Mind if we use the wee room for a brew up?"

'Please feel free, old chap. There's no one around for a couple of hours or so.'

'Great, man. Great vibe. This is a friend of mine, Christy. He's from the old sod as well. Christy, this is Smiley Bolger. Born and bred in this parish, has worked around Camden Market all his life.'

The detective and the security man smiled at each other and KP led Kennedy through to the cold and darkened venue.

There is something strangely serene about a venue awaiting audience and performers, Kennedy thought as he pulled his collar up. Kennedy felt he was intruding on hallowed ground as they walked through the auditorium. The raked seats and stage had been created and built entirely inside the shell of the one hundred and fifty year old building.

The structure was designed and built by Robert Dockray for the London North West Railway Company in1847 for a few bob over sixty grand. The building was constructed to house 23 proud engines and their tenders on a thirty-six foot turntable, enclosed inside its 160-foot circular walls. The Roundhouse continued as an engine shed until 1869, when it was leased to WS Gilbney and Sons as a Whiskey store. The Roundhouse closed in 1919 and reopened in 1964 as a concert venue.

KP guided Kennedy through the back exit, and into the cold air outside. It wasn't much warmer inside. They went down several steps and back into the Roundhouse by a small black door, which KP unlocked, using a key of his own. Inside the door KP fiddled around in the dark for a time until he located the 'house' torch.

After a few seconds in the dark Kennedy had lost all sense of direction. KP moved this way and that, picking his well-known route through the catacomb. He explained to Kennedy that the spaced created by the twenty-four bays had been used to store coke for the hungry tenders waiting thirteen feet above. Apparently they were in the building's undercroft.

Kennedy guessed they must have re-crossed the entire width of the venue. They reached another underground doorway cut through a thick, brick wall. KP unlocked the cast-iron door, solid and secure. Incredibly, this led to another brickwork corridor. Three feet further along there was a similar door, which KP also unlocked. KP flicked a light switch and revealed a small room. All surfaces, floor, walls and ceiling were tiled in matching white tiles.

'Come in and shut the door, man,' KP advised his companion. 'Keep the heat in.'

'What on earth is this place?' Kennedy replied, obeying the order.

'No one really knows. It's a space that doesn't exist. It doesn't show up on any of the plans. No one knows it's here apart from Smiley, a few mates, and myself. It's somewhere to escape to, bit of a home away from home.'

The room was furnished with two wine-coloured armchairs, a small coffee table and three beanbags. KP had already turned on the kettle and was washing out a couple of cups in a basin of water in the corner.

'No sound system?' Kennedy inquired, surprised.

'No way, man. We never wanted to risk being found out. We just use it for playing cards, chatting. You know, a Speakeasy type of vibe,' KP answered.

'Cards, you say?' Kennedy started. 'Tell me, did Wilko ever play cards down here?'

'Yeah, you bet, man. Whenever he wanted to escape the women.'

'Any women in particular?'

'Yeah, the Mc Sisters. The wife and her sister,' KP replied.

'Oh,' Kennedy said, unable to hide his disappointment.

'"Oh," he says,' KP replied, with a little devilment creeping across his well-lined face.

'Why?' asked. 'What do you know?'

'Can I tell you something?' KP began.

'Of course.'

'Our friend Wilko was doing the business – you know, the wild thing? With *both* the sisters of mercy.'

'What?'

'Well, actually I'm not sure he was doing it as much with his wife any more but he told me he just couldn't keep away from Tracey.'

'I'll be…this changes everything,' Kennedy looked at KP. 'How come you didn't tell me this before?'

'The thing was, it kinda seemed disrespectful to the deceased. But Sean and I were talking and we felt you should probably know.'

'Interesting, very interesting,' Kennedy said, recalling something that had been said earlier.

'What?' KP arched his eyebrows up until they nearly reached the brim of his vibrant blue skullcap.

'Oh nothing,' Kennedy replied. 'Now, where are we with this much talked about brew-up.'

Half an hour later, as they made their way back through the undercroft and up to the auditorium, Kennedy considered the atmosphere inside this aging brick shell. In three hours time it would be packed with an audience keen for entertainment and musicians eager to perform. Even in the autumn coldness, the air of anticipation was palpable. For KP it must really *have* been home away from home, confirmed when KP stopped at the main door and bade his farewell to Kennedy.

'I think I'll hang around here for a while, see you later perhaps. God bless you, man. Fare-thee-well.'

Nineteen

Kennedy raced back to North Bridge House. Upon entering his office he went straight to his notice board and marked up a few cards that he replaced on his green felt "Guinness is Good For You" notice board. His list of suspects now read: Susan Robertson (nee McGee), Tracey McGee, Richie Slattery (Wilko's Lawyer), Simon Peddington (Wilko's manager), Robert Clarke (Wilko's replacement in Circles), James MacDonald (Circles' Music Publisher). Was wife Susan jealous of her sister? Wilko said he couldn't keep away from her. What was all that about? As he sat on the edge of his desk Kennedy considered Tracey McGee.

She was plain and seemed to go out of her way to prove the point. Was that all a ruse for her sister? Did her sister know that she was cheating with Wilko? Why could Wilko not keep his hands off Tracey? And why on earth would Tracey cheat on her sister? Boredom? Lust? Adventure? Revenge?

What exactly was the relationship between Tracey and Susan? Could they possibly have conspired to murder Wilko and carried out the deed together? Tracey had volunteered, unasked as Kennedy recalled, that she and Susan had been together on the night Wilko was murdered. What was this thing about Wilko being murdered in a room locked from the inside?

What was all that about? Was it part of the plot or was it the entire smoke screen?

Because of the locked door, should the affable Kevin Paul also be on Kennedy's suspect list? Could KP have done the evil deed, come out of the dressing-room, locked the door, smashed it in and then placed the key back on the inside of the door? And if he did do that, then *why*?

Was there something out there that could connect KP and Wilko? Did KP fancy the sister-in-law? KP seemed like a good person. Can 'good people' murder their fellow man? This murder hadn't been a crime of passion, nor a killing in the heat of the moment. This had been premeditated and well planned. So, what reasons were there for a decent god-fearing, dope-smoking hippie like KP to kill Wilko Robertson? A person he had known and worked with for a couple of decades? What changed?

Wilko had rejoined Circles. Could that have anything to do with his death? Could either Rickie Slatterly, the lawyer, or Simple Simon Peddington, the ex-manager, have a reason to want to get rid of Wilko? And if so, what was it? Could James MacDonald, the music publisher, and Wilko been cooking up something? Perhaps something to persuade Sean to sign a new lucrative publishing deal; a deal both Wilko and James would benefit from? Had the conspiracy backfired and James needed to get rid of Wilko in order to protect himself and his position in the company?

The Circles songs were certainly proving to be worth a lot of money. Kennedy was finding this to be the case with a considerable number of the sixties and seventies groups selling-on their copyrights for sums in the millions. Could Robert Clarke feel aggrieved enough at losing his position in Circles to Wilko, to make him want to murder Wilko? If so, it had certainly been effective, because Sean was now planning to bring him back into the band again. So that couldn't be ruled out.

'What about Sean?' he found himself saying, aloud.

'What *about* Sean?'

Kennedy swung around in his chair to find Superintendent Thomas Castle with his head stuck around the office door, one hand still grasping the door handle the other resting on the door post.

'Oh, sorry, sir. I was miles away,' Kennedy replied quickly grounding from his astral travels.

'I'd say so. Is this the pop group mess you are working on? That thing up in Camden Lock?'

'Yes, in fact it is,' Kennedy replied quickly.

'Any progress on it?'

'A bit, I suppose.'

'What's this other thing you've got Taylor working on up at St Pancras Hospital?'

Kennedy explained his conversation with Rose Butler. 'How have you heard about it so quickly?'

'I've had some hospital authorities assuring me this is none of our business and that they'll be dealing with it as per standard procedure,' Castle replied.

'Very interesting, very interesting indeed. And...?' Kennedy fished.

'And...' Castle smiled, 'I think, if they're kicking up a stink this early that's justification enough for us to carry on.'

'Good. Just out of interest, sir, who was it you spoke to from the hospital authorities?'

'A Doctor Ranjee Shareef. Yes, as you say, Christy, very interesting. Very interesting indeed. Keep me posted.'

Twenty

'Ah, glad I found you.'

WPC Anne Coles approached Irvine, dressed in civvies. Loose-fitting black slacks, roll-neck white woollen jumper, black wind-breaker jacket and blonde hair tucked up and (sadly) hidden under a black ski-hat.

'Not quite soon enough' Irvine muttered, half under his breath.

'Pardon?'

'Sorry, nothing. What's up?' Irvine replied.

The WPC brought the DS up to date with the recent revelations of the McSisters. Kennedy wanted them visited immediately and interviewed separately.

'I'm not sure it's such a good idea,' Coles began as they walked down Delancey Street.

'What? What's not such a good idea?' Irvine replied. He seemed under-dressed for the weather. Donegal three-piece tweed suit, checked shirt, green tie, brown and white brogues. Although the wind was blowing furiously not one single copper-coloured hair was out of place. Coles considered her colleague as she answered his question.

'Well,' Coles began hesitantly. 'It's just that Susan Robertson has just learned about the death of her husband. She's being comforted and supported through these troubled times by her sister Tracey. Now we find out from KP that husband Wilko was sleeping with Tracey. Surely this is going to completely take the rug from under Susan's feet. We're going to take away the only stability she has left.'

'Yes, I see what's troubling you. I'm not sure I would worry about it as much as you do though,' Irvine sympathised.

'Oh, that's just…'

'If you're about to say, "That just because you're a man" I'll be very disappointed with you,' Irvine cut in.

'No, I was…' Coles struggled.

'There, you see? I knew…'

'No, you didn't,' Coles cut in indignantly. 'You didn't know what I was about to say. I was about to say, "That's because you're not a woman."'

'Oh, maybe you were correct, in part. But don't forget that one of these grieving sisters may have murdered Wilko. We must certainly consider it a possibility.'

'Well, I must say, that I find it quite hard to believe that anyone would have trouble keeping their hands off Tracey McGee,' Coles replied. 'She seemed very plain to me.'

'Perhaps that's what she wanted everyone to think. You know, just in case the sister was ever suspicious? There's also the possibility that it was a package deal, as it were. Wilko had a healthy sexual appetite and, well, you know, the sister helped her out?'

'Oh, please. That's disgusting. How can you even think that?'

'You're quite an innocent, aren't you?' Irvine laughed.

'I've had my moments, I'll have you know,' Coles replied mentally kicking herself for responding just a wee bit too quickly. His reply only served to confirm her worst fears.

'Oh, I've never doubted that.'

God, the WPC thought. How had she allowed the conversation to fall to such an unprofessional low? She prided herself on having an asexual relationship with her colleagues in

Camden Town CID. But here she was with DS James Irvine, complete with his James Bond accent and thermal underwear, admitting to her that he'd considered her sexually. Oh God, please make the ground swallow me up, she thought. Just then she remembered the best form of defence is attack, so attack she did.

'I suppose you've had you fair share of sisters,' she grandstanded. What?, she thought the second the words had left her lips. What kind of attack was that? Didn't she just go and dig herself into an even deeper hole?

'No, actually I wasn't speaking from experience,' Irvine replied. Coles wasn't sure, but she thought she sensed a wee bit of hurt in his voice. 'But it's not unheard of, in the outlying areas of Scotland, for sisters to share a man. Not just in Scotland. It's not as uncommon a situation as you might think, and I'm talking about long term relationships.'

'Incredible!' Coles said.

'Yes, I suppose so.'

'No, I mean that we are actually considering this,' Coles said, gaining her confidence again.

'Well, we're on an investigation, we have to consider everything, no matter how unpalatable,' Irvine said. They had arrived at the Robertson house and climbed the four tiled steps. 'So listen, do you want the wife or the mistress?'

'Oh, the mistress of course,' Coles replied, and rang the bell.

Twenty-One

The police couple introduced themselves to the sisters and Coles advised them that they had returned to ask a few more questions. Irvine suggested that the interviews be conducted separately. Susan seemed the more nervous of being with the police by herself but she wasn't given the time to worry about it. A few seconds later she and Irvine were seated around the kitchen table and Coles and Tracey in the sitting room. A brick wall and two closed doors separated the couples. Had a fifth person been eavesdropping on the conversations and been able to decipher the simultaneous parts of the conversations, this is what they would have heard:

Irvine: I'm sorry for your loss, Mrs. Robertson, Wilko sure was a fine singer.

Susan: Why thank you. Had you ever seen Circles?

Tracey: Why are you back so soon?

Irvine: Yes, as a matter of fact, I did. I saw them perform a sensational concert in The Barrowland, Glasgow. I was there in a profession capacity, but Circles were on-stage and I thought they were incredible.

Coles: Well, to be quite honest, Miss McGee, we picked up a new bit of information and we wanted to check it out with each of you.

Tracey: Oh, and what information would that be?

Irvine: As you know, in order to find out what happened to Wilko we need to delve into his past and see who was involved with him.

Susan: Yes?

Coles: Well, it's come to our attention that Wilko was having an affair.

Irvine: Yes, and there's no easy way to tell you this, particularly at a time like this, but we think we've found out that Wilko was having an affair.

Tracey: He was hardly a saint was our Wilko.

Susan: That will be news to none bar those on the Outer Hebrides.

Coles: I'm surprised you haven't asked me with whom he was having the affair.

Irvine: Perhaps. But, at the same time, perhaps the name of person he was having an affair with will be news.

Susan: (Laughing) Only if it were to be with our Tracey.

Tracey: I'd be interested in with whom Wilko didn't hit on, to be honest.

Coles: Well, we've heard it was you.

Irvine: Actually, it *was* your Tracey.

Tracey: (Nonchalantly) Oh, don't be stupid. Of course I wouldn't sleep with my sister's husband. (Then laughing) I know whom you heard that from. Kevin Paul, that little hippie shit. He hit on me once and I turned him down and he hasn't forgiven me since. His ego dreamt this idea that the only way I'd have been able to resist his charms was if I was involved in a ménage a trios with Susan and Wilko.

Susan: No, not... (Then bursts into a fit of uncontrollable sobbing).

Coles: We've received our information from more than one source, Ms McGee.

Tracey: You may have received your information from a hundred sources but that doesn't make it true. Unless someone

*saw Wilko and I making love, perish the thought. It's all
hearsay. Tell you what, love, you come back to me when you've
got something more concrete than that little shit's gossip, gossip
which spilt up the group in the first place.*

And with that, Tracey got up and left the room. The minute
she opened the door she could hear her sister crying, more like
wailing. Before WPC Coles had a chance to restrain her, Tracey
burst through the kitchen door and ran to her sister, who greeted
her with open arms at which point they both hugged, rocking
together gently.

Tracey McGee hissed over her shoulder at Coles and Irvine.

'Now look what you've done. Get the feck out of here
before you cause any more damage.'

Considering their interviews to be a disaster, they left the
sisters of mercy, both couples dejected. But the interviews
hadn't been a complete waste of time. There had been a
valuable piece of information given away during the course of
the interviews. But it was like Kennedy kept saying to his team,
"All the information is out there. It's waiting for us to collect.
Once we collect it, we have to realise what we have, and more
importantly, we have to know what to do with it."

Twenty-Two

Kennedy barely had time for Coles and Irvine's report. He considered what Susan *hadn't* said. Kennedy was convinced that KP was telling the truth, that Tracey had in fact had an affair with Wilko.

At seven-forty he exited North Bridge House with the unwholesome threesome on his mind. Did Tracey's being forbidden fruit turn on Wilko? Was Tracey the one to do the chasing? Had Susan Robertson set up the whole affair?

For heaven's sake, how could you sleep with your sister-in-law? How on earth could you ever look at her or you wife in the face again? Was rock-n-roll really as decadent as people made out?

Or perhaps this particular infidelity cost Wilko his life. Suppose Wilko was sleeping with Tracey. Could that have been the final straw, the thing which made Susan snap? She'd managed to overlook all the other affairs, but this one, literally on her doorstep, just pushed her over the edge. Kennedy considered another scenario. What if Wilko decided he didn't want to continue the affair with Tracey any longer? What if he wanted to return to his wife? Tracey, humiliated first by sleeping with her sister's husband, then losing him back to her sister again, couldn't take it any more and killed him.

He considered both sisters. He was happy to assume that

both had a motive. But, whichever sister it was, how on earth did she murder Wilko Robertson in the basement of Dingwalls Dancehall? How did they carry it out?

What if Tracey's accusation against KP was true, that he had been jealous of Wilko enjoying her favours? Was there any history there? If KP was a legit suspect then the crime itself became somewhat more explainable again. KP burst down the door before anyone else arrived and replaced the key. That worked. Didn't it really, Kennedy thought, as he crossed Regent's Park Road into Rothwell Street.

His ruminating came to an abrupt end when he noticed ann rea's maroon Ford Popular parked outside his house, number 16. The car was empty but his doorstep wasn't.

'In approximately forty-five seconds you would have been officially late,' ann rea scolded playfully.

'In other words, I'm early,' Kennedy replied, as he jumped the four steps in one and planted a peck on ann rea's cold cheek. Kennedy loved it when her cheeks were cold.

'Is that all I get after last night?' she teased, as he unlocked the solitary lock.

Kennedy said nothing. He caught her by the hand and playfully pulled her after him into his darkened hallway. When they were both clear of the door he turned, closed the door, and took ann rea in his arms and kissed her.

'We should split up more often,' she said as she pulled away. 'I'm thirsty, let's have something to drink.' She led him through to the kitchen and produced two bottles of cold white wine from her black canvas rucksack and presented them with a flourish.

As ever, ann rea dressed to thrill. She wore white skin-tight leggings under a deep blue micro skirt, a white satin shirt under a matching blue waistcoat. The head-turning ensemble had been concealed under a sober navy-blue duffel coat. The cold evening had given just a little hint of colour to her usual white cheeks, but it was the eyes that got Kennedy. They always did.

'Kennedy, don't go all sloppy on me, remember where that got us last time.'

'Oh, forget sloppy. This is my tongue on the ground look.'

'Yeah, the old white bra under a white shirt trick always got you going,' ann rea returned, noticing his line of vision.

'I'll say,' Kennedy replied, happier to keep the conversation on a lighter note, particularly this lighter note. Truth be told, he adored every inch of her body. She had, what was for Kennedy, the perfect body. Full figured, very full figured, but not plump.

'That'll have to do you for now, Kennedy. I've another hunger to satisfy first, so feed me.'

The detective smiled, admitting he'd been caught out. 'Okay, you go and put on some music and I'll start dinner.'

A couple of minutes later they were both sitting at his large well worn table, the hub of his kitchen, sipping their wine and listening to Van Morrison's Saint Dominic's Preview. In the oven Mr Marks and his good friend Mr Sparks were furiously whipping up another of their specialities of *le package*, Chicken Paramount, Potatoes Gratin and peas.

By the time they'd reached 'Listen to the Lion', the final track on side one of record, they were both so lost in the music that neither spoke for a while. The Belfast-born vocalist moved from singing the lyric to using his voice as an instrument; an instrument to weave around the arrangement, pulling your heart this way and that. Kennedy thought, with this music filling the room and this vision of ann rea before him, he would settle for what he had. No gripes, just grateful submission. By the time the song had ended Kennedy felt drained.

'That is so beautiful,' ann rea announced, as much to herself as to him.

'Aye, I know, but it'll never get on the Radio One Play list.'

'You're not wrong and you can thank God for that,' ann rea said.

As Kennedy laid out the food and replenished their wine glasses, ann rea returned to the study to put on a new cassette;

this time the sound of The Beatles' Revolver album filled the kitchen.

'This is class as well,' Kennedy nodded.

'So, how are you getting on with the Wilko murder?' ann rea began, as they settled down to their food.

'Well, we're making progress,' Kennedy replied. It wasn't exactly the direction he hoped the conversation would have taken. Nonetheless, he continued, 'Did you know that Wilko was having an affair with his wife's sister?'

ann rea stopped mid-bite.

'No!' she spat out. 'How gross. How low can you get?'

'The sister, Tracey McGee, denies it of course. But it does give us a couple more suspects.'

'The sisters?'

'At least,' Kennedy replied.

'You mean there are more?' ann rea quizzed.

'Well, Tracey claims the alleged affair is a figment of KP's imagination. She claims he started the rumours to protect his bruised ego when she turned him down.'

'But you think that's a bit of a smoke-screen?'

'Perhaps, but there *is* a certain logic to it,' Kennedy reflected.

'How so?'

'Well, if KP *did* murder Wilko, then the procedure with the locked door kind of makes sense. At the same time, I don't think he'd be the type of person who could murder anybody.'

'God, what a mess. Your own sister sleeping with your husband, or your own husband sleeping with your sister. I don't know which is worse. You see, that's the aspect of this whole love thing that I can't get to grips with.'

'What? People cheating on each other?' the detective replied, fearing this shift in their conversation.

'Well, obviously Wilko and his wife ...' ann rea hesitated.

'Susan,' Kennedy prompted.

'Yes, Susan. Well, obviously at one point in their

relationship they were in love, in love enough to get married. And then this happens. He has an affair; she gets jealous and then he ends up dead. It's like us in a way…'

'How on earth is it like us, ann rea?' Kennedy cut in, more than a little annoyed. 'You think that just because I was in love with you there is a possibility it was going to be dangerous to your health?'

'No, no, not at all,' she held up her hands, 'It's just that we were on that "happy ever after" road and I didn't want that, I didn't want all that cosiness. I love the way you lust after me. I'm not so sure I like the way you loved me.'

'And which way was that?' a mortally wounded Kennedy inquired. He wasn't sure that he wanted to hear the answer.

'The way that demands I love you too.'

'Oh, that's absolute rubbish. We met. I was attracted to you. We had a shaky start. At one point we were destined to become "just good friends…"'

'Yes, but just hold it there. Hold that thought. That is exactly what I wanted to be. Your friend. Not *just* your friend. If we are true friends the word "just" doesn't apply. I was happy to be your friend. I liked you, I liked you a lot. Then we got closer and closer and then this unresolved man – woman thing appeared and then it's "will we won't we?" For heaven's sake, I was thinking it, I knew *you* were thinking it…it wasn't as though you were just after one thing. If fact, if you had been, it would have been much easier.'

'What? You mean if you thought I was only interested in sleeping with you, it would have happened sooner?' Kennedy asked incredulously.

'Yes, Kennedy. If I thought you had been just after a bonk, we possibly would have a lot earlier. But you wanted so much more from me. You wanted so much of me you nearly scared me off. All the time, here am I wanting you as a friend and all the time we were growing closer and closer. I suppose it was inevitable we would end up in bed together. But I don't like to feel that my resistance has been worn down.'

'I can't believe you just said that,' Kennedy said, after an uneasy pause. He'd given up eating his food. 'Are you telling me that we only made love because I wore your resistance down?'

ann rea also appeared to have lost her appetite.

'Look, Christy,' ann rea began shakily, 'what I'm saying is that I started out wanting to be friends with you and we ended up lovers. I'm not complaining. It was beautiful. It *is* beautiful. But then it started to feel like being lovers wasn't enough for you. You were so in love with me, I couldn't love you the same way in return. Your love was so precious, so full, so committed, so sure, that anything less than a 100% return was going to be cheating you.'

'Hang on a minute there. I can't believe all of this. What happened to "boy meets girl, girl meets boy, they fall in love?" What's wrong with that? What's wrong with using that as a starting point as opposed to a finishing point? Being in love is not the end of your life, it doesn't mean it's all over. Being in love does mean being friends, different kind of friends, but friends. Friendship exists but there is also a passion you wouldn't have with a friend. But, for heaven's sake, it doesn't mean that the next point along the road is cheating and hurting each other. It's only the beginning, ann rea,' Kennedy paused for breath and continued.

'Yes, we met and became friends and grew close. And yes, I loved you. I mean just look at you, why on earth wouldn't I? But my love was not conditional on you loving me in return. I didn't tell you I loved you so that you would say "I love you, too." I told you that I loved you because I loved you. That was it. It wasn't meant to be a threat. Don't you see that?' Kennedy pleaded, continuing before she had a chance to get a word in edge ways. 'No, you obviously don't, because you say things like, "How is he so sure about his love?" or "I thought I was in love before but the guy turned out to be a shit. I could also be wrong about Kennedy," and on and on, tormenting us both. But not once do I remember demanding you to return my love. And now you to sit here and say we only made love because I wore your resistance down, I can't believe it.'

'Look, what can I tell you?' ann rea asked. 'I wanted to be your friend, period. Nothing else. We became friends. You were really nice to me but I didn't want to become your lover. I wanted to be your friend. Eventually we did become lovers, but I hadn't wanted to. So I look at it now and I have to think, either you wore my resistance down, or we wore my resistance down…'

'Or, possibly,' Kennedy added sternly, 'You wore your own resistance down.'

'Possibly, Kennedy. Possibly. But you have to see that's where all my doubts come from.'

'So, because of your continuous doubts we're not going to pass GO?' Kennedy pushed.

'Well, we're together right now.'

'But…'

'Oh, Kennedy, give me time. Please. I like us being back together again. I missed you. I missed not being with you and yes, I missed not being physically close to you. I don't want to be with anyone else but that doesn't mean that we take up the relationship where we left off. I still have all those doubts, but if the alternative is not seeing you then yes, I do want to see you. But I want to forget all this baggage for a while. Let's just deal with being with each other, caring for each other. Let's have some fun together and see where that gets us, shall we?'

'I never wanted anything else,' Kennedy replied. He felt he should be happier than he was.

Twenty minutes later as she led him up the stairs in the direction of the bedroom she said quietly, 'Christy, you said earlier that you loved me?'

'Mmm?'

'Well, that kind of implies the past tense. Does that mean....'

'Don't even dream of going there,' Kennedy warned in an even quieter voice.

Twenty-Three

A beautiful sunny Sunday morning, four weeks to Christmas, still far enough away for Kennedy not to have to worry about it. Presents, where to go for the holidays, and with whom? ann rea's recent attention didn't make the decision-making process any easier. In fact, he wasn't altogether sure he liked the new ann rea. Of course, he shared these thoughts with no one. There was no-one to share them with.

This was turning out to be a perfect Sunday for Kennedy. A bit of a late lie-in with ann rea, breakfast, a shower, good-byes, and then Primrose Hill by eleven. The sky was blue as far as the eye could see, the day was blustery but not cold, and it was perfect weather for a walk. Lots of seagulls squawking around. It was enough to clear Kennedy's head from all thoughts of ann rea and his two current cases.

Dr. Taylor had arranged to meet Kennedy at North Bridge House at one thirty for tea, shortbread and the verbal delivery of the autopsy on the late Sinead Sullivan. The timing couldn't be better, following a two-hour walk listening to Michael Parkinson on Radio 2 on his headset, a cup of tea would be just the thing for Kennedy. He was looking forward to hearing Taylor's report. He secretly hoped, for Rose Butler's sake, that there was something concrete in the report from which Kennedy could launch an official investigation.

The look on Taylor's face was not encouraging.

'He's a bit of a Dr Teflon is our Shareef,' Taylor said. 'Nothing's going to stick to him. That is, of course, if the suspicions of Nurse Butler are correct.'

'I'd a nasty feeling that was going to be the case,' Kennedy replied, losing some of his early morning pace.

'Miss Sinead Sullivan *did* indeed die as a result of a massive haemorrhage. The fatal haemorrhage *was* brought on as a result of Placenta Praevia…'

'So, where does that leave us?'

'Well, nowhere to be blunt. There are no records of Miss Sullivan being monitored. That is a choice she would have been free to make. If she wasn't being monitored the ailment wouldn't have been detected and she wouldn't have been treated.'

'Could this Prave…'

'Placenta Praevia.'

'Could Placenta Praevia been induced by any form of medication?'

'Something similar perhaps, but not really. This death was definitely caused as a result of Placenta Praevia. The Placenta was very low,' Taylor replied.

'OK. Say, for instance, a doctor with knowledge of the above was monitoring a young lady in private and he chose to ignore the symptoms. As a result the young lady dies,' Kennedy fished blindly.

'I see exactly where you're headed, old chap. But sadly, there is no way in a million years that you could prove it. She'd have to have been monitored officially, with proper notes and records kept. Should a doctor be clever enough to murder the girl as you suggest, I doubt he would leave incriminating notes lying around. It's possible, of course…' Taylor continued, as he refilled his tea cup, 'that the doctor in question was totally unaware of Miss Sullivan's predicament and is as troubled as the rest of us over her untimely death.'

'Yes, there's always that, isn't there?' Kennedy smiled. 'Did you discover anything else in the autopsy?'

'Only that Miss Sullivan recently had an abortion,' Taylor announced, 'Straight-forward procedure, no evidence of complications.'

'How recently?'

'Possibly the back end of twelve months ago.'

'Hold on a wee minute,' the detective began, suddenly revitalized. 'When Rose was running through the list of causes for Placenta Praevia I'm sure she mentioned recent abortions.'

'Yes, she would have,' Taylor nodded.

'So, if we assumed Sinead became pregnant by Dr Ranjesus…'

'Who?' Taylor interrupted.

'The nurses call him Ranjesus because he thinks he's God's gift to women. But say he finds out she's pregnant and aborts her. From what Rose says about Sinead, the young nurse would have felt very guilty about this. Probably even felt she'd committed a mortal sin. Say she gets pregnant again as soon as possible. Only this time she doesn't tell the doctor.'

'Possible,' Taylor acknowledged.

'So, she informs Ranjesus about their baby, but only when it's too late to do anything about it. Tell me,' Kennedy paused. 'At what point in a pregnancy would it be impossible to have an abortion?'

'Eight weeks, maybe twelve weeks. If the mother's health was at risk, then possibly as late as twenty-four weeks, but the patient would have to be in extreme danger,' Taylor said.

Kennedy paced his office.

'The doctor worries, but decides to bide his time. He monitors her, discovers the Placenta Pree…'

'Praevia.'

'Praevia, right, and he lets nature take its course. It rids him of two problems,' Kennedy replied excitedly.

'Yes, old chap. It works. But, again, you are never, ever,

going to be able to prove it,' Taylor sympathized with his friend.

'Perhaps not, Doctor, perhaps not. But in the meantime, I intend to carry out a high-profile investigation into our Dr Ranjee Shareef. Somewhere, someone on the hospital staff, the hotel staff, somewhere, must know something.'

Kennedy closed Taylor's autopsy report and placed it in his top right-hand drawer.

'Well, just be careful. That's all I ask of you, Christy, just be careful. He's got some influential friends, our Dr Shareef,' Taylor said, rising.

'I hear you, Leonard. I hear you. But I can't just sit around and ignore what's happened.'

'What you *think* has happened,' Taylor corrected.

'No. What I'm *convinced* happened.'

Twenty-Four

'Hey man, what's the vibe?' KP announced, recognizing Kennedy's voice.

'Oh, it's a fresh-week a.m. vibe, man.' Kennedy tried to imitate KP-speak. First thing Monday morning, before most of his team had arrived, Kennedy had Kevin Paul on the phone.

'You mean it's a "I don't like Mondays" scene, man. Hey, I've been on the old Philip Marlowe trip myself over the weekend,' KP jived back.

'Really?'

'Yeah man, I've been trying to figure out why Sean brought Wilko back into the band.'

'Any progress?' Kennedy inquired. This same question had been burning a hole in the detective's brain the previous afternoon.

'Hey, it's kind of complicated, but I think there might be…'

'You've got my attention, KP.'

'At this stage, I've got but one piece of information for you, man.'

'Which is?'

'I think Colette Green may be involved in this somewhere. I've been up all night tracking down a few leads. I like all the darkness and shadows vibe, man. Makes me more of a Camden Dick Noir than the employees of North Bridge House.'

'Or a vampire,' Kennedy said, recalling KP's slight frame, white skin and dark clothes.

'Very dry. My contract says I get all the funny lines. Please remember that, Detective, if we're going to get team vibe going. Paul and Kennedy, doesn't really roll off the tongue like Watson and Holmes, Dodi and Di, bangers and mash…'

'Nah, you're right. There's no natural connection between the two names. Perhaps it just wasn't meant to be,' Kennedy cut in. 'But I hear Lewis has left Morse; perhaps there's an opening for you there?'

'I'm not into the Swan Song vibe man. Anyway, as I was saying before I was interrupted, I've been up all night. I'm wrecked. I'm going to bed for a couple of hours and then I'm meeting someone at twelve. Why don't we hook up at two o'clock for a late lunch.'

'Sounds good to me.'

'Let's meet in the back room at Trattoria Lucca. Cool vibe man, see you later.' KP disappeared off the line, leaving Kennedy with a rather large grin on his face.

A grin which disappeared twenty seconds later when WPC Anne Coles and DS Irvine marched into his office, ready, willing and able for the week ahead.

'OK, we've a busy day ahead of us. Let's get stuck straight in. We need to talk to Leslie Russell, Sean Green, the McSisters, Wilko's lawyer Slatterly, Simon Peddington, Kevin Paul, James MacDonald and Robert Clarke. And that's just before lunch-time,' Kennedy joked.

'No problem,' Irvine came back, quick as a flash, 'And what are you two going to be doing while I'm looking after that lot?'

'Seriously though, there *is* something taking shape here. I'm just not quite sure what it is yet. At this point I think we're doing okay. Right, let's divide up and get on with it,' Kennedy suggested.

They spent a few minutes working out who was going to see who and with whom. Irvine took Allaway with him, leaving

Constable Tony West to work with Coles. A decision that had Allaway turning up his nose and West trying hard to contain himself.

The McSisters, as Irvine had christened them, were first on Kennedy's list of people to be interviewed. If they had been upset about the previous day's visit from Coles and Irvine, they certainly weren't showing it. Susan seemed in high spirits, all things considered, and even Tracey had managed to doll herself up in her Sunday best.

Kennedy chose, for the time being, to ignore the alleged infidelities of Wilko. He accepted their kind offer of tea and, while Susan was out preparing it, inquired as to her well being.

'Oh, as well as can be expected under the circumstances. As she mentioned to you last time, they were no longer emotionally close, so perhaps it's not as bad as it might have been for her. There's probably still a little bit of anger there that Susan's using to fight off the sense of loss,' Tracey replied.

Kennedy was a little taken aback at how comfortable she appeared to be with him, as a policeman, in light of her recent confrontation with the Camden CID.

'But at the same time, from her last conversation with me, I got the feeling she still had a soft spot for him,' he said. 'You know, respected the fact that he still felt it important to look after her and all that.'

'Oh yes, definitely. We both respected him for that quality. He knew his responsibilities, did our Wilko. But at the same time, our Susan, you know, she'd never have divorced him. She wouldn't have thought it correct. Now with Wilko gone though, I suppose she feels, to some degree, she can make a new start. I think that's why she's feeling all right. I think...'

'You two seem to be quite cosy,' Susan interrupted, as she entered the room carrying a tray laden with cups, saucers, biscuits, milk and sugar.

'Well, he's not your average peeler, is he now Susan?' Tracey laughed.

The two women enjoyed a sisterly giggle, while Susan played mother with the tea.

'I was just wondering how you were getting on really,' Kennedy offered gently.

'Oh, you know. So-so,' Susan replied immediately. 'But I have to tell you, perhaps I'm having a delayed reaction, but I feel better than I think I should feel. Is it crude to say that?'

'Certainly not,' Kennedy comforted. 'It's an unknown area for you. We're all a lot more resilient than we expect – we have to be. We have to deal with this loss, and I think we always prepare ourselves for it being worse than it actually is.'

Kennedy wasn't altogether sure he believed himself. He'd been to houses to announce the death of a husband, wife, brother, sister, mother, child, and he had witnessed the bottom completely fall out of people's worlds. He'd seen people lose, completely, their will to live. But he felt it was important that Susan didn't feel guilty over the "easiness" at dealing with her loss. For all he knew there may be another reason for it. Relief perhaps. This relief would make it easier to keep the conversation on an up and the more up the conversation the easier it was going to be to collect his vital information.

'Are you okay to answer a few questions about Wilko?' Kennedy inquired.

'Sure,' Susan answered, as she stole a look at her sister.

'It's just, I'm trying to work out why Sean would have Wilko back in the group?'

'Shouldn't you asked Sean that question?' Tracey asked.

'Well, I have. He says it was because he wanted to have another go at Circles breaking America and he thought they'd have a better chance with the original singer,' Kennedy replied.

'You don't believe him?' Susan asked.

'Well, not exactly. Everyone says that the replacement singer, although he was no Wilko, worked well in the group. Some say Circles would have had as good a chance in America with Robert Clarke.'

'Maybe even better. He was a lot younger than Wilko and well, you know Wilko wasn't exactly aging well,' Susan offered, making Kennedy's job all the easier.

'Yes, Robert was a bit of a looker,' Tracey agreed.

'So my point would be, with all you've just said and the added financial attraction – I'm assuming here Robert wasn't receiving as much money as Wilko – why did Sean want Wilko back in the group? I can see all the advantages for Wilko, but I don't see any up-side from Sean's point of view, at all,' Kennedy said.

Neither Susan nor Tracey spoke.

'Would there be any other reason you could think of?' Kennedy pushed.

'I think you have to realize how long Wilko and Sean were together,' Susan answered. 'You have to realize how much they depended on each other, how much they needed each other at the beginning. They covered each other's weaknesses. They lived in each other's pockets in the early days, when they were penniless. Sharing a tin of cold baked beans can bring you very close together. That's a bond that goes way beyond money. Goes way beyond the fights and squabbles. They were closer than brothers, hell, closer than husbands and wives. Poor Colette and me were always the rock widows.'

'Poor Colette nothing,' Tracey cut in, 'She got what she wanted, always.'

'Ah, she's not as bad as you think. She's been great in all of this,' Susan continued, addressing first her sister and then the detective. 'She's been around here twice a day, offering support; saying she and Sean will do whatever we need. Saying that Sean has said I'll never have to worry about money for the rest of my life. They don't need to be like that. They could get away with just sending flowers and cards. But there's Colette, raising a family and she's coming around here all the time making sure everything is okay. That's the bond I'm talking about. Yes, Wilko dumped on Sean when he left the group, but

Sean didn't feel bitter about it. He always said it was the break that got him off his arse and got Circles going again. Perhaps he would have felt different if Wilko had gone on to greater success as a solo artist. Maybe it was easy for Sean to be so generous, generous enough to offer Wilko his gig back again.'

'Maybe he felt it would be good for his profile, you know, "Look what a great chap I am, bringing Wilko back into my group."' Tracey cut in. 'He was always the master of PR, our Sean.'

'Aye, that's correct and we can all thank God he was,' Susan shot back. 'Without his drive I'd hate to think where the band would have gone. Let's not forget that. A good number of people – musicians, crew, wives and girlfriends and Kevin Paul – all enjoyed a good life out of Sean and his ability to drive the group.'

Kennedy noticed the emphasis Susan put on KP's name. It was more dismissive than vicious. He decided to leave the subject lurking somewhere beneath the surface, for now anyway.

'So, you think it's as simple as that? Sean brought Wilko back into the group because of all their history together?' Kennedy asked.

'Well, it certainly could be one explanation. I'm not sure I can think of any others. Can you, Tracey?'

'Not really, no. But what about you, Inspector? Surely you must have a few theories at this stage.'

'We're still gathering our information.'

'Is that police-speak for, "you have your suspicions but nothing you wish to divulge at this moment"?' Tracey pushed.

'Something like that.'

'Well I suppose it is better than, "Someone is helping us with our inquiries." That always means a suspect is in custody, doesn't it?'

'Ah, come on, give him a break. I'm forever telling you that you watch too much telly,' Susan cut back in.

'Tell me, what were you were both doing on the Thursday evening last?' Kennedy asked suddenly.

'I have a confession to make,' Tracey offered, breaking the seven seconds silence since Kennedy's question.

'Oh?' Kennedy had noticed that Susan was doing everything possible to avoid eye contact with both himself and her sister.

'Mmm, yes. The other evening when I said we were together, I'm afraid that I lied to you. It was really a spur of them moment thing. I don't know what I was thinking, really. Probably felt I was protecting her.'

'So where were you on Thursday?' Kennedy repeated, looking at Susan.

'*I* was here, all evening,' Susan said quietly, looking directly at her sister. 'By myself.'

'Did anyone drop in?'

'Nope.'

'Did anyone call you?'

'Not a dickey bird.'

'Did you ring anyone?'

'Not a soul. I'm sorry, detective. I don't exactly have a large circle of friends or a heavy social life. I suppose that leaves me without an alibi?'

'Oh, I'm not sure alibis are all they're cracked up to be,' Kennedy admitted.

Susan Robertson appeared to take little comfort in Kennedy's generous remark.

'And yourself?' he tuned his head to the sister, 'Miss McGee, what were you doing on Thursday evening?'

'Well,' Tracey began nervously, 'I was at the Circles gig at Dingwalls Dancehall.'

'I couldn't swear to it but I don't think your name was on the list of people we interviewed after the gig,' Kennedy stated, after a lengthy pause.

'Ah, no,' Tracey began, appearing somewhat more confident now. 'That would be because I wasn't there at the end, you see. I always thought that instrumental they do as one big ego-trip, all the musicians getting a chance to show off their musical legs, as it were. It's all very well for the band and their egos but boring as watching paint dry for the audience. I suppose Wilko and Sean needed a bit of a breather at that point in the show.'

'Actually,' Susan began, 'Wilko needed the break to change out of his sweaty clothes. At that point he was always soaked through to the skin.'

'Yes, whatever. I'm sure they could have done something without him anyway. An instrumental version of one of the songs. But there was no need for Sean to leave the stage as well. He didn't have to prance around the stage all night, working up a sweat. He just sat behind his keyboards like Lord Muck. Anyway, as I was saying, I left just as they took the break,' Tracey said.

'Did you often go to their gigs?' was Kennedy's next question.

'All the time, they're a great band and they play so rarely these days you have to take every opportunity you can.'

'What about you, Mrs. Robertson. Did you not go to all the concerts?'

'No. Wilko preferred me not to. Said he was always more nervous when he knew I was out there. He said I knew who he really was and that there'd always be one person out there who knew it was all an act. I'd sometimes slip in to the bigger shows, when he wouldn't know I was there, but Dingwalls was too small for that…'

'Yes,' her sister interrupted, 'I don't really know why they were playing such a small place at all. It was so packed, you couldn't move in there. I mean, I've been to Dingwalls lots. It's an okay place, but it's mostly for comedy these days. But Circles could have easily sold out the Albert Hall. This still had an audience and they hadn't played in town for ages.'

'Tell me, Mrs Robertson,' Kennedy began, 'did you know that your sister was going to see Circles?'

'Mmm, well, I'm not her keeper you know, only the little sister,' Susan replied, forcing a laugh.

'So, you didn't know that she was going to see your husband perform on Thursday evening last?'

'No, Inspector, I did not know she was going to see Circles that evening.'

'Did you see Sean in the crowd walking around during the break, Miss McGee?'

'No, Inspector. As I have already told you, I left before the jam session.'

'Yes, sorry. So you did. I was wondering did Wilko know you were going to be attending the concert?' Kennedy continued, directing his question once more at Tracey McGee.

'Well he would, wouldn't he? He gave me a lift down to the show.'

'But I thought your sister didn't know you were going to the concert?'

'She didn't,' Tracey replied abruptly. 'We didn't leave from here, you see. The band had a long soundcheck to do.'

'Soundcheck?'

'You know, all that "testing, one, two" routine that they go through to make sure the sound is perfect. They hadn't played for a good time, so Sean was putting them all though their paces. A bit of rehearsing as well as sound checking. Anyway, I met Wilko at The Engineer. It's not far, a quick walk down the canal path from Dingwalls.'

'And you went to the gig together?'

'Yes.'

'But I thought you said he gave you a lift.'

'He did.'

'But you just said that you walked along the canal path.'

'No, I was just telling you how to get there from Dingwalls. With all the fans and that, Wilko wasn't going to walk along the canal path and straight in the front door, now was he?' Tracey replied calmly.

'No, I suppose not. It's just that it would seem, by car, to be quite a long and complicated journey, because of the railway track and such. Perhaps as much as ten minutes, whereas it would only be a couple of minute's walk,' Kennedy persisted. Something there was niggling him, he wasn't exactly sure what.

'The price, and inconvenience, of fame, Detective Inspector. What can I tell you?' Tracey replied.

Kennedy tried a new approach.

'Tell me, Miss McGee, what time did the soundcheck finish?'

'About five-thirty.'

'So you were there. You were at the soundcheck?'

'Yes, I've just told you I was.'

'No, not exactly. You told me you met him at The Engineer and he gave you a lift back to Dingwalls.'

'And that's also correct. I was at the soundcheck. I walked to the Engineer and he gave me a lift back to the venue,' Tracey stated. If Kennedy's questions were getting to her she certainly was making a good job of hiding it.

'OK, good. I'm with you now. So, tell me, what time did Circles go on stage?'

'Nine p.m. Sean's a stickler for time keeping and when the schedule says "On stage: nine p.m." that's when he wants the band on stage. None of this rubbish about building up tension in the audience by keeping them waiting.'

'So when would you have left The Engineer to get back to Dingwalls?'

'Eight thirty sharp. Wilko had to change and he didn't want Sean on his case. He was nervous enough about it being a London show.'

'That would mean you spent about two and one half hours together?'

Kennedy made his point, which was noted by Susan as well. A Susan refusing to make eye contact with her sister.

'Yes, in fact it would,' Tracey confirmed innocently.

'And you spent all that time at The Engineer?'

'Well, where else would we have spent it?'

'No, it's just that I was wondering, you know, with what you were saying and all that, with The Engineer being so close to Dingwalls, well, surely there must have been some fans in the Engineer and wouldn't they have been bugging Wilko.'

'No. As I said, it is close to the gig but it's the other side of the tracks, just far enough away. That crowd would have been drinking at The Dublin Castle or The Fusilier & Firkin, or even Dingwalls itself.'

'That means you sat drinking and talking in The Engineer for two and one half hours?' Kennedy smiled.

The McSisters' reaction to each other was something to consider. Even if Tracey had managed to persuade her sister that there was nothing to Irvine and Coles allegations, Kennedy was sure she have some explaining to do the second he left. He also imagined that if KP's report, that Wilko could not keep his hands off Tracey, was accurate then they wouldn't have sat for two and one half hours in the pub having a cosy little chat. Kennedy needed more information from KP before he pressed that line of questioning any further.

He was sure he sensed a major sigh of relief from the McSisters when he announced, 'Well, that's all for now. I may need to see you later today, though.'

'Oh, you know where we are. You'll be most welcome,' Susan replied warmly, and added. 'Anytime!'

'Thanks for your hospitality,' Kennedy said, equally warmly, as he left the McSisters to their own little discussion. Oh, how he'd have loved to be a fly on the wall during that chat.

Twenty-Five

While Kennedy had been pursuing his own line of questioning, other members of Camden Town CID were also gathering information on the death of Wilko Robertson. Detective Sergeant James Irvine and Constable Allaway were sitting down to talk with Rickie Slatterly, former legal advisor and representative for the same Wilko Robertson.

Richie Slatterly sat in his a plush set of offices in Delancey Street, quite close to the Edinboro Castle Pub. He was frightfully English in a Noel Coward way, but without the camp. In fact, Irvine noted, if he'd managed the trademark-gap between the top two teeth he could have passed for Terry Thomas. He was wearing a dark blue two-piece suit, pink shirt, ice blue tie, black loafer shoes and pink socks to match his shirt. His naturally wavy hair was held in place with what looked like gallons of Brylcream, which continuously reflected the ceiling strip lighting into Irvine's eyes.

His walls were bare and a little faded, save for a framed diploma of some sort above the mantelpiece. The office consisted of a partner's desk and a large swivel chair at either side. Irvine sat in one chair, Slatterly in the other. Allaway shared a sofa with several piles of files, all tied up neatly with red ribbons. Most of the Royal Blue carpet was hidden under similar piles.

Slatterly had a file on the desk in front of him. He untied the ribbon and opened the file. He was ready to address the officers, but made no offer of refreshment to them. A half remaining cup of tea or coffee may encourage the police to linger on a while longer than was necessary.

'We're trying to gather as much information as possible on one of your former clients, Mr Wilko Robertson,' Irvine began.

'Yes?'

Irvine suspected that the solicitor was not going to offer up any information without prompting.

'Right,' Irvine began. 'Did Wilko have any financial problems that you were aware of?'

'It was all a bit of a mess, actually. There was money all over the place. What Simon Peddington and myself tried to do was simplify his affairs, put everything all under the one roof as it were. When he left Circles, money was coming in from everywhere and it was hard to keep tabs on everything.'

'Did you ever carry out an audit?' Irvine asked.

The solicitor spent a few second checking through his file before answering.

'Yes, as it happens. We audited them on three separate occasions.'

'Find an discrepancies?'

Again Slatterly checked his file.

'Actually, no. The audits didn't turn up anything substantial.'

'When you say they didn't turn up anything substantial, do you mean that the audits turned up insubstantial amounts?' Irvine inquired.

The file was checked once more. Irvine knew that Slatterly had the answers to these questions, so why did he persist on checking the file?

'No. No discrepancies were found.'

Irvine decided it was time to move on.

'In the time you were his representative did Wilko have any problems with drugs?'

'None that I was ever called upon to help him with.'

'Are you saying that there were or there weren't any?' Irvine asked.

'I'm saying that there might have been, but because I was never called upon to represent him at those times, I have no first-hand knowledge. I can neither confirm nor deny,' Slatterly clarified.

'What about Sean and Wilko? What were they like together?'

'I never worked with both of them. I've never actually met Sean. All my dealing on Wilko's behalf has been with Sean's representative, Mr Leslie Russell.'

'Did Wilko like Sean?' Irvine asked.

'Frankly, I'm not sure there was any love lost between them. However, I've never heard Wilko speak badly of Sean. They'd been in the group for a long time, been in each other's pockets for years. To be quite honest, they were probably quite relieved to be apart, when the split eventually came,' Slatterly answered.

'Why, then, did Wilko rejoin the band?'

'His own career was a disaster. Simon couldn't get anything going for him and, really, it was the only place left for him to go.'

'Why do you think Sean had Wilko back in the band?'

'An altogether more difficult question. I could never work that one out myself.'

'Financially speaking, did Wilko need to rejoin the band?' Irvine asked.

'Absolutely,' Slatterly replied quickly, and then, after a moment of thought, 'He had the life-style of a pop star but not the income. Money flowed through his hands like sand. He'd never listen to Simon, his accountant, or myself. He was convinced there would always be another cheque, simply because there always had been before. But at the time we stopped working together, which would have been just before he rejoined the band, he wasn't exactly flush.'

'Why did you stop representing him?' Irvine asked.

'Very simply, he stopped paying my bills.' Slatterly smiled.

'We'd heard he was annoyed that you and Simon bought back his solo album from his record company yourselves?' Irvine stated repeating some of the gossip they'd picked up.

'Yes, I heard that little tale as well,' Slatterly replied. 'Basically, I negotiated with the record company for them to return the masters to Wilko. Wilko, Simon and I discussed the deal in great depth in this office. When push came to shove, Wilko wouldn't come up with the money. He said they were his songs and they should be given back to him free. When that didn't fly, he wanted Simon to buy them back for him. Simon, quite simply, said that he wouldn't buy them back for Wilko. The only way he could justify such expense would be to buy them back himself, as an investment, and pay Wilko a percentage from any sale of the masters. Wilko was desperate and he agreed, in a huff. I finalised the deal. I was not party to the deal and Simon Peddington paid me for my time.'

'Are there any pending lawsuits out against Wilko?'

'Actually, I can only speak for when I finished working with him. There was always a list of paternity suits, but I think that's common with a lot of pop stars, and he rarely was taken to court, mainly because the other side's brief would find out there was no gold at the end of that particular rainbow.'

'If he was that tight for money, how did he manage to get by?' The DS asked.

'You tell me. It's a phenomenon known only in the entertainment business. I see television stars, movie stars and pop stars, none of whom have worked for years and yet, they still have this lifestyle that doesn't seem to change. I could never work it out. Wilko did occasionally receive funds from Sean Green, but not enough to keep him in the manner to which he'd become accustomed.'

'Does that mean he'd lots of creditors?'

'Some, I suppose, but none who ever wanted to do anything legal about it, or I would have been involved.' Slatterly smiled. 'Simon would probably be a better man to answer that question.'

'Was Wilko easy to deal with?' Irvine asked what he hoped would be his final question.

'Oh, he was okay. He'd get frustrated sometimes when things weren't going his way. He didn't pay enough attention to the contracts, he'd sign anything. That was dangerous for me, it leaves me open to a charge of malpractice at a later date. But you know, he was a pop star, you can't expect too much.'

'Yes, indeed. That's all for now, sir. Thanks for your time' Irvine replied, looking at the very thin file Richard Slatterly was closing.

Meanwhile, Simon Peddington and Coles were discussing the pros and cons of the music business and puzzling over Wilko's inability to crack the charts.

'You see, the main difference,' Simon Peddington began. 'Between the artist and their public, is that the audience will always listen to the song, but the artist will listen to the recording.'

'Are they not both the same thing?' Coles inquired. They were sitting in Peddington's dark, comfortable offices in Regent's Park Road, the end near the Chalk Farm bridge, in the company of Constable Tony West.

'Ah, they're most definitely not. They are entirely different,' Peddington replied. 'The song is pure. It'll either connect with the listener, or not. The artists will listen to the recording and hear only the shortcomings. The voice is too quiet, or too loud, the drums are too noisy, they can't hear the choir, the keyboards are drowning out the harmony vocals and on and on and on. That was the problem with Wilko's songs. They just weren't great and he wasted loads of money trying to make them something they could never be. He was trying to make hits and they never came.'

'There aren't people who help the artists with this?'

'Yes, we can give our opinions, but in the end it's down to the artist. And it's tough for them, because everyone in the business is a critic. Managers, record company twits, publishers, girlfriends, roadies, radio producers, and our good friends in the press.'

Simon Peddington looked like he ought to have known what he was talking about. One wall of his entire office was given up to stacks and stacks of records. About a third were singles, the balance were standard, original vinyl records. Not a CD in sight.

'So, could you not have found Wilko some good songs elsewhere which might have become hits?' Constable West asked. 'Lots of people seems to have hits with covers these days.'

'Good point, and in fact one of Circles' biggest hits was their cover of "Together Again," a Buddy Holly song. But they'd already had several hits of their own. Wilko wanted to go out on a solo career with his own songs. He felt he'd a lot to prove! Maybe he had. Circles were a very successful group, he had a lot to live up to,' Simon replied.

'But didn't the fact that he was the lead singer of a very successful group count in his favour?' West again.

'*Formerly* a successful group. Don't forget, when Wilko left Circles they were washed-up,' Simon reminded West.

'How was Wilko off for money?' Coles asked.

'Houdini wasn't half the magician our Wilko was. Personally, I don't know how he got by on his income. I knew what was coming in and believe me it was a whole lot less than what was going out.'

'So, where *was* the difference coming from?'

'Search me.'

'You've no idea?'

'Well in the beginning, his accounts were such a mess that

no one noticed the deficit. But then, when a few of my invoices were ignored, I chased down the accountant and we started to put some kind of order to it.'

'There were large debts out there?' West asked.

'Well, there should have been. But no, he was always able to make ends meet.'

Coles thought for a moment. She just about managed to make her own finances work. Police pay was not great, by any means, and after mortgage payments, buying clothes, food and the few bits and pieces which made one's life easier, she nearly zeroed herself out each month. How did Wilko manage it?

'Is there any chance he could have had another source of income, interest from some inheritance or something?' she asked.

'I doubt it. The reality was, he had trouble keeping money. He thought it was for spending and positively loved to spend it.'

'Why did Wilko rejoin Circles?' West asked.

'See all of the above.' Again a simple reply from the manager.

'Why did Sean want him back in the group?'

'Now, I couldn't work that one out at all. Either Sean Green is a very generous and forgiving guy or…'

'Or?' Coles coaxed.

'Well, I suppose there would be a certain logic to Wilko rejoining the group if he, you know, had something on Sean and, well…'

'Wilko might have been blackmailing Sean Green?' West asked incredulously.

'Maybe not as strong as blackmail. But you have to admit, it has a certain logic about it.'

'OK,' Coles said, enthusiastically. 'What could Wilko have been blackmailing Sean about?'

'Now there *is* a question,' Peddington replied.

'What were you doing, Sir, on Thursday evening last?'

'On Thursday evening last I was having dinner with a client

of mine. A singer/songwriter from Dublin, who was in town for a couple of days. I hung out with him all Thursday from about seven o'clock until way after midnight. He's a great artist, a cross between Van Morrison and Ronan Keating. He's called G. B. Shaw.'

West felt compelled to asked the inevitable question.

'What, as in George Bernard?'

'Sadly, no. Gary Brian. We're hoping for a big success though.'

Twenty-Six

WPC Coles and DS Irvine were about to commence an interview with a solicitor, Irvine's second lawyer of the day, Mr. Leslie Russell.

'Now then,' Russell began, after shaking hands warmly and inquiring about Kennedy's well-being, 'what can I do for you two on this cold and frosty day?'

'We're just doing some follow-up work on Wilko Robertson,' Irvine offered, trying to find comfort in his modern chair. 'And we've a few follow-up questions for you.'

'Fire away.'

'Well,' Coles began, 'From what we can gather, Wilko was living well beyond his means. There was more going out than coming in. But he was still keeping his head above water. Is there any chance Sean Green was helping him out?'

'I suppose it's possible, but I rather doubt it. Sean would be charging it against some account, so I'm sure it would have crossed my desk at some time.'

'Did Sean ever discuss bringing Wilko back into the group?' Coles asked.

'Yes, he felt that the band would have a better chance in the States with the original line-up. There seemed to be a certain logic in that.'

'We believe you and Sean were still negotiating the deal with Wilko?' Irvine asked.

'Yes. With Wilko and his new solicitor, Richard Scott.'

'And had you hit any snags?' Again Coles.

'No, not really.'

'Then why was it taking so long?' Coles persisted.

'As a matter of fact, in terms of legal negotiations it *wasn't*, but there was a bit of posturing going on, on their side. We insisted that Wilko had independent legal representation, and his solicitor, Slatterly, was trying to prove that he was worth his fee.'

'And I bet he had the meter running all the time,' Irvine chipped in.

'I'm afraid it would be unprofessional of me to comment on that,' Russell said, smiling.

'What sort of things were you discussing?' Coles inquired.

'Mostly merchandising issues,' Russell replied.

'The swag, you mean?' Irvine laughed.

'Precisely,' Russell continued. 'We're talking serious money. At a place like Wembley for instance which holds eleven thousand people who each spend pay up to sixteen pounds on merchandise for something like Cliff, or down to a minimum of say, one pound and fifty pence per head for an artist with a less committed audience.'

'Where would Circles fit into the scale of things?' Coles inquired.

'Oh, at their peak I'd say we were grossing about four pounds and sixty pence a head.'

'So, Richard Scott is right to drag his heals over crossing the T's and dotting the I's?'

'Absolutely. That's why we recommended Wilko get outside legal advice in the first place. He was happy enough to be back in the group, earning real money and still have everything paid for by the group. In the end, to make sure it was all above board, Sean even agreed to pay his legal bill,' Russell told them.

'What? Sean paid Wilko's solicitor's bill so that the solicitor could negotiate a contract with Sean?' Coles inquired.

'Yes.'

'But isn't that a conflict of interest?'

'I can assure you it's both ethical and common practice. It happens all the time in deals with music publishers and record companies. Obviously when they are signing an unknown act, the act isn't able to afford the legal bills. Equally, if the act doesn't take legal advice then the contract could be deemed null and void,' Russell explained.

'Is Sean Green an easy man to deal with?' Irvine asked, fishing in a different stream.

'I doubt if one could use the word "easy" to describe Sean. However, if you do your job properly, as he pays you to, he's fine. This firm have represented him for a very long time and I suppose that says something in itself.'

'Did he and Wilko ever have a falling-out or a disagreement?' Irvine asked.

'Not that I'm aware of.'

'Is there anyone you know who would have wanted to harm Wilko?' Irvine asked, a wee bit desperate.

'I've racked my brains since it happened, but I can't for the life of me think of one person. However, ' Russell said. 'This morning, I received a copy of the record company's sales figures for the Circles' catalogue, particularly the Greatest Hits, and…well, they've gone through the roof. I imagine there will be three Circles' albums in next week's top-twenty and the Greatest Hits might even make it to number one. So, I suppose, there is at least one group of people who are benefiting from Wilko's death,' Russell revealed.

'Surely Sean Green will reap the same rewards?' Coles inquired.

'I suppose so,' Russell conceded. Coles was convinced by his inflection that he was trying to persuade the police that this was the first time such an idea had swam through the troubled waters of this particular solicitor's mind.

'Can we talk for a bit about this other publishing deal? You know, the one that both James MacDonald and Wilko were up for, and Sean wasn't?' Irvine asked.

'Yes.'

'Why did Sean not want to do the deal? It was a great deal I hear,' Irvine continued.

'Yes, you are quite correct. It was a sweetheart of a deal. They were offering a staggering three million pounds up front for the entire song catalogue,' Russell announced.

That got their attention.

'Holy shit,' Irvine gasped in open envy. 'Sean Green turned down three million pounds?'

'Yes, but it was a calculated business decision made in the cold light of day by Sean and, you know, under scrutiny it does bear up. Remember the story about John and Paul being offered Northern Songs for £20,000,000,' Russell began. He had the ability to take you off on a tangent, but by the way his delivery changed gear, you knew his story was going to be a compelling one. 'These were songs Lennon and McCartney had written for free, you need to remember. They had formed a company with Dick James, who was, up to that point, famous only for singing and writing the theme song to the TV series Robin Hood. Anyway, even though it was supposedly their own company, they were still only on a 50/50 royalty which they continuously asked Dick James to increase. They were the most successful song-writing team in the world and their deal was crap, but would their friend agree to a change. Not on you life.'

The solicitor paused to ensure his audience was still with him. He needn't have worried. 'Not only had they made him rich beyond his wildest dreams, but when he decided he wanted to get out of the business – this would have been in the late sixties – he didn't even tell them he was selling out. They most definitely would have raised the £3,000,000 he sold his shares to Lew Grade's ATV music for, but he didn't even give them a call to let them know what was happening. That was in 1969. It didn't end there. That's the thing about this business, no matter how legit it's meant to be, artists, on all levels, are always being shafted. Even artists such as the Beatles were not beyond being on the sharp end of the stick. In 1981 ATV decided they were going to sell Northern Songs for the aforementioned £20,000,000. Lew Grade, having come from the old school, proved to be more honourable and rang Paul McCartney up to offer him first refusal. This time Paul decided he would go for it. At that point, John, sadly, was dead. Paul decided the most honourable thing for him to do would was to ring up Yoko, who controlled John's estate, with a view to them doing a deal together. Paul reports that Yoko said it was too expensive and she would get her people onto it and secure it for five million quid. Obviously the deal fell through and an Australian bit ATV's hand off to win the deal. Yoko obviously needed the money for one of her other then current passions; purchasing prize cows. She would have been au fait with the pedigrees, some say. Sadly it doesn't even end there. In 1985 Wacko Jacko bought Northern Songs for fifty three million dollars, which then would have been about forty million pounds, in real money. Again McCartney had no knowledge about the deal until after it was done. So, you see, Sean holding out on the deal for his catalogue, proved that he'd learnt something from the Beatles' misfortune, which really had to be the crime of the millennium.'

'I'd read bits and pieces about it in the papers over the years, but I'd never realised it was as obscene as that. Mind you, I'm not so sure you should be comparing the Circles' catalogue to The Beatles' catalogue. If you are, never let Detective Inspector Kennedy hear you say it,' Irvine offered.

'No, no I wouldn't, and he'd be correct. But my points would have to be this. One: Sean Green is not short of money. If someone is prepared to offer that kind of money then they must reckon that it is possible to make a profit on it in the long run. So, from Sean's point of view, as he doesn't need the money today, why should he not hold on to his songs and make the original three million, plus a lot more besides? In ten years time, God knows what it will be worth,' Russell said, and then added as an afterthought, 'Particularly considering the sales they've enjoyed over the last couple of days.'

'Well,' announced Irvine rising from his chair, 'On that very high note, we'll leave you.'

Five minutes later, Coles and Irvine were in the car, driving back to the station.

'It would all be make a lot more sense if it was Sean Green who'd been murdered. We'd have two great suspects in Wilko Robertson and his publisher. What did Leslie Russell advise us they would have made from the sale?'

'One hundred and fifty thousand pounds for Wilko and seventy-five grand for James MacDonald,' Coles replied, as she negotiated the very heavy traffic at the junction of Chalk Farm Road and Camden High Street. Not a million miles from Dingwalls Dancehall, in fact.

'You see, now that is a lot of money. Some scavengers would murder their mothers for a lot less than that.'

'It's a lot of money, but not as much as three million,' Coles said.

'Sorry?'

'OK. It's just a theory, but...'

'I'm listening,' Irvine said.

'Sean Green gets offered three million pounds for the Circles' songs. He realises what the potential is. He decides, rather than sell out to another company, he will not only keep the catalogue, but also increase its value.'

'So how was he going to do that?' Irvine inquired.

'Simple. He brings Wilko back into the group and makes a bit of a fuss about it so that his name, Wilko Robertson, is publicly connected with the group again. He then murders Wilko at a gig, he knows it's sure to receive a lot of attention, and then he sits back and watches the sales go through the roof. Look at Hendrix, Lennon, The Doors, Otis Redding. Following their deaths their sales increased tenfold and their records just keep selling and selling. I know that Circles are not in the same league, but even a small percentage of what those artists are turning over these days would float a small country or two.'

'I wonder,' Irvine said as they pulled into the Car Park at North Bridge House, 'Interesting theory, float it past DI Kennedy and see what he thinks.'

I'll take great pleasure in doing exactly that, Coles thought.

Twenty-Seven

Detective Inspector Christy Kennedy was tired, hungry and early as he waited for Kevin Paul at the back of Trattoria Lucca. Frank, the owner, showed him to his seat, enthusing over Arsenal's current form, 'If we could just keep winning matches the way Manchester United do, we'd win the league again.'

'Footy-vibe, man,' was KP's greeting, on over-hearing the conversation. 'Give me a Bestie any day of the week. Now he was so good I'd almost forgive him for doing those adverts for Cookstown Sausages.'

'How's it going?' Kennedy asked. There was no one else in the rear section of the comfortable restaurant, so they could enjoy total privacy.

'Oh, it's a stressed-vibe, this detective work. I can tell you. I used to think that all you did was a Columbo type vibe. You know, just bumble around, looking cross-eyed in a tatty gabbo and a cool car, finishing every interview with a, "Oh, just one final thing.",' KP answered.

'Aye, that's an approach, I suppose,' Kennedy laughed. He felt a tickle in his throat. He swallowed again quickly and it disappeared.

'Now, this is a totally different trip altogether, man. You earn your dosh, I can tell you,' KP enthused.

'Why, thank you Kevin.'

Frank returned to take their order. Kennedy had his usual spaghetti with pesto sauce and peas and a cup of tea to wash it down. This drew a up-turned nose from KP.

'You are one weird detective, man. Pesto and Peas! Ever thought about going on telly and telling all your stories?'

Frank hovered over his order pad.

'And yourself, sir?'

'Love the polite-vibe, man. Ah, I'll have the potato and leek soup and a Fountain Salad, whatever that it. I just love the name. Oh, and a glass of your finest white wine, Landlord.'

'OK, Kevin. First off I need to ask you about this Wilko and Tracey affair,' Kennedy started, the minute Frank had left. 'You see, Tracey denies it, Susan said it was impossible and Tracey said you made the claim because you wanted to go to bed with her.'

'And I *did* go to bed with her and what's more it was truly wonderful. Then we didn't anymore because she'd found someone else and that someone else she found was Wilko. She made me promise that I'd never tell Wilko she and I had a scene. I think, as much as anything else, she needed to talk to someone about it. She knew it was wrong but she had fallen for him and he for her, supposedly. Well he would, wouldn't he? She was a woman. And boy, what a woman,' KP announced.

'How long did they date?' Kennedy asked.

'Well, it wasn't really a "dating" vibe, man, if you know what I mean. It was kinda difficult with the wife in the background and the fact that the wife was also the sister, the same sister who wanted Tracey to move in with her and Wilko. They had, shall we say, a scene for the last eight years or so.'

'You're kidding?' Kennedy gasped.

'No, I'm not kidding. And it was an awkward situation for me because I'd have to cover for both of them, a go-between kind of vibe. They'd both confide in me. I know for a fact that they were still at it up to the day he died, literally!'

'Pardon?'

'She came down to the soundcheck to meet up with him and they went off to the Britannia Hotel for a couple of hours. I know, man, because it was me who picked them up and brought them back to the gig.'

KP must have spotted some doubt in Kennedy's eyes.

'I can prove it as well, because I paid their bill on Circles AMEX. It's known in show business terms as a day room, so it's a legit expense. But besides, I've got the itemised bill back at my pad if you want to see it. It details food and drink for two.'

'When you picked them up, how did they seem?'

'Yea, cool-vibe, man. They seemed fine to me. We dropped her off at the front and Wilko went on one of his guilt trips with me, "God, I know I should stop but I just can't keep my hands off her." I'd always thought it wasn't his hands he should have been worried about. All he had to do, allegedly, was to look at a girl and she'd get pregnant.'

'But he and Susan didn't have any children,' Kennedy added, as the food arrived.

'Sadly, Susan couldn't have kids. I think that was why Wilko went around on his wild-oats vibe. He wanted to prove to everyone that he could cut the mustard. Bit too much of a macho trip for me man, but each to their own. This is delicious soup, man.'

'So, when they came out of the hotel, they didn't look like they were arguing?' Kennedy continued.

'No, not really. I mean, I wasn't really tuned in to them. My mind was more on the gig,' KP answered. He was about to swallow another spoonful of soup, when something stopped him. 'There's one thing though, and it might be nothing.'

'Yeah?' Kennedy asked.

'Well, I didn't really think about it as being strange at the time, but when I went back to the Britannia to pick them up they were waiting for me in the lobby. That's unusual for them, I usually have to pry them out of the room,' KP recalled.

'You weren't late or anything?'

'No, as I said, they were usually impossible to get out of the room, so I was always early. If he misses a gig, it's not his fault; it's my fault for not getting them there on time. So, I always allow myself an extra twenty minutes or so with Wilko. Sean, now he's completely the opposite. He's always on time, or five minutes ahead. He'd be the first on the tour bus and, God bless him, he doesn't sit there moaning about all the latecomers. And Wilko was *always* late,' KP broke into another of his grins.

'Reminds me of when we started. I'd drive everyone and the equipment in a Ford Transit. Which was okay but by the time we did the gig and come back to London – we could rarely afford hotel rooms in those days – it would be the early hours and there'd be a fight as to who'd be dropped off first. Wilko usually shouted the loudest. But the thing about Wilko was he could sleep on a tupenny stamp. He'd jump in the van when we picked him up, he'd say a quick hello lean his head against the window and be out like a light. Not wake up until we arrived at the gig. One day, I think we were playing the Boat Club in Nottingham and we'd been driving for hours, Wilko woke up in darkness, jumped up and shouted, "KP don't forget to drop me off first, man." "For goodness sake, head." I replied, "We haven't even reached Nottingham yet to play the gig." He'd just lost all sense of time,' KP offered by way of explanation.

'So, they were waiting for you in the lounge of the hotel. Can you remember anything about them, anything all?'

'Like?' KP asked.

'Were they sitting together on a sofa? Were they standing apart? Any signs of intimacy? Or hostility?' Kennedy coaxed.

'Well now, let's think about this for a moment, man. I can see it's important to you. Yea, okay I remember. When I arrived at the hotel Wilko was sitting by the door in an easy chair. He said that Tracey had just gone to get a newspaper. When I was laying down the plastic with the cashier she came over to me, minus a newspaper. I didn't think about it at the time, but now

I come to think of it, she didn't have a newspaper. Does that mean anything?'

'How did she seem?'

'She seemed okay to me. I mean they were quiet in the back of the car on the way back to Dingwalls but I just put that down to pre-gig nerves on Wilko's part and her allowing him his space. He said we should drop Tracey off first, near the front door, and when we did, he laid his guilt-trip on me again.'

KP helped himself to a generous swig of wine and turned to his Fountain Salad, so named because of its presentation. Three whole carrots standing upright in the middle of the plate, surrounded by an array of yoghurt coated nuts, lettuce, grapes, bananas, avocado, scallions and miniature boiled potatoes, still in their skins, peppered around the perimeter of the plate.

'Totally wild vibe man,' KP pronounced with evident joy. 'A bit more colour in it and it would be truly wonderful. My compliments to the chef, landlord.'

'So, were you badly cut up over the thing with Tracey?' Kennedy asked.

'Not really, regretfully. I mean regretfully, because the sex had been truly wonderful. On our first night together I counted at least seven things she did to me which are probably illegal in some countries. But if I was being totally honest, man, there was nothing between us other than the sex.'

Kennedy considered Tracey McGee. A sex goddess? He didn't think so. But then, Wilko couldn't keep his hands off her and, eight years later, KP still recalls her with more than a twinkle in his eye. You simply never know, do you?

'Oh, I get the motive vibe, man,' KP announced, mouth full of salad. 'You're wondering could I possibly have harboured a grudge against Wilko for the last eight years, and topped him to get Tracey back for myself.'

'A possibility, you have to admit,' Kennedy replied, hoping a smile would dilute the seriousness of the question.

KP considered this for a time and eventually said, 'Yes, I'd have to give you that. In a different set of circumstances, it could have been a possibility. I'd have to have been hopelessly in love though, a flaw I do not think I carry in my baggage. I'd have to have been able to bear a grudge for eight years, allowing it fester and ferment away, all the time growing into a carbuncle vibe. Finally, I would have to have been someone who could take someone else's life. I'm not religious. Hippie yes, religious no, but I could never end someone's life. I'd never have the bottle, for one thing.'

'Who do you know who would have the bottle?' Kennedy continued.

'Well I've been thinking about that a lot and I think I might be on to something,' KP boasted.

'Please tell?'

'Not yet. I'm still waiting for a few loose ends to be tied up. Let's wait to see if it pans out, then I'll give you the low-down.'

Kennedy wanted more, but KP was playing his cards close to his chest. What could KP possibly have uncovered? Some of the manager's dealings? The band and their finances were complex, but Kennedy's investigation he hadn't uncovered even a hint of fraud.

It was starting to get dark outside. Kennedy paid the bill, no resistance offered from KP, and they headed out into the overcast winter afternoon. Kennedy planned to see Sean Green and possibly his wife, Colette, next.

Kennedy noticed that, even an a hour or so before the offices closed, The Spread Eagle was filling up. As the detective had discovered this particular pub was beginning to buzz increasingly with Camden Town's music business types. He asked, by way of conversation, 'Do you lot ever go there?'

'Nah,' KP answered quick as a flash, 'No one ever goes there. It's always too crowded.'

For once, Kevin Paul failed to realise the wit of his words. The detective shook KP's hand warmly as they parted. Kennedy took comfort in that he had met someone, albeit under the adverse conditions of a murder investigation, who he liked, a lot in fact. He hoped to get to know this particular Camden Town character better when the case was solved.

'See you later, Kevin.'

'God bless you man, see you later.'

Kennedy felt another tickle in his throat. He imagined an unwanted cold lurking in the back ground, or even worse the beginnings of a flu. There were not many things in Kennedy's life he hated, but having the flu was definitely one of them. The detective enjoyed his life and his work so much that he detested anything, such as catching a cold, or worse still, a flu, which interfered with his enjoyment of it. Kennedy made do with a call to the chemist and he purchased three wonder cures for his impending aliments. The grey skies had disappeared and the sun broke through for the remains of the day. At this time of the year, Camden Town with it's fiery red skies drifting past the multi coloured skyline was simply a pleasure to behold. Particularly this year with the fresh white fall of a snow helping to cover up all the bits the council would like to sweep under the carpet. Sadly this white carpet was but a temporary solution to their problem. A problem that would return, in aces, when the snow was replaced by slush. However, for now, it was a picture-postcard fit to rival all, and any, Woody Allen might take of his beloved Manhattan. Kennedy took comfort in the red stormy skies; they usually meant the following day was going to be a good weather day. And a good weather day would be helpful in beating the imminent flu germs into an early submission.

Twenty-Eight

WPC Coles and DS Irvine had spilt up again, despite the fact they both would have liked to interview witnesses together. They were becoming a good team, but the current work-load dictated that as Kennedy was on his way to the Green residence, Irvine was knocking on the front door of Robert Clarke's residence and Coles was being shown into James Mac Donald's office.

Mac Donald's greeting was warm and friendly.

'Sorry to have to trouble you again, but we've a few more questions we needed to ask you,' Coles started.

'Fire away, by all means. We at Goode Olde Songs have nothing to hide.'

'Speaking of Goode Olde Songs, I understand you were offered three million quid for the company. That's quite an offer.' Coles opened her mental briefcase and removed the first question card.

'You unearthed the figure. I thought you would.'

'I'm sure it's not really a secret, Mr. MacDonald. BTV Music is a publicly owned company. The board would have had to clear any offer made. Were you not even in the slightest tempted by the offer?'

'Tempted?! I would have thrown in my first born as part of the deal as well.' MacDonald laughed bitterly.

'So?' Coles prompted.

'It wasn't my call. I did the negotiations,' MacDonald boasted, 'but, at the end of the day, Sean Green has the final say. It *is* his company.'

'Tell me, your share of the three million – how much would that have been?' Coles asked.

'Three hundred grand, give or take,' MacDonald responded, exaggerating six fold if Russell's figure was accurate, give or take.

'That is a lot of change. Had you thought what you'd do with it?' Coles asked.

'Funnily enough, I had,' MacDonald started. 'I was going to see if I could form another company inside GOS, with Sean as an equal partner. Call it something like GOS/Other Artists, invest some of my money and sign some other acts. I've got all the contacts now, you know. I know how to do it.'

'Did you and Wilko ever to change Sean's mind?' Coles asked presenting one of her trump questions.

'Well that wasn't really the way with Sean. When Sean didn't want to do something, he wouldn't come right out and say it. He'd say something like, "I'll get back to you on that." But he never would. End of subject. I know that Wilko and his solicitor brought it up at one of the meetings, but it didn't fly there, either. I think Sean had something else in mind, he just wouldn't ever say what. If Sean had only come to us with his plan and said look, "Here's how I see it, here's how I want to do it." that would have been okay, you know?'

'But did he need to do that with you or Wilko? Were you partners? Surely if you *were* partners he would have had included you in the decision-making process,' Coles asked.

'Well no, not exactly.'

'What *exactly* do you mean?'

'I'm employed by Sean to run his company. He pays me a wage and also a small percentage of his company.' MacDonald just about managed to let the words escape through his gritted teeth.

'So, could GOS shareholders, you, Wilko and Leslie Russell, not club together and vote some sense in Sean's head?'

'No, not really.'

'And why's that?' Coles asked, noticing for the first time how badly bitten MacDonald's fingernails were.

'Well, you see, they're not really those kind of shares. They're more profit-related bonuses I suppose.'

'Oh, I see,' Coles announced, as much to West as to McDonald. 'So you really aren't a shareholder at all, more of a manager, really. I guess there was really nothing you or Wilko could do about it then, was there?'

He turned on her, humiliated and angry.

'Ah. Well now, that's what you think.'

'Well, there seems to be no other conclusions.'

'You see that's where you're mistaken. Wilko had another way. A back door in, as it were. A casting vote, so to speak. A pillow persuader, if you will,' MacDonald said. He looked disappointed, as if he'd hoped to take greater pleasure from the disclosure.

'What, you mean…you don't mean Colette Green?' Coles threw away the rest of her questions.

'I'm not saying another word,' he replied, defeated.

But you already have you bastard, Coles thought. You think you've already done the damage don't you?

'Just one more question before we go, Mr MacDonald,' Coles said, as she rose from her chair. 'Can you tell us where you were last Thursday evening, between the hours of eight p.m. and midnight?'

'I can as it happens,' he returned smugly. 'I was in Birmingham, to see one of these new writers I've been telling you about. One I hope to sign. He was playing in a hotel, the Central. I caught the 17.05 train from Euston which got me in to New Street at 18.55 I went straight to the Central, where I checked-in, watched telly for a bit, and then met the writer, a Mr Tommy Flowers, at about eight o'clock. He did his show at nine, I was a wee bit disappointed to be honest. You expect songs to be better live than on cassette; they weren't. We had dinner; I got back to my hotel room about a quarter to midnight, crashed out and caught the 07.42 train back to Euston Friday morning. I got into London at 09.25 and was at my desk working by ten a.m.'

Twenty-Nine

And then it was Irvine's turn.

Robert Clarke lived, financially and geographically, at the other end of Camden Town. He shared a second floor flat in Camden Square. It turned out his flat-mates were in when Irvine and Allaway called, so Clarke led them into his bedroom so that they would have some peace and quiet to carry out the interview. Irvine was shocked at the response Clarke received from Valerie Bower when he requested she and her ex-boyfriend (the third flat-mate) go down the pub while he chatted with the police. 'Fob off down the pub yourself; I'm doing me noodles. It's my flat as well, you know, and I don't give a shit who's around.'

Long gone were the days when the police were treated with respect and warmth, not to mention a little fear.

Robert Clarke's bedroom was so neat, tidy and clean the chambermaids at the Savoy Hotel would have been proud to say it was on their round. The room was positively cavernous with high ceilings and the illusion of space was further enhanced with a coat or two of white paint. The bare floorboards were honey coloured and coated with a clear varnish. The large bay window afforded a panoramic view of Camden Square. Robert used the bay window as a workspace. He'd filled it with a desk, computer, synth-keyboard, cassette

Recorder, lots of paper and lots of light. To the right of that, in the alcove, was a shelving system packed floor to ceiling with albums, singles, CDs, cassettes and books. Then came a fireplace, complete with gas fire and pretend flames. Above the fireplace was a Circles poster with Robert's face, centre position beaming from ear to ear. Set in the alcove on the opposite side of the fireplace was the head of his double bed with a blue eiderdown. A pair of black velvet trousers were neatly draped over the back of the room's one easy chair. Clarke removed the trousers, put them on a wooden coat hanger and hung them in the large pine wardrobe which was packed to overflowing and positioned in the centre of the remaining wall. He offered the easy chair to Irvine, spun around the chair at the workspace for Allaway and positioned himself on the bed.

Robert Clarke was dressed in a well-worn, but classic, black suit with a Daz white shirt. Before hopping on the bed, he had unbuttoned his jacket and yanked his trousers up slightly at the knees. He was a tall, fit man with well-chiselled features, with longish but styled blonde hair. The overall appearance was more North American than North London.

'I know what you're thinking,' Clarke began nervously, 'Pop star, member of big group and he still shares a bedsit?'

'Actually, to be honest, I'd been thinking how tidy your bedroom is,' Irvine admitted.

'Why, thank you,' Clarke replied, displaying just a slight hint of campness. 'No. Mmm, as I was saying, I know people expect me to be in a mansion. You have to remember that I was an employee of Circles. I wasn't on a percentage. The wages were good, I grant you, and Sean Green is more than generous with his bonuses, but my mum always told me to live within my means, so, rather than mortgage myself up to the eyeballs, I just put a lot of it away. Ernie, my little nest egg, is growing all the time. I'm trying to get my own record deal, and, if that comes together I'll be able to do a publishing deal. I know I'll need the advance from the record company to float my career, but well, the publishing money I'm hoping to use that, along with Ernie, to buy somewhere nice, maybe over in Islington. Islington, now that's the happening place. I've got friends over there. And this one girl, well two actually, two partners I mean. They bought a place in Amell Street, they got it, oh let's see, Lordy it must be about six years ago now, yes it would have been six years because I was in Circles at the time and that's how I met them. Well I didn't meet them through Circles, but because I was in Circles I was invited to this dinner party and Anita and Pauline were there and they were so nice to me, so genuine. Where was I? Oh yes, anyway, they bought this place about six years ago for seventy five grand and, yes they did spend a bit doing it up. They did it up wonderfully, they've got such good taste, actually Pauline is the one with the exquisite taste, Anita tends to coast along on her coat tails as it were. So, anyways, an identical flat, two doors down, recently came on the market. I know this because Pauline rang me up to tell me. She knew I was looking, but the truth is I wasn't quite ready to buy, but all my friends keep tipping me off on places. Lordy it's such good fun going around to see all these places, you get such wonderful ideas for your own places, when you get one that is. But you'll never guess how much they were looking for this other flat?'

'No?' Irvine who'd sat stunned through all of this barrage was glad to get his first words in edgeways, or anyways for that matter. You could tell Robert was a musician by the beat of his conversation. Irvine figured if they had long enough, he and Allaway simply needed to sit there and eventually Clarke would have told them everything they needed to know.

'Two hundred and thirty five grand,' Robert screamed, and, throwing caution to the wind, moved to high camp. 'Lordy, I mean it's fine for me. Well, really, it's not even fine for me. But when I think about a young family starting off with two children, how on earth could they afford it? I'm going to be fine of course. I've got some great songs. Pauline, the one with the taste, I was telling you about, you know Anita's friend. Friend, now that's a good word isn't it? They're not really friends, they're life partners. You know, let's call a spade a spade. However, I'm not quite sure because Pauline, well you see, she's older, much older and Anita well I kind of think, this is a personal view of course, I think she's still got some wild oats to sow, so it might be difficult. However, you see, that's where Pauline's canniness comes in. She knows that Anita has got to get this out of her system so she's been encouraging her to, Lordy this is so embarrassing, discussing this with members of the local police force. How do I ever get myself into these situations,' Clarke rattled on.

At this juncture, Irvine was convinced Clarke was going to blush. He regained his composure and continued uninterrupted. Uninterrupted because the police were still so shell-shocked they didn't offer even a mutter of resistance.

'Where was I? Oh Yes. Lordy, she's only been encouraging Anita to sow some wild oats. But I've told Pauline this is a two-edge sword. I said to her, I said, "Pauline you're playing with fire." Because she is, you know, playing with fire. But anyways as I was saying, oh yes, two points, Pauline loves my material. It's kind of confessional stuff, you know, and Pauline said, "Robbie." she calls me Robbie you know, I'd never dream of letting anyone else call me Robbie and you must promise not to tell anyone that Pauline's nickname for me is, Robbie. Anyway, she said, "Robbie, you're very brave to bare you soul like that. Most males can't. I think you're really in touch with you femininity." Can you believe she said that to me? I'm in touch with my feminine side. Anyway, I'll play you some of the songs before you leave, but the other point was that I'm okay with my songs to be able, eventually, to pay that kind of money for a place, but what about young couples starting. Now if they hadn't built the Dome, they could have spent all that money making homes easier to buy, married couples with children or first time buyers but, please, don't get me started on the Dome.

Mind you, that Peter Mandelson is nice, I'd love to see him with a moustache, though.'

Silence. Beautiful silence, Irvine thought. He hardly wanted to spoil the silence with a question of his own.

'Were you surprised when Sean brought Wilko back into the group?'

'Lordy no. You see, Sean Green, now he is a wonderful man. I have the feeling he may be in touch with his feminine side as well. I keep meaning to ask Pauline about that. She'd probably think it had something to do with his stature. Well, come on, let's admit it, he's hardly going to be a professional basketball player now is he? Come on!' Robert Clarke claimed and laughed effeminately. 'Lordy, I am awful, but I'm sure you won't tell him. Anyway. He was always up-front with me. Told me at the beginning that it was a tour-by-tour thing. Although he did pay me retainers in the downtime. Now he didn't need to do that. But he said he wanted first call on me. No one had ever wanted first call on me before, so he was welcome. However, I thought it was going okay with me in the band. I've got more of a vocal range than Wilko ever had. I can ape his voice, near perfect, on the belters, but then I can also go up a register and work with Sean on the harmonies. People were saying that the harmonies had never sounded so good. But, you see, Sean Green is great at working out strategy. He's probably a brilliant chess player. He can plan so many moves ahead. I'll let you into a little secret here. The reason Circles were so successful and continued to be so was down entirely to Sean Green. He did the majority of the song writing. Yes, I know, occasionally Wilko would have thrown in a word or two, like on "Colette Calls". And, let me tell this, you for a set of Wilko lyrics, they are very good. Mostly though it's Sean. But, apart from the song writing, he knows how to work the music business. He knows all the games which have to be played and, more importantly, how to play them. He beats them at their own game every time, but the really clever part is that they don't even know he's stroking them.'

'Will I take that as a no?' Allaway interrupted.

'Sorr -ie. What was the original question?' Clarke rejoined, shooting the constable a "You bitch" look.

'Were you surprised Sean introduced Wilko back into the group?' Allaway replied.

'Oh yes, sorry. You really must cut me off you know. Lordy I'm likely to rattle on here all day. I just adore a good natter, don't you? Anyway, I was gutted. But then you get to think it wasn't meant to be. You know, it was a sign for me to get on with my own career. Sadly I was to find out, to my cost, that being a member of Circles wasn't particularly good for one's CV. So, you know, every cloud has a silver lining and if I had remained in the band too much longer maybe I wouldn't have been able to get my own career started.'

'Yes, it's seems hard to do that doesn't it. I mean, Wilko tried didn't he?'

'Crap songs. Wilko had crap songs. And I can tell you, you're never going to get anywhere in this business with crap songs. And the place that you can get to with crap songs, and the record company hype which invariably goes with that particular station, is not somewhere you would want to go to,' Clarke lectured, waving the index finger of his right hand from side to side.

'Have you worked out why Sean brought Wilko back into the group?' Irvine asked, pushing his luck one further time.

'A momentary lapse in sanity,' Clarke replied, and then erupted in one of his girlish squeals again, 'No, sorry, just kidding. No, really. I've been thinking about it and I've been discussing this very subject a lot with Pauline but neither of us can come up with a solid reason for it. Although, as I have said, Sean is a great planner, and somewhere in there he would have had something clever worked out.'

'Were you at the show on Thursday?' Allaway asked.

'Oh, clever. Lordy, Lordy, very clever,' Clarke smiled back immediately, bouncing on his bed as if threatening to embark on the first flight of mankind. 'That's a very subtle way of asking me if I have an alibi for the night of the murder.'

'No,' Allaway replied indignantly, 'I was simply asking you, were you at the show on Thursday night last.'

'Oh, okay. Maybe I was crediting you with too...anyway. No, Lordy, no. I couldn't have abided it. I'm sure it would have been very high on the butt-clenching scale of embarrassments. A bunch of us got together at Anita and Pauline's for a kind of Broken Circles' party. I got absolutely hammered and spent the night over there and positively have the crow's feet to prove it.'

'Have you heard from Sean Green since that night?' Irvine continued.

'Well actually, I know it was very forward of me, but as I said, I did like Sean, so I rang him up the following day to say how sorry I was,' Clarke offered his shortest reply of the session.

'How did he seem?' The DS asked.

'Weird. I mean, he told me all about how Wilko had been found stabbed in the dressing-room with the door locked from the inside. I said it sounded frightfully Agatha Christie and do you know what he said?' Clarke again offered a short one.

'Go on?' Irvine took the bait. 'Tell us?'

'He said, "Oh well, when they come to make the movie, you can play the part of Wilko." Now is that macabre or what? Apart from that he seemed okay. I thought that perhaps he might still be in shock, so I gave my condolences; I mean I knew Sean was close to Wilko's family. I don't really know the wives or anything.'

'Had you ever met him? Met Wilko?' Irvine asked.

'I had actually, about three times. Once backstage at a Circles gig in the early days. I was a fan and wanted to get to meet them. The second time was when I was in the group and KP introduced me to him. KP, now there's a sweet guy. Don't get me wrong, not my type. I mean more sweet in as much as he was a hippie, a true hippie.'

Clarke paused appearing to be choosing his words carefully before continuing. Irvine guessed it was another tangent and so cut him off at the pass with, 'And the third time?'

The singer appeared uncertain, like someone who'd been woken suddenly from a light sleep.

'Sorry? The third time? The third time was when I was 'round at Leslie Russell's office picking up my final cheque and sorting out my National Insurance and all that stuff. As I was leaving the office, Wilko and his solicitor were entering. He was very gracious. He didn't need to be. I told him there was no ill feelings and wished him all the best. He asked what I was going to do and when I told him he said the best bit of advice he could give me, was to make sure I worked with the right people. We shook hands and parted on a very warm basis. I was quite happy at that you know. I can't abide all these ugly scenes and people throwing shapes, and that's just the road crews,' again Clarke paused to shriek at his own joke, testing the springs of his mattress a bit more. When he saw the two members of Camden Town CID were not joining in his party he continued,

'But they've all been really nice to me since I left. Sean told me I could ring him up anytime if I needed any info or help. Now I know a lot of people in this business say that, and then when you ring up they won't take your calls, but God bless him, Sean has always taken my calls and he's steered me on the right path a couple of times, even got me down-time at a studio he uses, so I could do my demos. Oh yes, that reminds me, I did promise you I'd play you a couple of tracks,' Clarke concluded as he launched himself off the bed and ran across the room to his music system to press the play button, before either policeman could offer a word in protest.

Obviously a well rehearsed routine, Irvine thought, allowing his cynical side to show through.

Ten minutes and three songs later he felt bad for having had such thoughts. The tape was brilliant; even PC Allaway was nodding approval. Irvine thought that the songs were just so good that most people with an ear for music would like them. He was also convinced that this man, this unassuming camp man, was going to be a success. Yes, Irvine thought, the songs were confessional in the way the early Elton John songs were, but they also seemed to have so much heart and soul. On top of which the songs still managed to have an instant appeal and had hooks the likes of which Celine Dion would die for.

Irvine nervously congratulated Robert Clarke on his songs. The DS felt somewhat inadequate in communicating to the singer just how good he felt the songs were.

'If they move people, that's all I ask for,' Clarke replied humbly, 'Lordy, of course I'd like you to buy them as well, that's if they ever get released on a CD.'

Irvine would have bet money that they would be. However, he also knew that Sean Green was about to invite Clarke to rejoin Circles. It was Irvine's opinion that if he accepted the invitation, Robert Clarke would be making the biggest mistake of his life.

Thirty

'Kennedy here.'

'Hi, KP here.'

'Hello how's…'

'Listen man, no time for niceties. I think I've cracked this. I can't really talk at the minute but can we meet later, say eleven, in the Golden Grill?' KP asked.

'Sure, what have you got?'

'I think I've solved your case. Not very pleasant though. I'm just playing this blu– Look, sorry, man. Gotta go, see you at eleven. God bless,' KP concluded the conversation in nearly a whisper and hung up the phone.

Kennedy assumed it was because someone had come into the room, wherever that was.

Thirty-One

Kennedy rang the doorbell of the Green residence and was greeted by the lady of the house herself. She apologised to Kennedy for her husband's absence, he'd been called out on urgent business, and she didn't know where he was.

'Actually, I also wanted a chat with yourself,' he announced, hands deep in pockets and collar pulled up against the cold.

'Goodness me!' she exclaimed, wiping her hands on her apron before offering one to the Detective Inspector. She used her handshake to pull him into the house, 'In that case you'd better come in. Do you mind if we go downstairs to the kitchen, it's just I'm in the middle of baking...'

'No, no that would be perfect,' Kennedy replied. He would much prefer to talk to her in the casualness of her kitchen than the formality of Sean's study, one flight above. About halfway down the hallway, the smell of baking pastry hit Kennedy's nostrils. Kennedy continued down the hallway, closer and closer to the smell and, with his sweet tooth, closer and closer to danger.

'Would you like a cup of tea or something?' Colette offered Kennedy, as she turned the radio down to a barely audible level.

"Is the Pope a Catholic?" Kennedy thought as he said, 'That would be nice.'

'Do you mind if I get you to make it yourself? I'm at a

crucial stage in this and I don't want it to be a disaster. Of course, if you need my undivided attention, I could scrap the lot and start again once you've gone,' Colette volunteered. Her accent was Scottish, but softened by many years away from the motherland.

'Heavens no,' Kennedy immediately replied, 'Just point me in the right direction and I'll happily make my own. Would you like one too?'

'A self-sufficient man. Great. And here's me thinking that you were totally extinct,' Colette replied.

'Ah, no. One of the joys of bachelorhood,' he replied.

'And a bachelor as well. A bachelor who can look after himself. God, leave your name on the notice board over there. Some, if not all, of my girlfriends will be forming a queue outside your door.'

Kennedy smiled but said nothing.

'The tea's in the cupboard directly above your head, behind you. The milk is in the fridge. The cups and saucers are in the cupboard, to the right of the fridge. The spoons are in the drawer to the left of the sink. The plug is in the wall by the cooker, the water is in the tap over the sink…'

'Truce, truce. Please,' Kennedy laughingly pleaded.

'Okay, and just to show my truce is not offered with a forked tongue, I'll even supply you with a couple of my speciality, Cheesecakes. But you mustn't tell Sean. I'll have to steal them from his stash and they're his favourites. Promise?'

'Promise.'

So, while Colette Green went about her baking business. Kennedy prepared the tea.

The space was about ten-foot by ten-foot and, although it wasn't really properly separated from the rest of the basement, it was a sort of fort, or refuge, with counters forming a square against the far wall from the stairwell. In pride of position, against the wall, was an old cream Aga. The counters were used for preparation and serving purposes, broken only by an entrance and a double sink unit. The cupboard doors and tops were all made of old teak wood and the overall effect, probably very expensive to recreate, was of a rustic farmhouse kitchen.

When Kennedy had completed his bit, he sat on one of the three high-stools guarding the counter. Kennedy watched as she unconsciously and energetically beat and coaxed the dough into submission with her bare hands. She then thinned it out with a rolling pin. Next she placed it over a large flat-rimmed soup dish, trimmed the pastry up to the edge, and placed in a generous helping of peeled apples.

'Sean likes his home cooked food. He's got a bit of a sweet tooth but he likes to know what he's eating. I'm not complaining, though. I love baking. It's very therapeutic.'

Colette then covered the contents of the dish with another layer of pastry, which again she trimmed to the edge. She matted it into the lower pastry along the flat rim, using of a fork, poked a few holes into the top of the pastry with the same fork and then took it proudly to her oven. She slid the dish into the oven and removed another before shutting the door again. She had done her long hair up into some kind of crazy bun, more for cooking than style.

'For a man with a sweet tooth, Sean doesn't appear to put on a lot of weight,' Kennedy said.

'I know, unforgivable isn't it?'

'Has he always been so slight?'

'For as long as I've known him. My son, William, can even pick him up. Sean gets very embarrassed and doesn't allow it any more, but it was very funny.'

'I suppose Sean's hair makes him appear bigger than he is?'

'Yep, but can I get him to change it? I keep reminding him of his age, but all he says is that it is part of his image now, and he has to keep it. I tried to get him to at least get rid of the 'tashe, but no way. Ah well, as my father used to say, a leopard never changes his spots. You said you wanted to speak to me.'

Colette left him to serve the tea and moved towards another

cupboard to take out a Tupperware container from which she removed four cheesecakes.

'Excuse the fingers.'

'Thank you,' Kennedy replied, taking one of the cakes. 'I'm trying to find out more about Wilko.'

'Yes?'

'It seems he was a bit of a character.'

'Aye he was that. A bit of a character,' Colette laughed. 'But he was more as well. A lot of people only got to see the rock and roll side of him. But he was a very sensitive man as well. Very warm, very giving. Maybe he was *too* giving. When he had some money the spongers would be around him like bears at the honey pot. He'd always buy the round, the dinner, the tickets or whatever. He was generous to a fault. That's why I left him,' Colette dropped a bombshell.

'Sorry?' Kennedy said. 'You left him? I mean, you were together?'

'Well, yes,' she said, offering him a generous smile as she brushed a few crumbs from the side of her mouth, 'Before you can leave someone, you first have to have been with them.'

'But, I thought…' Kennedy said. He didn't really know what he thought.

'Oh, I thought you might have found out by now. Yes, Wilkenson and I were together. William is his son. Tressa is Sean's daughter. That's how I met Sean – through Wilko. He was a good man, detective. Now he's dead I feel kind of numb. I've not been able to discuss it with anyone; no one wants to talk about it. Sean's being very clinical about it all. I'm trying to work out should I be grieving or celebrating.'

'God, I didn't know. I'm sorry, I'm very sorry,' Kennedy said, not really knowing where to put himself.

'And here I am talking to the police about it. Doesn't that show you the state of the world we live in? The father of my first child is dead, murdered, and the only person I can talk to about it is a policeman,' Colette hesitated, she looked like she was considering saying what was on her mind. 'You look like you care. Listen, Inspector, I'll tell whoever you want, the peelers *are* good for the community.'

'How did you meet?' Kennedy asked.

'We met in Scotland, in Glasgow, in The Barrowland Ballroom. It was a Circles gig, probably twenty years ago now. They were brilliant; the audience were as noisy as the band, singing along to all the hits. It was a wonderful night. I was out with a few girlfriends and we were in such high spirits that we decided to go on to a hotel we knew which had a late bar; we wanted a few more drinks and a bit more fun. And guess who was in the bar, buying the rounds? Wilkenson Robertson. He made a bee-line for one of my mates, Neen, a stunner. But she didn't want to know.'

Kennedy noticed that Colette had finished her tea, well before him, so he poured her another cup as she continued.

'I wasn't even his second choice. Mave was next. Problem number two for Wilko, she'd a steady boyfriend whom she was engaged to. Then it was my turn. Well, I can tell you, I was quite drunk and I let him have it right between those bushy Rob Roy eyebrows. Egged on by my drunken girlfriends, I told him, he had a cheek. I told him we weren't his groupies and that he'd made a huge mistake, I told him to wise-up and to get a proper job. I told him to get some manners. I tore him to pieces and then, when the others weren't watching, I gave him my telephone number.'

Another pause and another smile from Colette.

'He rang me up the next day,' she continued. 'Invited me out for tea that afternoon, and, you know what? Sober he was a perfect gentleman. He told me I been completely correct to give him a hard time the night before, that a lot of the things I'd said were absolutely true. He told me that my friends and I had disproved the rock and roll theory that one out of every two women will bonk a pop star. I took a playful swing at him, which connected and knocked him off his chair. He always said that was the punch that knocked some sense into him and made him fall in love with me. I went to the gig that night again, they were doing four nights at the Barrowland. It was the first time he'd done a concert without a drink in years. We met up afterwards and we started dating. I made him do it the old fashioned way. Took it really slow with him. He'd been used to girls throwing themselves at him, so I thought I'd make him work at it. It was great for ages. We moved in together, but then he went back to his old ways. I had heard my father give the same excuses to my mother.'

Kennedy looked at her closely. He wasn't sure if she was close to tears or not, but she looked quite sad. He decided to keep quiet – the only noise in the kitchen was the clock on the wall ticking away the time.

'I gave him every chance possible, Inspector. I really wanted it to work. There was a decent man there, for all his faults. A working-class lad who'd struck gold and didn't know how to cope with it. The problem was, he just couldn't use the word "No" when it came to women. And on the road there are lots of women who want the buzz of sharing some time with a celebrity. They'd waltz around town the next morning feeling ten foot tall because they'd spent the night with someone who'd been on Top of the Pops, while everyone would be calling them slags behind their back. It didn't mean anything to Wilko, he claimed. He claimed he loved only me and the others didn't count. But I wasn't going to end up another casualty, just like my mum. I warned him three times. When he cheated on me the forth time, with Susan in fact, I left him. Went back to Scotland. He followed me up and proposed to me. It was all very painful and a very sad time for me. Part of me wanted to marry him more than anything else in the world but deep down I knew if we did, my life would turn out to be a series of miseries and tears. So I turned him away. It took all the resolve that I had, but I managed to do it.'

'How did you and Sean...How did you meet up?' Kennedy asked, quietly.

'Well, obviously through Wilko. Sean was always a real gentleman with me. We'd always got on well at the concerts and events and he'd always spend time with me. Not hitting on me or anything like that, just chatting. We had great chats.' Colette allowed herself a smile, thinking back to better days.

'When Wilko and I split up, Sean rang me up to say how sorry he was that it hadn't worked out and how much he hoped we'd continue to be friends. That's what I liked about him. He was solid. After I'd seen what an absolute shit my dad was to my mum, followed by Wilko and all his promises, what I wanted most in the world was a dependable guy. I wanted a lot more than just a good time in bed,' Colette said, without the slightest hint of embarrassment.

'Hang on, I'm a bit confused here,' Kennedy cut across the thread. 'Wilko and Susan got married. Yet you told me that Wilko was William's father.'

'Good point, Inspector.'

'You and Sean were becoming friends. Wilko and Susan were...were what exactly?' Kennedy asked.

'Nothing had happened between Sean and I. As I said, he was being the perfect gentleman. He'd take me out to dinner sometimes when I was down in London or he was up in Scotland – Wilko and Susan were still getting it together. One night I'm at home in Glasgow, I get a call from Wilko. He's in Scotland for some reason or other. He rings, we chat. It was a good chat. He invites me out to dinner. No strings, he'd just like some company. We go out have a great dinner, We'd a few bottles of wine. He looks after me, puts me in a taxi, says he'll drop me off a home. He does, even keeps the taxi waiting outside. He leaves me to the door I feel sorry for him because he'd been so nice and he hasn't tried anything on. I decided to give him a goodnight kiss at the door. During the goodnight kiss all my old feelings come rushing back. I hadn't been with any other man since Wilko, so one thing leads to another and we end up in my bed making love. Out of it William is conceived. I tell Wilko, but also tell him nothing has changed. I've decided that I want the child but that doesn't mean I want him. Sean was very supportive throughout the pregnancy. William was born. Sean comes to Glasgow for a couple of week around the time of the birth. We're growing very fond of each other and it's getting better and better all the time, getting closer and closer. Does this sound too weird?'

'No, I don't think so. What happened between you and Sean?'

'Well, actually,' Colette started, and then stopped. 'If I'm going to be having this kind of conversation with you I'm having a glass of wine. Do you fancy one?'

'Yes, that would be very nice,' Kennedy replied, hoping she'd feel more comfortable if he did.

'Good on you,' Colette replied. She rose from her stool and fetched two glasses and an opened bottle of wine from the fridge. 'Good on you, Detective Inspector Christy Kennedy.'

After pouring both each of them a generous glass, she raised hers with a, 'Here's to the member's of Camden Town CID.'

Kennedy clinked her glass and raised the wine glass to his lips. He wet his lips but didn't sip. 'How about, "Here's to love,"' he said by way of distraction.

'Love? Ah now, I don't think the get into that one until the final episode. I don't think they've even written the script yet.' Colette had a little giggle and a rather large swig of wine before continuing.

'During all our long conversations, I'd probe Sean about the women in his life. By now, we were on the phone to each other every day. I was using him as a life-line, but I wanted him to feel free to be looking elsewhere for love. He'd always reply that he was much too busy. I even started to think he was gay. I remember having this bizarre conversation with him one night, I told him I didn't mind gay men, that by and large I found them very sensitive and caring. In effect I was trying to tell him that, if he was gay, it was OK to tell me. But he never bit, and I thought then that he was either straight, or so deeply stuck in the closet he wasn't coming out. Anyway, time passes. I'm having William's first birthday party and decide to invite Uncle Sean up for it. In my life at this point there are no other men, you have to realise. I've been with one man, Wilko, once in nearly three years. So I decide to seduce Sean when he comes up for the party. He stayed that night in our house, and I'm determined. I let him go to bed. I wait five minutes, undress, and go into his room. I slip under the sheets with him, and it's wonderful. He tells me he's wanted to be with me since we first met, but because I had been Wilko's girlfriend and then his friend he didn't want to make the first move. I told him that I could always have said no. But he said that it could have spoiled our friendship and that, more than anything, he wanted to protect our friendship. After that we hung out everywhere together. After about six months he proposed, I accepted. He was exactly what I was looking for. Dependable, good with kids, a decent chap, and faithful. I loved that.'

'Do you love *Sean*?' Kennedy regretted the brazenness of the question the minute it had left his lips.

'Oh, I don't know. I feel we are working towards it, if that doesn't sound too weird after a marriage and one child,' Colette replied as honestly as she could.

'So how was Wilko about all of this?' The detective chose what he hoped would be an easier question.

Colette refilled her empty glass as she replied. When she directed the bottle towards Kennedy's glass he put the fingers of his right hand over the top of it. She didn't even notice that he'd not touched a drop.

'Wilko. How was Wilko? Well, at this point he and Susan were wed. So wed he was on his fifth affair. That's exactly what I'd been trying to avoid. We never spoke about it, to be honest. Wilko wished Sean all the best, he said I was the best he'd ever

met but that he wasn't a big enough man to keep me. I think
Wilko was happy Sean was going to be a father to William.
Wilko knew, better than most, what Sean's qualities are. We
invited Wilko and Susan to the wedding and they turned up. I
was half-expecting an embarrassing drunken affair. But in the
end it was fine. It was all very civil. A well organised event.
Sean's great at organising things, and our wedding was one of
his major triumphs.'

'So that would have been close to the time Wilko left the
band?' Kennedy asked.

'Yea, he left about a year or so later. Yes, it would have been
after Tressa was born,' Colette answered, before taking another
sip of wine.

'And it wouldn't have had anything to do with you and Sean
getting married?' Kennedy chanced.

'Goodness no. Wilko thought the band was finished. Sean
had other ideas. But I think he felt, for his ideas to work, it
could no longer be a partnership. Wilko kind of offered it on a
plate to Sean by inviting him to buy him out, Sean did, and he
offered Wilco a lot of money. I had a go at Sean about that. I
thought he was offering Wilko too much money. Maybe I
agreed with Wilko, that the band was over, and I hated to see
Sean throw all that good money after bad. The point I was
going to make to you was, when I had a go at Sean about how
much he was paying Wilko as a settlement he said it was vitally
important that William wouldn't think Sean had cheated his
father. So I couldn't argue any more on that one, could I? You
see, that is the thing about Sean, he has a logic for everything
he does and by sticking to his logic, things usually work out for
him. Take me for instance, he was incredibly patient with me,
when I didn't even know he was being patient, but he got what
he wanted. But that's Sean for you, he always gets what he
wants.'

The noise of a key turning in a door above them followed by
footsteps and a voice calling, 'Colette, where are you?'

signalled that the man who always gets what he wants had returned home.

'I'm down here, baking and having a glass of wine with this very nice man from Camden CID.'

'Did you see Kevin then, love?' Colette said to her husband as he came into the kitchen.

'No, actually he didn't show up. Good afternoon, Inspector. How is your investigation progressing?'

'Good afternoon, Sean. Oh, I suppose we're getting there, slowly,' Kennedy replied. Sean and Colette gave each other a brief peck on the cheek. The detective noticed Colette had dispensed with her shoes immediately, the minute she had heard her husband enter the house.

'Darling, why don't you take the Inspector up to your study and leave me to finish my baking? You'll have more peace and quiet up there,' Colette suggested, as she rinsed out her empty wine glass. Kennedy did the same with his – still untouched – glass and placed it upside-down on the draining board. The gesture went unnoticed by both Colette and her husband.

'Good idea,' Sean agreed, 'Would you like some tea or coffee, Inspector?'

'Of course he would, Sean. The man's parched with all the talking we've been doing. I'll bring you both up some in a few minutes.'

'Had a good chat with the missus then?' Sean said, as he led the detective up two flights of stairs.

'Oh, very interesting. Was that Kevin Paul you were meant to meet?' Kennedy said, watching the wee man in his high platforms carefully negotiate the numerous stairs.

'Sorry? Oh no. No, another friend of ours from Scotland. Mind you, it's usual for him not to turn up, he's very unreliable,' Sean replied, and then added, 'Here we are, sit yourself down. Now, what can I do to help?'

'Well, there are still a few bits of this I'm trying to piece together. It's hard to get anyone to talk about Wilko. It would seem that people just didn't know him. Although your wife's been a great help.'

'Really? What did she tell you?'

'Oh, about how she and you met.'

'Yes?'

'And about how she and Wilko met.'

'Really?'

'Yes, she's filled me in on all of that.'

'So now perhaps you know better why I brought him back into the group. I understand from Leslie Russell that you were intrigued by that.'

'Well I suppose it makes a bit of sense,' Kennedy replied, hoping Green would elaborate.

'When you realise that Wilko was the father of William – the brother of my daughter – well of course I'm going to want to look after him aren't I? I'd hate William to grow up and accuse me of not being fair to his father. When he finds out, that is,' Sean offered.

'He doesn't realise that Wilko was his dad?' Kennedy asked.

'No. Colette and Wilko's decision of course, nothing to do with me. But I was perfectly willing to honour it. Colette's thing was that he was only the biological father, never anything more, and she didn't want to confuse William. If we hadn't got married she probably would have told him by now. But she's a great believer in the family unit and she thought it would be better for both William and Tressa to wait a bit.'

'So, you brought Wilko back into the group because he was William's father?' Kennedy probed.

'Well, no, not entirely. I'd hate you to think that I'm too much of a goody-two-shoes. Wilko was a great singer. He'd been with the band for a long time. His face was well known. Him fronting the original line up would probably work a lot better in the USA. His attempts at a solo career had flopped, he was down on his luck. He had, however, done me a very large favour in leaving the band when he did.'

'He did?' Kennedy asked.

'Yes, well, he allowed me the freedom to put all the band's affairs in order. Ah, here's our tea and coffee,' Sean said, as Colette emerged from the floor below. Her hair had now been released from its restrictive clasps and fell long, flowing and naturally around her shoulders. She had also removed the shapeless apron to reveal a flowing blue dress which hung loosely about her body as she moved.

Sean stole a seductive glance at his wife – a glance of unbridled lust. He clearly still found his wife ravishing and was proud of her looks. Sean looked at Kennedy to see if he was he also enjoying the vision and was saddened to find the detective's eyes not on his wife but on him. Green looked back at his wife once more.

'Where are William and Tressa, dear?' Sean asked.

'Oh, they're on a sleep-over with Simon and Georgie.' Colette then addressed Kennedy, 'They're the children of friends of ours over in Richmond. They all get on great. It means sometimes we can have breathing space and sometimes their parents can. It's important you know.'

"Perhaps we'll have a glass of wine after I've finished here with the detective,' Green suggested.

'Yes, that would be nice, love,' Colette smiled, 'I'll leave you to it.'

Kennedy wondered if "Perhaps we'll have a glass of wine." was similar to "Honey have you flossed yet?", Clint Eastwood's code for horizontal entertainment.

'Beautiful woman, isn't she,' Green stated.

Kennedy got back to the investigation.

'So, it all makes a lot more sense now, that Wilko wrote "Colette Calls". I couldn't quite figure that one out.'

'Shows you were on the right path though, doesn't it?' Sean agreed.

'I'm not sure I would have made the connection without the help.'

'Yes,' Green replied.

'Which brings me back to my original question – why would anyone want to murder Wilko?'

'I was discussing that very subject recently with KP,' Sean said.

'And did you come to any conclusions?'

'It's a bit like that old "pick a number, any number" game,' Green replied.

Of all the replies Kennedy had expected Sean to give to his question, that one wouldn't have made the top hundred.

What would have been in the top hundred? Kennedy considered this puzzle. Something like "you should look at Simon Peddington, Susan Robertson, Tracey McGee, Richard Slatterly or Robert Clarke." Well, that would have been Kennedy's top five. But if he could get Mr. Sean Green – the man who currently only had the hots for his wife on his mind and couldn't wait for Kennedy to leave so that he could check with his wife, "Have you flossed yet, Honey?" a couple of times – to disclose his top five suspects who would be on the list and in what order? Would KP be there?

Could it be possible that there might be a name which might be top of Sean's list who Kennedy and his colleagues were totally unaware of at this point in time? It's all to do with digging. Kennedy recalled his first visit to the Green residence. That really had been nothing more than a show, hadn't it? All happy families. But now, now that he had some of the truth, the picture was entirely different now. There was a history between Colette and Wilko. Colette had seemed quite relaxed about giving out the information. Was this because she knew Kennedy would have eventually found it out and by volunteering the information it took a bit of the suspicion away from her? Did this mean she should be under suspicion? Could Colette Green be on her husband's list of murder suspects? Yes, she was being quite casual about it now, but was it really all dead and gone? Was it all done and dusted? When Kennedy had asked her was she in love with Sean, she'd given a very clever, thought provoking answer. But was that just a smokescreen for the fact that in pure and simple terms she didn't love him and this was a very cute way to tell the detective. Did she still love Wilkenson Robertson at the time of his death? She'd never denied loving him. Then again, Kennedy hadn't come right out and asked her the question, had he? She'd said she wanted to be with him with all her heart, but equally she could foresee her life would be a misery if she had chosen to be with him. How big a misery, however, had her life been separated from Wilko?

It's OK to say you can't be with someone because you know that they are going to make your life a misery, but what if your life is going to be an even bigger misery away from them? What then? Could you consider that it might be better to go for the lesser of the two evils? Yes, Wilko could have been a two-timing shit, but what if you knew that and accepted that, could you deal with it? Could you deal with the person you loved being with someone else, knowing that it didn't really mean anything to them and could you keep allowing them to come back? Susan Robertson seemed to have had her fill of Wilko. She said herself that what she felt at his death was more relief than grief. Did you just get to the point where you've heard the same old story so many times that you just go, "You know what, I don't give a shit anymore. On your bike."? Could it really end up like that? Would Colette have concluded that being with Sean, a decent guy you didn't love, was better than being in love with Wilko, a waster you *did* love? Not an easy call.

'Do you think there is any chance Robert Clarke could have killed Wilko?' Kennedy ventured.

'Well,' Sean Green began, 'You have to realise that Robert had his own agenda. He was happy to be in Circles. It paid the rent, it got him on stage. It gave him a profile, of sorts. But, in the end, he's got bigger plans than Circles. He has his own songs, great songs, and wanted his own career. He realised that the longer he stayed with us the harder it was going to be to make a break, and the harder it was going to be to succeed. He saw exactly how bad Wilko's solo career was going. Mind you, I would have to repeat the fact that Robert, unlike Wilko, has a fine bunch of songs. Does he have an alibi?'

'That's being checked,' Kennedy replied. 'What about KP?'

'Still fishing?' Sean said, offering a grin. 'No motive, no "bad vibes."'

'What about Wilko stealing Tracey McGee?'

'You *have* been doing your work, haven't you?' Green laughed. 'I still couldn't see it. I can't see what any of them see in her, to be honest. But each to their own.'

'So, you don't think it might be a possibility?'

'Hey, you're the detective. You tell me.'

'You don't exactly have an alibi yourself, Sir, do you?' Kennedy wasn't sure he was throwing down another ace, but he fancied a bit of a bluff at this stage in the game.

'Ah, now you're not suggesting that someone with as light a frame as myself could over power a fiery Scot like Wilko, are you?' was Sean Green's simple reply.

'Well, I think that's it for now, Sir.' Kennedy wasn't sure that Colette had been eaves-dropping, but a few seconds later she re-appeared from the stair-well.

'Ah, you're leaving us, Inspector. I was just about to offer you both a fresh pot of tea,' she said as she joined her husband. They followed the detective down the stairs, hand in hand.

A few seconds later Kennedy was standing on the other side of their front door in England's Lane, buttoning up his Crombie. If the sounds from directly inside the door were anything to go by, "Honey" wasn't going to have time for flossing.

Thirty-Two

The lights of North Bridge House welcomed Kennedy as he arrived there twenty minutes later. He summoned Irvine, Allaway, Lundy and Coles to his office and they gathered around his notice board.

'So, our friend James MacDonald thinks Colette Green may have been Wilko's spin-doctor in the Circles camp?' Kennedy suggested, as he wrote a few more names on cards and tacked them on the notice board.

'I think that's what he was suggesting,' Coles said. 'Do you think there is anything in the fight between KP and Wilko, over Tracey McGee?'

'Well, I have to admit it's gathering credence all the time,' Kennedy replied. 'Clarke, MacDonald and Slatterly all checked out, so I suppose we should drop them from our notice board entirely. Same for Edwards. Let's dig for more information on Susan Robertson and her sister, Tracey. And Sean Green and his wife. And KP. Let's now put our brains to the method of murder. If we can work that out, we might take a giant step. If KP is the culprit, then the locked door thing all fits, but if it's not him then why was the door locked, first off? And how was the door locked?'

How could someone possibly have entered the room, stuck a sharp needle into Wilko's heart, placed the murder weapon neatly amongst his sweaty clothes, and disappear through the walls of the dressing-room? Impossible! There has to be a simpler solution. Was the locked door meant to distract us from something? And if so, what?

'Okay, let's get back into this. There's more out there waiting for us. Let's meet back here at seven and see what we have,' Kennedy bid them all good-bye.

Kennedy's mind flashed to Rose Butler. Seeing Irvine had made him think of her again. He felt guilty for not having devoted more time to Sinead Sullivan's death. Now that he had this Rose Butler/Dr Ranjesus problem on his desk again he needed to focus on it. After his meeting with Dr Taylor, however, he was no longer convinced that the Doctor could be brought to justice. Consequently, he was delaying meeting Ranjesus because he was unsure how to handle it knowing that if he handled the meeting wrong the doctor would scarper. On top of which, he was us to his eyeballs with the Wilko Robertson murder. He was seriously considering an immediate visit to Ranjesus when his phone rang.

It was Irvine, he'd been waylaid in the reception of the station house. A Geordie by the name of Larkin had been hauled in on suspicion. He'd been asking too many questions around Camden Town about another murder victim thereby drawing suspicion on himself. Irvine was fine and said everything checked out, he just wanted Kennedy to give him the once-over before he let him go. Kennedy was fine with it. He encouraged Irvine to give the Geordie as much help as possible. He was obviously distraught and on an important agenda of his own.

With two hours to spare until his next meeting, Kennedy toyed with the idea of visiting Dr. Ranjesus. He still wasn't sure how to deal with the situation, but at least he had the germ of an idea. A long shot, but it might work. He decided to visit Dingwalls

Dancehall before returning to the North Bridge House for the seven o'clock meeting. On his walk to the Dancehall, he pondered the mysterious eleven o'clock meeting with KP.

Ten minutes later, he stood in front of Dingwalls Dancehall, just like five or six hundred other people that night. Kennedy, though, was there to visit the scene of a crime. The several hundred patrons were on their way to see Ireland's latest sensation, Sharon Shannon, the Jimi Hendrix of the accordion. When Kennedy read this notice on the poster outside the venue, he wondered was she going to pour lighter fuel on her instrument and set it alight.

'Excuse me, Guv. Can I help you?'

Kennedy flashed his warrant card to the bouncer, a stocky chap in a shiny black bomber jacket, black chinos, gleaming black shoes, black hair and a black mobile glued to his ear.

'Yes. Sir, can I help you?' He was six foot four, at least.

'Is this the only way into the back stage area?' Kennedy asked, shutting the security door behind him.

'Yes, Guv, this way or over the stage.'

'Do one of your chaps cover this spot every night?'

'Correct, Guv. Four of us every night – one on the door by the box office, one each end of the long bar and me here back stage.'

'Do you move around? You know, relieve each other?'

'The other three do, but I'm the only one cleared to deal with the actual artists, so I always do the back-stage door.'

'Were you working last Thursday evening?' Kennedy inquired. He had to raise his voice slightly as the band had started into another number.

'Yes indeed, Guv. Sad night for that band, wasn't it?'

'Tell me, sorry, what's you name?' Kennedy asked.

'I'm Philip Silver.'

'Good to meet you. Tell me, Philip, on Thursday night, do you remember anyone coming back here during the concert?'

'No, not a one,' Silver replied confidently.

'You're absolutely sure about that?' Kennedy continued.

'Yes, well except for the tour manager. I remember his name, he just had two initials, KP. He told me that no one should get backstage during the concert. He came in and out of here several times during the show, but no one else passed me that night, I'm absolutely sure of it. I told all this to one of your officers on the night.'

'Are you sure it was KP and not someone else? One of the musicians, say? Sean Green?'

'What the little geezer with the handlebars and the Hendrix haircut?' The bouncer laughed.

'Yes,' Kennedy replied hopefully.

'Nah, definitely not. He's the boss, isn't he, I'd recognise him even in daylight. But no, the only person to come through here during the show was the tour manager, KP.'

'Is it okay if I go back through to the dressing-rooms?' Kennedy requested.

'Course you can, Guv, you'd only go and get a warrant if I said no anyway, wouldn't you.'

'Thanks,' Kennedy made his way past Philip Silver and back along the full length of the venue, underneath the dance floor, going further and further away from the stage. Eventually he came to the dressing-room area. The racket above him, five hundred pairs of feet doing a Michael Flatley, was creating quite a din.

Kennedy felt uneasy being there. He felt Wilko's presence, he was sure if it.

The dressing-room door was still to be repaired and so Kennedy opened the door and walked in. It was pretty much as it had been the last time he'd been down there. Except now all the Circles' clothes had been removed and replaced with Sharon Shannon's band's clothes that were much less flamboyant that Circles's clothes. Replace the platforms and flares and wide collar shirts with Doc Martin shoes and denim, and denim, and denim. He looked around the room. A fiddle case here, a battered accordion case there. A few CDs, and some other trinkets, and a guitar case on the floor close to the dumb waiter. A dumb waiter who had the nights off when it's base was used as a dressing-room for the visiting attractions.

Kennedy paced the room in all directions. The bouncer was convinced that no one other than Kevin Paul had passed him back stage last Thursday evening. The only other route back-stage was the very public route over the stage. Kennedy wandered around the dressing-room, deep in thought. He was reluctant to accept the mounting evidence, but he had to accept the facts. And the facts suggested that Kevin Paul had murdered Wilko Robertson.

He had the opportunity.

He had the motive.

He imagined KP in the corridor that night, banging on the door trying to raise Wilko's attention. How many times would he have tried before he burst the door down? The security man was only two minutes away on the backstage security door. Why did KP not first go to him and get a key to the dressing-room door? Why did he not seek the help of the six foot four strapping security man to burst the door down? KP was, at best, slight of frame.

No, Kennedy reluctantly had to admit, the murderer had to be KP. He had the opportunity and the motive. It had to be Kevin.

Then another thought hit Kennedy. How should he play his eleven o'clock meeting with KP? KP claimed to have a lead. Was it a wild goose chase, to take Kennedy off the path and further away from the tour manager? Kennedy wondered how he could get KP to admit he was the culprit. He liked him, so he felt shitty trying to trap him. Kennedy insisted his brain run that one by him again. "He like him, so he felt shitty trying to trap him."

'For heaven's sake, man,' he warned himself out loud. 'Get

a grip. This nice hippie chap of yours has just gone and fecking murdered someone, so get out of this feeling shitty vibe.'

KP was the murderer and Kennedy would have to use all his suss to catch him and secure a confession. Any other considerations were irrelevant. He closed the dressing-room door behind him, thanked Philip Silver for his help, and stepped out into the cold night. He decided he'd better bring Irvine with him to the eleven o'clock meeting with KP.

Thirty-Three

'So, you're convinced it's Kevin Paul then?'

At ten-twenty Kennedy and Irvine were sitting down to a late night snack in the crowded Golden Grill. Cafes or restaurants in Camden Town who take late orders were rare. Good ones were even rarer. In fact, Camden's finest were quite possibly sitting down in Camden's finest late night diner. The tickle in Kennedy's throat was developing and he felt his eyes getting heavy. Working on the theory of "starve a cold and feed a flu", he ordered the works. Two eggs, crispy bacon, hash browns, a couple of sausages, and wheaten toast. All to be washed down with a mug of tea.

Irvine went for a much more sensible diet of hot whiskey – double at that. He was working on his own theory, "you can't have too much of a good thing." Strictly speaking, Irvine wasn't drinking on duty. His shift had ended at six.

'Sadly, yes. It can't be anyone else,' Kennedy replied as his breakfast arrived, either fifteen hours late or nine hours too early.

'But, is that enough? You know the fact that it couldn't be anyone else?' Irvine prodded.

'It must be him. I really would like it to be anyone else other than KP. But he was the only one with backstage access. He was the only one who could be at the scene of the crime. Only two people left the stage during the concert. Wilko went straight back to the dressing-room to change and Sean hopped off the front of the stage into the audience, where he remained until the end of the instrumental. So, the *only* person with access to Wilko during the vital time was KP. Also, he had a motive. Wilko had stolen his girl.'

'But he wouldn't surely murder a man over a woman, would he?'

'Well, you know, it wouldn't be the first time a sensible chap lost his head over a woman. You see, KP's been on the road a long, long time. Perhaps the thing he wanted most in his life was a home and a family to come home to. If you're KP, a simple no-nonsense Irish guy, you're not going to be impressed by the rock and roll groupie scene. Yeah, they're great to look at and maybe even something more, but you're not going to bring them home to meet the mammy, are you?'

'Aye, sir. I know exactly what you're on about,' Irvine agreed.

'In the middle of all this madness KP meets and falls for Tracey McGee,' Kennedy continued. 'She's from a down-to-earth Scottish family. She's...well, he was attracted to her. Maybe he even, you know with too many late nights alone, nothing but dope or pills, or whatever, felt that she was the one for him. She was the one to mother his children. The person to make a home with. He was probably bursting to get back from some tour to proclaim his undying, hash-influenced love for her, and to whisk her off to the land of happy ever after. Then he finds out she's fallen for Wilko. Her sister's husband, no less! That was probably when the evil rot set in. Wilko was married. KP knew his wife. KP knew exactly what devilment Wilko was getting up to on the road behind Tracey's back, the woman he was *already* seeing behind Susan's back. Say KP wanted Tracey McGee for himself. I mean, get this, on the day of Wilko's death, KP drove him and Tracey to a hotel for an hour in bed before his concert in Dingwalls. Perhaps that was the straw which broke his frail back.'

They sat in silence for a few minutes, both deep in their thoughts and Kennedy helping himself to his breakfast.

'Goodness, Sir. Would you look at the vision that has just walked into my life,' Irvine said, as a stunning young woman stepped up to the service counter.

'It looks like Vange has beaten you to this one,' Kennedy replied. They watched Vange step in and work his charm on the delighted object of desire.

'No, it's OK. I'll come back later. When he's in the kitchen washing the dishes I'll step in and she'll be mine,' Irvine grinned confidently.

They spent the next few minutes involved in small talk with Irvine continuously monitoring Vange's progress with the young woman. His concentration was broken by a bit of a racket at the door and the entrance of a rubber man. He made his way, very unsteadily, to Vange and the girl. Rubberman started to hit on the young woman, ignoring Vange. It seemed he knew her. It was equally obvious that she didn't want to have anything to do with him. It was one of those scenes which was bordering on ugly. Irvine stood up and made his way across to try and defuse the situation. Kennedy also thought that his DS was more than happy to jump to the girl's defence.

'Come on, Sir. Leave these people alone. There are lots of other tables,' Irvine started.

'Nah, we don't want him in here. He's a troublemaker. Get out, Tommy, you know you're barred,' Vange offered confidently. The situation was still a friendly, but one teetering on a razor's edge ready to tumble over into nastiness with the first nudge.

'You know my name's not Tommy, mate,' the Rubberman spluttered, spittle flying everywhere.

'Come on, you heard him Tommy. Leave them alone. With Vange's personality he needs all the help he can get with the ladies,' Irvine offered light-heartedly, winking at the girl. Kennedy clocked the first eye contact between them. It looked like Irvine's irresistible charm was going to prove to be just that.

Rubberman turned around and focused his attention on Irvine, 'Ah, a Jock, and if the smell on your breath is anything to go by, I'd say a drunk one at that. You're a drunk!'

'Yes, Sir. And you're ugly. However, tomorrow morning I'll be sober but you'll still be ugly!' Irvine replied, using one of the classics he kept up his sleeve. At that point the situation could have gone either way but a few people in the café overheard the conversation and started to laugh. Then the young lady started to laugh as well.

Kennedy thought, you've cracked it with her, Irvine. You may get your head kicked in, but you've cracked it with the girl.

When the Rubberman joined in the laughter, the tense situation was defused.

Irvine returned to Kennedy's table just as his superior was finishing his meal. Irvine noticed the tea cup was empty.

'Vange,' Irvine called out, happy to interrupt. 'Two more teas over here please, *mate.*'

The tea arrived, and Kennedy checked his watch. It was seven past eleven and still no sign of KP. Unusual for KP to be late, Kennedy thought. He's usually early.

By eleven-thirty Irvine was starting to get itchy feet. He kept looking at his watch and glancing over at Vange and the young woman.

'Listen, I think he's blown us off for tonight. Maybe he's sussed we're on to him,' Kennedy started.

'Should we go and pick him up?' Irvine offered helpfully.

'No, I'll wander around Camden for a while maybe call by his house. If he's in, I'll give Flynn a call and we'll get a car.' Kennedy paused as he glanced over at Vange and the young lady. Two more people had just entered the café and Vange made a move to give them a couple of menus. 'Here's your opening now. Good Luck. I'll see you in the morning.'

Thirty-Four

Kennedy walked towards Camden Lock. The pubs were closed, supposedly, and the streets were packed with funsters. A blanket of snow offset the darkness around Camden Town. There was no aggression in the air, the way there was sometimes at the weekend. The lights from fast food joints splattered their colours onto the fresh fall of snow as he crunched his way past the market and in the direction of Dingwalls. The snow covered the sight and smell of the market rubbish. It was nice, Kennedy thought, not to have to smell the rotting vegetables and fruit.

Characters lurked on the street corners talking their jive, clipping their feet and waiting for something to happen. What were all these people waiting around for? Is this what life was all about? You went to school, you were educated, you secured a job and then you stood around the late night streets of Camden Town? Could that have been the reason KP wanted things to work out so desperately with Tracey McGee? He wanted to avoid all of this?

Kennedy felt bad for KP, in spite of himself. Had someone like Coles or Irvine been party to this thought process how would Kennedy possibly have justified it? Wasn't he constantly telling them, "Never allow yourself to become personally involved in a case. Keep a distance. Keeping a distance will not only help you, but it will allow you to do your job better."

He was just passing Compendium Books and about to cross the bridge over the canal. He stopped to look over the bridge on the Dingwalls side. The moonlight was sparkling on the water. The water was still, so still it looked solid enough to walk on. A couple of people were standing below the bridge by the side of the canal. Both were male, middle-aged and dressed in dark clothes. For heaven's sake, thought Kennedy what are they doing standing there in zero degrees, rabbiting away close to the midnight hour. Dingwalls was closed and Sharon Shannon and her band were probably well gone, probably playing a late night session somewhere else.

Perhaps that's where KP was, perhaps he'd joined up with the band and they'd gone off for a session somewhere. Kennedy couldn't begrudge KP that, his last night of freedom. Where better to spend it than having a session somewhere with Sharon Shannon and her musicians.

Had KP been trying to tell Kennedy that he was setting up a bluff? Or was he just giving Kennedy the run-around, throwing up dust clouds to confuse the detective? Kennedy forced himself away from these thoughts. He had finally unearthed the man who'd murdered Wilko Robertson. It would be only a matter of time before he caught up with him.

The main difference between Camden Town during market hours and the hours of darkness was the clientele. The daytime community were not all angels; more a case of likeable rogues, but an honourable chap amongst the night-time mob was as rare as an original song on a Baron Knights set list. Or at least it looked that way. Everyone acted suspiciously and itchy when someone they didn't know passed their turf. This always made Kennedy wonder was there a deal of some kind going down. On the other hand, they could all have been God fearing patrons who were as wary of Kennedy, in his smart threads, as he was of them. Many are the sins which blossom in ignorance, Kennedy thought, as he walked cautiously on.

Kennedy was now heading towards Chalk Farm. He intended to drop in at KP's flat, just in case. At the last moment, he turned left into the Roundhouse, suddenly remembering the watchman and thinking it just might be profitable to check whether he'd seen KP in the recent hours.

'Evening, Sir,' the watchman said, recognising Kennedy instantly.

'Evening. It's a cold one' Kennedy replied.

'Coldest one yet, if you ask me.'

'Yea, you might just be right. Listen, you haven't by any chance seen KP tonight have you?'

'Yes, he's downstairs. Been down there all evening he has.'

'Oh,' Kennedy did a quick reassessment of the situation. 'We were meant to meet earlier, do you mind if I go down and see him?'

'No problem, here's a torch. You'll need it. I'd take you down myself but I'm not meant to leave my post. But you know where it is, don't you?'

'Yea, it's underneath at the other side of the theatre, isn't it?' Kennedy recalled.

'Indeed. All routes eventually lead there – you'll probably smell the brew-up before you see him.'

A few minutes later, Kennedy wasn't so sure this had been such a good idea. He'd already come eye to eye with two rats. He felt like stopping and tucking his trousers into his socks. He didn't fancy rats using his trousers legs for drain-pipe practise.

What seemed like ages later, he was too far in to turn back, but not close enough to feel comfortable continuing. The problem was, that each turn took him into an identical brick corridor to the one he'd just left. There wasn't a sound to be heard, except for the crunching of his own footsteps. He was treading through water and mush. He *hoped* it was mush. Kennedy started to whistle.

It might be the basement of Camden's much loved venue, Kennedy thought, but there was a definite spooky vibe around these vaults tonight. He thought of all the men who had once worked down there, turning the large turntable above them so that the trains could go out the way they came in. He wondered if any of those men were ever accidentally killed while working down here in this dungeon? Kennedy knew he was spooking himself.

He realised he must have done about three circuits of the perimeter of the Roundhouse. Was the outer wall to the right or the left? If he knew which was the outer wall, then all he had to do was to keep checking for a break. He reached the point where he thought he'd first entered the maze. So he took the exit to the right, only to find himself in yet another corridor. This one however didn't have steps to take him back up from the basement. He decided to stick to this new corridor for a while. He might as well try something new, rather than continue to walk around in circles

Hang on, he thought, his light-beam reflecting off something. He'd found it. It was the outer stainless steel door which lead to KP's hideaway. He opened it and the torch immediately picked up the inner identical door. He tried the second door. It was locked from the inside. Kennedy sighed a sigh of relief. He'd discovered why KP had failed to keep their appointment. It wasn't through guilt. No, it was because he had fallen asleep in his secret hideaway, comfortably snuggled up in his chair.

Kennedy tapped on the door. No reply. He kicked it, still no sound from within. He banged it one more time, as loudly as he could. He put his shoulder to it and pushed. There was no give. He remembered the bolt of the lock being mid-door. It wasn't exactly a substantial lock, merely a bolt and hook, more one to afford privacy than security. He raised his foot, aimed carefully and kicked the door with all his might. With a few creaks and groans the door gave way to his force, but still some of the lock's screws held on. He gave the door another massive kick. It sprung open. Immediately he was in the white room. The lights were off. He turned them on.

He spotted Kevin Paul.

KP was sitting, flopped out in the chair, head bent down towards his chest and arms spread out over the sides of the chair. He looked like a puppet waiting for his master to activate the life-giving strings.

These dopeheads, Kennedy thought. Even the racket with the door couldn't disturb their cannabis-induced slumber.

'KP?' Kennedy began, his voice echoing around the white tiled room, 'Do you realise how late it is? I've been waiting for you down in the Golden Grill.'

Kennedy found himself barely whispering the words. This was silly. What was he scared of now?

'KP,' he said again, his voice gaining confidence. 'Come on mate, time to wake up. Let's go and have a warm cup of tea somewhere.'

He moved his hand to shake KP, to wake him up. The minute Kennedy touched his shoulder, the tour manager keeled over and fell off the chair. He fell with a dull thud, a bit like a sack of potatoes hitting the ground. Kennedy froze, and then he jerked back. He tried to help KP back into the chair and his hand accidentally brushed the stone cold skin of KP's face. This time the eyes were open.

'Oh, God.'

Detective Inspector Christy Kennedy touched Kevin Paul's neck, searching for a pulse.

Thirty-Five

Kennedy found no signs of life. There were no noticeable wounds. On the table he noticed KP's mobile and he dialled North Bridge House. Sgt. Tim Flynn was on night-duty and Kennedy left him to get a team down to the Roundhouse. Kennedy stood in the small room, opposite KP.

Within five minutes, members of the team started to arrive and Kennedy watched the scene evolve around him. The only thing static in the room was Kennedy. He couldn't remember the last time he'd considered a corpse so thoroughly. Usually the detective would remain around the body for only as long as was professionally necessary. But Kevin Paul was different. Kennedy felt there was a possibility KP could still be alive if he had done his job differently. What had KP found?

The pathologist, Dr Leonard Taylor, was the last to arrive on the scene. The team was now complete.

'I say, old chap, these locations are getting stranger and stranger.' Taylor knelt down beside KP. 'No obvious marks to hands, face, head or neck,' he concluded, following his initial examination. 'Is this the same fellow who discovered the singer the other evening?'

Kennedy nodded in the affirmative and saw the doctor glance at the door with the catch for the bolt of the lock busted from it's holding.

'Not another locked room murder?' he proclaimed.

'Yes indeed, Leonard. Only this time, I was the first on the scene and I can confirm that the door was locked from the inside when I got here.'

'How extraordinary. I've read about such scenes but never actually been on one until last Thursday evening. And now a second one. In that case, let's check...' Taylor pulled up KP's black sweater, unbuttoned his black shirt, and finally hiked up the black t-shirt, revealing the palest skin Kennedy had ever seen.

'There wasn't much to him,' WPC Coles uttered when she saw how thin he was.

'Now that's where you're wrong,' Kennedy smiled sadly, 'There was more to him than anyone I've met for a very long time.'

'Good Lord, Yes. Extraordinary. It's exactly the same,' Taylor gasped.

Kennedy looked at Taylor but said nothing.

'See here?' Taylor said, pointing to a tiny speck on the chest. 'A single drop of blood. I'll have to carry out a full examination you understand, but it is my guess that our friend here was murdered *exactly* the same way as your singer fellow. A thin sharp object, or blade, straight into the heart.'

KP's body was prepared for removal. Hands and feet sealed in plastic bags, contents of pockets emptied into separate bags with labels to denote the origin of the contents. His mobile phone was also bagged and would make its way back to North Bridge House with all the other bits and pieces.

'Can we get an itemised list of the calls KP made this afternoon?' Kennedy asked Coles, examining the contents of the plastic bags as he spoke.

KP, on his final journey, had one hundred and thirty pounds in notes; three pounds and forty-two pence in change; a Jordan Grand Prix cigarette lighter; a packet of cigarette papers; a small Woodbine tin, old and original, containing an ample supply of hash; a small black telephone book; a few scraps of paper containing illegible scribbles; a Wonderland Lottery key ring, containing three keys, two Yales and one Chubb; a couple of cinema ticket stubs – for the Odeon Camden Town to see Divorcing Jack – a small, leather wallet containing a Mastercard in KP's name and an American Express Platinum card with "Circles Touring" as holder, and finally, believe it or not, three marbles.

'Are you okay?' Taylor asked the detective.

'It's just that…I knew him, or was getting to know him. He was a bit of a character,' Kennedy started.

'And you feel that if you had acted quicker or…differently' Taylor sympathised.

'Yes, well you see…'

'Don't, old chap. You can't beat yourself up about this. If I started to think like that, I'd be a mess. And you would be too.'

'Thanks,' Kennedy replied, comforted by his friend's words.

'Not at all. Now, let's get on with our jobs. Aren't you meant to ask me, "And what time did he die?"'

'Yes, something like that,' Kennedy agreed, recharged somewhat by Taylor's charm.

'Okay, in that case I'd hazard a guess of no earlier than teatime today. Probably six hours ago, at most. Of course, old chap, I'll give you a more accurate, similar, guess after I've carried out the autopsy.'

And with that, the portly doctor departed the room of death, which was now being examined with a fine tooth comb by Kennedy's team. Within five minutes, Coles discovered something at the entrance door.

'Look, Sir. Over here.'

'What have you found?'

'See,' Coles began, pointing her plastic gloved finger to the bolt of the lock. 'Here, Sir. I just saw it by accident as the light caught it. It's plastic or something.'

'It's a fishing line,' Irvine, who also joined them, offered.

'Yes indeed,' Kennedy smiled as he examined the bolt closely. Some very fine, transparent fishing line had been tied to the handle of the lock's bolt. 'Very clever. Very clever indeed. You've just solved the mystery of one of our locked rooms, Constable. Well done.'

'What, sorry? I'm afraid you've lost me, Sir,' Coles replied in bewilderment.

'Obviously our murderer had less time to plan this one,' Kennedy began. 'It's not as elaborately done as the dressing-room at Dingwalls. This trick wouldn't have worked there anyway – that was a Chubb lock. But here it's just a bolt and catch. What our magician has done is place the bolt in the middle position between these two rests, tie the fishing line to the bolt, close the door behind him taking the fishing line outside with him, and pull the fishing line after him. The bolt slides into place and locks the door from the inside. There was a very good chance we were going to miss this because it is so small and if the light doesn't catch it you can't see it. You can't see it unless you have the eagle eyes of our WPC here. Well spotted.'

'Had you seen this done before, Sir?'

'No. But it makes sense,' Kennedy replied.

'But why lock the door at all, Sir?' Irvine asked.

'Well, the watchman knew KP was down here. KP always checked in with him on the way in. This was his den. He brought me here once. So, if the watchman came down and the doors were locked from the outside he'd have know something was wrong, because he wouldn't have seen KP pass him on the way out again. The watchman takes his job very seriously, he sticks to his system like glue. However, if he found the door locked from the inside he'd obviously assume KP was enjoying himself and leave him to it. This would buy our killer plenty of time to get away.'

'That must mean that the watchman saw our murderer come down and go out again,' Coles said.

'Possibly, let's check it out,' Kennedy said.

Smiley Bolger, the watchman, was long past his bedtime and his usually smiling face was grey and drawn. He was visibly upset by the death of his friend.

'Ah now, he was a good boy, was our KP. Never a bad word to say about anyone. Always the time of day for me. Aye, and I tell you, he did a mean cup of tea and he wasn't selfish with his mates. Who'd ever wish to top such a gentle soul?' Smiley asked.

'That's what we're trying to find out,' Kennedy answered. 'What time did you say Kevin arrived at?'

'Must have been about five-thirty. He was all business, you know, like one of his big deals was going down. He was always doing a deal. "It's the big one, Smiley." he'd always say. There were forever people dropping off things for him here. You know, one day, a gross of yo-yos, the next a couple of gross of Michael Bolton CD's. Said they'd fallen off the back of a lorry. I told him they didn't look all that damaged to me. He said, "Smiley, wait till you hear the bleedin' music vibe man, then you'll realise just how damaged they are." He laughed his bleedin' socks off at that one I can tell you.'

'Did he tell you what type of deal he was doing today?'

'Nope. Just said he was setting something up. Said it was a bit of a "Sherlock Holmes vibe." He didn't hang around for long. Said he had a lot of work to do, down below in the office.'

'Did anyone else go down with him?' Kennedy pushed.

'No, but he said someone would be arriving for him at six.'

'And did they?' Kennedy coaxed.

'Yeah, this woman arrived about six. I'd never seen her before but she said she knew where to go, so she must have been down there before.'

'Can you describe her?'

'Well, she must have been cold, because she was well

wrapped up in a long grey coat. Her head was well protected in a large black scarf. The only part of her face I could see were her eyes. She had a pair of big glasses.'

'Did she speak to you?'

'Just said she was going down to see KP, said he was expecting her and that she knew where to go. With that she hobbled down the stairs.'

'Hobbled?' Kennedy asked, grasping at straws.

'Yea, she must have had a bad leg or something because she had a walking stick and she leaned on it heavily as she went down the stairs. She was a bit wobbly, I can tell you,' Smiley offered hopefully.

'What about her hair? What style? What colour?' Kennedy continued.

'Don't know, Sir. Couldn't see any of it because of her scarf.'

'What about her voice? Did she have an accent? How did she speak?'

'It was high-pitched, but not much more than a kind of whisper. I got the impression she was quite frail what with her bad leg and her having trouble getting her breath,' Smiley replied. He was really trying to find something pertinent to say.

'Is there anything else you remember about her? What about bags? Was she carrying a bag, a hand bag, a shopping bag, or anything else like that?' Kennedy was about to give up. He knew that Smiley had seen what someone had wanted him to see.

'No Sir, as I said she was having trouble enough moving along without anything else to hinder her.'

'How long did she stay down there?'

'I don't know.'

'Sorry?'

'I said, I don't know,'

'But I thought everyone would have had to come in and out through this door.'

'No. She'd have to have come in this way, as would KP. But at six o'clock, when they are preparing for the theatre audience, they take the chains off the fire doors – the emergency exits. So after that point she could have gone out through the theatre by pushing one of the fire doors open. The indoor security would have spotted it within a few minutes or so and secured the door again from the inside. For all I knew KP could have gone out that way too. He'd normally have come and said cheerio to me though. He's never going to do that again, is he now, Sir?'

Kennedy could do nothing but reach out his left hand and pat Smiley a couple of times in the centre of his back.

'We'll let you get off to your bed now. We may need to speak more tomorrow, or over the next couple of days. Thanks a million for all your help. I really appreciate it,' Kennedy said as he turned and left Smiley furiously wrapping his arms around himself to try and shake the chill from his bones.

Thirty-Six

Breakfast time is a good time to observe how smoothly a household works, Kennedy thought, as he may his way to the home of one Dr Ranjee Shareef.

He rang the door bell. A maid answered and Kennedy introduced himself. He'd like to have a word with Dr Shareef, if possible. The very same maid arrived not more than one minute later with a message from the doctor who claimed to be busy with his family. If Kennedy cared to ring his office at the hospital the doctor's PA would try to put something in the book for him.

'Would she indeed,' Kennedy said. 'Could you tell Dr Shareef that I am from Camden Town CID and I am investigating the mysterious death of Miss Sinead Sullivan. Could you further tell him that this is police business which won't wait.'

'He said that under no circumstances was he to be disturbed again, I'm sorry, mister, but he'll shout at me if I go back in again and tell him you're still here.'

Okay, let's make this a lot easier for you, young lady. Sorry, what's your name?'

'Jane,' she replied politely, betraying her Yorkshire roots for the first time.

'Jane, could you please tell Dr Shareef that if he refuses to see me then I'll summon reinforcements in the shape of several officers in several marked cars. Tell him we'll then remove him physically from his grand house here to the police station for questioning,' Kennedy was trying hard not to boil over.

Jane from Yorkshire seemed to take joy in the detective's attitude.

'Why don't you come and wait in the front room, mister? I'll take great pleasure in delivering your message, Detective Inspector.'

Kennedy was expecting an ugly piece of work, and Ranjesus didn't disappoint. Two and one half minutes later, the front room door crashed open and a tubby little man stormed in. He had a large pot-belly, and wore pin-striped, flannel trousers which were supported by the large belly and a pair of red braces. He had an expensive pink shirt and a blue polka dot tie. The sleeves of the shirt were gathered up above his elbows by two elasticised gold bands. He had a matching gold bar fastening the tie to the shirt, about three inches above the point where the polka dots disappeared into the trousers. He had a full head of black hair and Kennedy pegged him at being in his mid-forties. The thing which puzzled the detective was what could make a beautiful young Irish nurse fall for such a toad.

'How dare you? How dare you barge into my house uninvited? Who on earth do you think you are?'

'Good morning to you, Dr Shareef,' Kennedy replied.

'Don't...Don't you good morning me,' and he spat the "me" for extra emphasis, if indeed extra emphasis was required.

'Well, in view of your position Dr Shareef, I thought you'd prefer to answer questions here rather than up at North Bridge House,' Kennedy began. 'But please believe me, Sir. You *will* answer my questions. It's entirely up to you where you answer them.'

The toad of Ulster Terrace was pacing up and down in front of his fire place using his hand to rest on the mantelpiece giving himself some support.

'You are in trouble, ' Shareef spat violently. 'You mark my words, Sir. You are in trouble. The shit is going to hit the fan when I get on to your superiors, and I do mean big lumps of shit.'

'Be that as it may,' Kennedy replied, 'In the meantime perhaps we could get to the questions?'

Shareef merely grunted.

'I believe you knew a nurse, a Miss Sinead Sullivan?'

'Nurse O' Sullivan? No, can't say that I do. So, could you please leave my house immediately.'

'No sir, not Nurse *O*'Sullivan…'

'But you just *said* Nurse O'Sullivan!'

'No Sir, not correct. I said Nurse Sinead Sullivan.'

Shareef looked at him.

'What does it matter? Sullivan or O'Sullivan, I know neither of them. Now, will you please leave my house?'

'You see, Sir, I'm having difficulty here because I know for a fact that you and Miss Sullivan were acquainted. I have people who will swear in a court of law that you and she were seen going to a room together in the White House Hotel,' Kennedy lied.

Shareef lost a bit of his bravado at that point. Kennedy was totally mystified as to why a young nurse from Ireland, or anyone else come to that, would have anything to do with Shareef, let alone kiss him, let alone sleep with him, let alone become pregnant with a child of his, *twice*. He must be a brilliant doctor, Kennedy thought. There must be magic in those hands.

'Last week, Nurse Sullivan died as a result of a complication related to her pregnancy. We have reason to believe that you were the father of her unborn child. We also have reason to believe that this was the second time she was pregnant by you. The pregnancy was terminated the first time,' Kennedy noted that, although Shareef had stopped blowing hot air, he was showing absolutely no outward signs of agreement or disagreement with what Kennedy was saying.

'We know you'd been seeing her for quite some time, Doctor,' Kennedy continued. 'And had become quite close. All her friends knew she was pregnant and they knew who the father was. They also knew that when she refused treatment and monitoring from the hospital, that you must have been attending her. We believe when she developed a complication in her pregnancy, a complication called Placenta Praevia, where…'

'I know what Placenta Praevia is,' Shareef cut in.

Kennedy was silently relieved. He wasn't entirely sure he'd mastered Rose Butler's theory himself. So, the complicated bit over, he continued.

'You would have been aware of her condition. Then you know that a person with this complication will haemorrhage and die.'

Shareef sat in silence. When he assumed that Kennedy had finished, he rose from his seat, stood in front of his fireplace and dug his hands deep into his pockets.

'Okay, Detective Inspector, you have barged into my house. You have had your say now I will have mine. Perhaps I had an affair with this nurse. That is my business and my business alone. This girl may or may not have been pregnant with my child. But that's not the issue here. That, Detective Inspector, is where your hypothetical case runs out. She definitely was not being treated by me. A fact which can easily be proven by the hospital records. I was certainly unaware of any and all complications, including this Placenta Praevia. If she chose not to be monitored by the hospital then she and she alone made that decision. If she died because she neglected her own well-being then, I'm afraid that's very sad, but it has absolutely nothing whatsoever to do with me.'

Having regained his composure, and his ground, Shareef concluded with, 'And now Detective Inspector, if that is all you have to discuss with me, I'm afraid I must ready myself for the hospital. Were I to be late, I'm sure you'd agree, it is quite possible that some patient might just not receive the attention they require. I believe you'd be as annoyed as myself were such a thing to happen.'

Kennedy was about to say something, but anything he had said would have meant nothing. The doctor was clever. Following his initial claim of ignorance of Sinead Sullivan and her sad situation, he had accepted that he did have a relationship with the nurse. He also acknowledged that there was a chance he could be the father of the child. But he would accept no blame beyond that. And Kennedy had no proof of anything beyond that. Should the Doctor have denied that he'd fathered the child, then Kennedy was sure he could have forced him to give a blood sample and he was sure that such a sample would have proved Rose Butler's words to be true. But there was no need for such a sample. Dr Ranjesus had not denied the possibility that the child could have been his.

Kennedy didn't want to let it go there. But the "big lumps" would certainly be flying in his direction if he overstepped the mark with the doctor. Kennedy crossed the room to the closed door.

'As I said, we are currently investigating this case and I may need to ask you further questions.' And with that, Kennedy departed Ulster Terrace, fuming. He knew from the doctor's attitude that even if Rose Butler's accusation was correct, and Kennedy believed it was, there was no proof with which to continue the investigation.

Or did he? By the time he reached the Cumberland Gate exit to Regent's Park, he was forming a plan which just might work. By the time he reached the Fountain of Sorrow, the plan was in place. He resolved to contact Rose Butler as soon as possible and see would she be prepared to play a part, a vital part, in Kennedy's plan.

Three minutes later, as he walked up the steps to North Bridge House, the deaths of Wilko Robertson and Kevin Paul were back on the front burner.

Thirty-Seven

Kennedy felt a lot happier back on the friendly grounds of his office, surrounded by his team. Even his Super, Thomas Castle, had joined in. Kennedy re-arranged his notice board, moving KP's name from the suspect list to the victim list.

KP got too close to the killer and had lost his life as a result. Why hadn't Kennedy forced him to give him more information on the phone yesterday? In reality, he didn't have much of an opportunity. KP had been cut short in his conversation with Kennedy and had to disconnect. Could that have meant that the person KP was bluffing, or setting the trap for, was walking into the trap? The timing seemed to work. Kennedy had spoken to KP on the phone around six o'clock. Smiley Polger advised Kennedy that KP's visitor to the white room, the lady with the walking stick, had arrived around that time.

Another point worth noting, Kennedy thought, and mentioned to the team as he was bringing everyone up to date, was that when Kennedy turned up at Sean Green's, shortly thereafter, to interview both green and his wife, Green was out. When he returned, Colette had asked Sean if he had seen Kevin. Kennedy had also asked Sean Green if he'd been to see KP. Sean replied that it wasn't KP he'd been to see but another friend called Kevin, perhaps the Undertones cousin?

'So,' Kennedy began, 'we have to go back to our original

inquiries. People who would have had a reason for getting rid of Wilko.'

'And they are?" Castle inquired.

'Well...' Kennedy opened the floor.

'Susan Robertson, Wilko's wife?' Irvine called out.

'Motive? WPC Coles?' Kennedy asked.

'Uh...She found out that Wilko was sleeping with her sister?' Coles offered.

'Good. Who else? Allaway?'

'Tracey McGee, Susan's sister,' Allaway answered.

'The motive, Constable?'

The constable shook his head. Kennedy answered his own question.

'Either Wilko wasn't prepared to dump his wife or he was threatening to split up with Tracey herself. At any rate, we still have to find a way of putting our killer both at the scene of the crime, and also in and out of a locked room.'

'Oh,' Castle piped up with a smile on his face, 'From what I've heard about yesterday evening you're becoming a bit of an expert at solving the old locked room murder mysteries.'

There were a few muttering of approval around the room, all of which made Kennedy a little embarrassed. Compliments were not something he was good at dealing with, a point ann rea was constantly drawing attention to.

'You're too kind, Sir, but you should credit Coles with that one.'

'What about *this* one?' Castle prompted.

'Well this one's a lot more complicated. First off, the only people backstage were Wilko, who'd come off the stage, and KP, who had a pass to get there. No one else was allowed there, not even the venue staff were allowed there during a performance,' Kennedy said, seeing the scene develop in his mind's eye. Something interesting was forming. Castle interrupted again.

'Well, man, any theories so far?'

'I'm still working on it, Sir, but you'll be the first to know. In the meantime,' Kennedy addressed his team. 'Let's go back over this stuff again. Let's plough through all the witness statements from the night of the Wilko murder. There must be something there that we're missing. I still want to have another chat with Susan and Tracey, but separately. There's definitely something going on there.'

'Could they possibly be in it together?' Coles asked.

'Possibly. Or there might be something else there, waiting for us to find,' Kennedy replied. He thought in silence for a few minutes. His concentration was broken by some mutterings at the back.

'I hope you're discussing leads for this case,' Kennedy said, interrupting their chatter and losing his thread. 'Sean Green. I wonder if there's anything else there. He was supposedly in the audience. The security guy swears no one passed him, but someone in the audience must have seen Sean during his walkabout in the audience.'

'And his motive?' Castle asked, with a shrug of his shoulders, hands clasped in front of him.

'Well now, WPC Coles came up with a very interesting theory for that one, didn't you?' Kennedy smiled at the WPC, who was, as usual, sitting beside Irvine, as he waited for her to explain her elaborate theory. Kennedy wondered if there was anything going on between those two.

'Well,' Coles advised the meeting, 'quite simply, as I see it, he brings Wilko back into the band, raising their profile, and murders him, increasing the profile still further. The band not only enjoy incredible record sales but he also greatly increases the worth of both his recordings and the publishing catalogue.'

'These pop stars, they're not normal sort of people, are they? They're a bit weird,' Castle agreed, adding his own weight. 'Remember that chap, Pauley Valentini? He was so annoyed at Radio One not playing his records that he hijacked that radio station, GLR, forcing them to play his music. His sales went through the roof. I bought some of them myself and I can tell you I don't know what the fuss was all about. I understand perfectly well why Radio One didn't play his music. No, never as good as Neil Diamond. Now there is a chap with great songs, mind you, the missus tells me Radio One don't play his music either.'

'Nor the Beatles, Sir,' Kennedy felt compelled to answer.

'The Beatles, what have they got to do with this case?' Castle inquired, shaking his head as thought he was shaking himself out of a dream.

'Radio One don't play the Beatles either, Sir.'

'Yes, exactly, and they don't go hijacking a radio station, do they? No, of course not. They're like Neil Diamond, they've got good songs, they don't need to got hijacking radio stations,' Castle replied not exactly tying the matter up but at least taking it back to a point where Kennedy could pull in the reins again.

'Now back to Sean Green,' Kennedy said. 'There may be other things involved here, as well. It seems that Sean's wife was once Wilko's lover.'

Castle's jaw dropped in shock. He was about to say something but before he could, Kennedy continued.

'In fact, she had Wilko's child, William, who now lives with his mother and Sean Green. So, is there something there? And, if we are going to look at Sean, we also have to look at his wife. She openly admits she would have liked things to have worked out with Wilko. Perhaps she was even instrumental in persuading Sean to take him back into Circles. But she saw what a problem he was going to be, so she dumped him and married Sean. I don't know. Maybe we're clutching at straws. We need to find out what KP was on to. What had he discovered? Who was the disguised lady with the bad leg? Do Susan or Tracey or Colette limp, did anyone notice?'

Kennedy sent everyone off under instruction to re-interview the leading suspects and witnesses. The only people remaining in Kennedy's office were the Superintendent and the Detective Inspector.

'On another matter, Christy,' Castle began as Constable Allaway left the office, shutting the door behind him, 'Any progress on the Doctor Shareef thing?'

'No. Sadly not. I met him this morning. I'm afraid I didn't get much out of him. I'm convinced he did as Rose Butler suspects, but I think he's too clever a man by far to have left anything for us to trap him with. I'm thinking of getting Rose Butler to wear a wire and send her in to see him and see what that produces,' Kennedy replied, running the idea up the pole to see if he'd get Castle's support.

Castle was, all things considered, extremely supportive.

'Yes, I suppose it's got to be worth a try, but if it doesn't work, we're going to have to let this one go. Hell, I'm not even sure what we could charge him with. He didn't actually *do anything*, did he?'

'That's exactly it, Sir. He did nothing. But surely he was duty-bound to do something, given the circumstances.'

'Maybe he'd be struck off or something, but I'm not sure it would go much further than that. Let's wait and see what we get from the Rose Butler wiretap. Keep me posted, eh? And be careful, please. He's got lots of influential friends,' Castle said, making his way to the door. As he opened it he turned with a wink, 'But don't be too worried about his friends, he's got quite a few enemies as well.'

Thirty-Eight

Kennedy sat at his desk and looked at the plastic bags before him. Inside each one were the bits and pieces taken from KP's person when he was found.

Then there was the mobile phone. He'd deal with that later, he thought. He searched through the plastic bags until he found the one he was after. It contained two pieces of note paper, or one large piece of paper torn in two. He pulled a spare pair of surgical gloves from his desk drawer and shook his head in amazement at KP's handwriting.

The top of first page had tear marks along the top, showing that it came from a spiral pad. On the left hand side, written from left to right and spilling off the page, was the word "Prat". Then what looked like the beginning of a star drawn beside it and continuing off the page. Next to that was 0171 387 5080, the number of North Bridge House and a scribble which looked like it might just be the word "Kennedy". "Kennedy 0171 387 5080." Okay so far, but that was the easy part, that was his own name and telephone number.

"Prat." Kennedy turned the word over in his head. Prat.

The middle section of the right hand side of the page had a bird's eye view of what looked like a room. There were three rectangles in what looked like an arc around a line with a tick at each end. In the top rectangle were the letters CH, in the next

~~RAE~~

(2 MIN
BREAK

McGEE
NOT IN
TREZURE

McGEE!
LOVES
WILKO
LOVES
?

~~CLARKEY~~
~~McDONALD~~
~~STAFFERLY~~

DINGWALLS

TETLEYS
ORANGES
FLORAL
SPUDS
COOKIES
PIZZA B
HOOVERS
2 PACKS of LADIES BRIGHTKINED[M]
BULBS x 3 x 60 WATT
~~BANK~~ — DOSH f 200 BANK

SAINSB

one down was AI, and in the bottom one RS. CHAIRS. The dressing-room in Dingwalls? Then there would be six chairs rather than the three. In the top right hand corner of the room, if indeed it was a room, he'd had drawn another rectangle along the top and reaching almost into the corner. In this rectangle were the letters LUXOG with a little arrow heading out of the room, in the direction of the top of the page.

The bottom of the same page had a stroke come in at about forty-five degrees, then an O then an L, and an arrow pointing to the name Wilko with a question mark.

The bottom matching side of the same page had a rough sketch of what looked like seven musicians on a stage. A couple of the little figures looked like they may have guitars around their necks. But as KP's artistic influences took after the hangman style, the little figures had both their arms up in the air, away from their would-be guitars. There was a mess at the back which could have been a drum kit, and another which looked like a bath on high legs at the front which could have been Sean Green's keyboard. Underneath the band he had drawn a line and underneath that he had written the word WHERE?

On the first sheet, dead centre, was a large heart. Inside the heart KP had written:

McGEE!

L

WILKO

L

?

Due to the close proximity of the heart, Kennedy assumed the L stood for love. On the top left of the page and heavily scored out, was the word FRAC or it might even have been TRAC.

TRACEY McGEE.

Underneath, close to the bottom of the heart, was the note:

McGEE NOT IN TRY TWICE.

On the top right hand side of the heart was
    12 MINBREAK
and underneath that, bottom right of the heart,
    CLARKEY
    MACDONALD
    SLATTERLY
All had pen lines through the middle. Across the bottom of the heart was a large
    DINGWALLS?
with a thick wavy line underneath completing that part of the paper.

So KP had ruled out Robert Clarke, James MacDonald and Slatterly from his list of suspects. But why where they on their in the first place? What, in KP's mind, had made them suspects in the first place? Had he being trying to ring Tracey McGee? Was she out when he rang? Or, more like, she just wasn't in for KP? Perhaps KP was aware of this because he made a note to himself to try her twice. 12 MIN BREAK. Did this refer to the length of time Wilko was off stage and consequently the amount of time the murderer had to work with? And why DINGWALLS? Was KP, indeed, saying, "why Dingwalls?"? Did this mean, why were Circles playing Dingwalls? Or did it mean why was Dingwalls used as the murder venue?

On the bottom section of the paper, KP had written the following list:
TETLEYS, SAINSB ORANGES, SPUDS, COOKIES, PITTAB, HOMOUS, 2 PACS LADIES NICKS x MED, M & S BULBS x 3 x 60 WATT, R.J. WELCH, DOSH – 200 QUID BANK

Even in the midst of his trauma, KP had managed to jot down his shopping list. The Marks and Sparks item, which is what he assumed the M & S line referred to, intrigued Kennedy.

And that was it. Somewhere on those scraps of paper was a clue.

* * *

'It's as expected, Christy,' Taylor began. He was on the phone to North Bridge House mid-Tuesday morning. 'Same as Mr Robertson. Stabbed straight in the heart with an extremely thin sharp instrument. The heart was punctured. He would have died very quickly.'

'Oh,' Kennedy wasn't sure there was much comfort to be taken from that. 'And the time of death?'

'As we predicted, I'd say he died at the latest six-thirty yesterday afternoon.'

'Anything else?' Kennedy continued asking another of his routine questions in his routine fashion.

'Well, not really. Unless, of course you would consider the fact that he was wearing ladies underwear to be of interest.'

'Pardon?'

'Yes, I believe it's more common than we might think and I understand it's a lot more comfortable, although I'm not sure they come in my size.'

'Doctor!'

'Just kidding. But I am serious about KP.'

'Thanks,' Kennedy said. 'See you later.'

Kennedy set the phone down absent-mindedly. You just never know about people, do you?

Coles returned to Kennedy's office shortly thereafter to advise him that KP had made 12 calls during his final day.

1.	11.53	North Bridge House	3 minutes
2.	11.58	Sean Green	6 minutes
3.	12.05	Robertson household	1 minute
4.	13.02	Leslie Russell	11 minutes
5.	13.30	Robertson household	1 minute
6.	15.02	Sean Green	17 minutes
7.	15.20	Dingwalls	5 minutes
8.	15.45	Robertson household	3 minutes
9.	15.47	Leslie Russell	10 minutes
10.	17.00	Parkway Pizza	5 minutes

11.	17.15	Sean Green	7 minutes
12.	18.03	North Bridge House	2 minutes

At least part of Kennedy's assessment of the scribbling was correct – the bits concerning the calls to Tracey McGee and himself. But the other's – what information had KP gather as his day progressed? In the middle of all of his hectic day KP still had time for food. Once with Kennedy and once at the Parkway Pizza. And his call to Dingwalls, what was that all about? Kennedy felt sure that there was something to be learned from these calls and their sequence. But where to start?

Kennedy had scored three items from KP's telephone list. Two to North Bridge House, and one to the Parkway Pizza. Next he called the number listed for Dingwalls and was put through to Miss Violet Rodgers, the same person he believe KP would have been put through to the previous day.

'Yes, Kevin Paul did ring here yesterday.'

'Do you remember what he wanted?'

'Yes, I do as a matter of fact,' the owner of Dingwalls replied. 'He asked me if I ever noticed any members of Circles coming into the club. I told him the only two members of the band I would recognise would be Sean Green and Wilko Robertson and Wilko never came here, he did all his drinking up in the Spread Eagle, but Sean used to come in here quite a bit to check out the new bands.'

'Did he ask you anything else?'

'He asked me did we ever use any dressing-rooms apart from the one we gave Circles on the night Wilko died?'

Good question, Kennedy thought to himself and he put a star next to Dingwalls name on the list, 'And do you?'

'No, that's the only one we have for now. When the venue was rebuilt about eight years ago we thought we were going to specialise in comedy. Comedians tend not to need a dressing-room as much as musicians. They just need their own corner of the bar and they're happy. But now that we're getting into lots of live bands we do need proper dressing-rooms and, equally important, we also need the store room we currently use as a makeshift dressing-room, back as a store room. It's the only one with a dumb waiter and so when that room is being used as a dressing-room one of the lads has to carry the various brands of liquid refreshments up the stairs.

'What I'm planning to do is convert the space at back of the back of the venue, just above the artist's entrance, into a couple of dressing-rooms with showers and toilets. That's what I told Kevin. He was so polite, I like him very much, he has a real twinkle in his eye, you know?'

Kennedy advised the owner that sadly KP was now also dead. Violette Rodgers was gutted, as Steve Davies would have said, but Kennedy had a funny feeling the owner of Dingwalls Dancehall really meant it.

He considered the list further. The remaining eight calls were spread over three people, or so he thought. He sought out Leslie Russell number and dialled it but hung up before it connected. He stood up from his desk, grabbed his coat and went to look for Coles. He found her around by Flynn's desk. Kennedy asked her to fetch a car.

He had decided to interview the other three names on the list in person. He wanted to see their faces when he was discussing KP's death.

Thirty-Nine

As ever, Leslie Russell offered Kennedy a warm welcome and paid more than a little attention to WPC Coles.

Kennedy wasn't sure what KP and Russell had been talking about on the phone, but he knew the solicitor would relay it more or less word for word. He was a lot more sceptical about his next two stops, at the Green household and the Robertson household. Russell had already heard the news about KP and was deeply saddened. He told Kennedy how fond he was of KP. They'd worked closely together over the years.

'Have you any idea who did it?'

'We're working on a few leads,' Kennedy said, and mentioned KP's calls the previous day.

'Yes indeed, Kevin rang me twice yesterday,' Leslie Russell advised the police.

'May we ask you what he was ringing you about?' Kennedy asked.

'Of course. He wanted to know if Wilko had signed his new deal with the band. As I've told you before,' Russell nodded to Kennedy, 'that deal had yet to be signed. He asked me what were the major sticking points in the contract, why it hadn't been signed. I told him that it all just had to be finalised at that stage. All the main points had been agreed. Wilko had got what he wanted, money payments, percentages and bonuses, and he didn't really care about the rest.'

'And what else did you and KP discuss?' Coles inquired.

'Well, let's see. He asked me where we stood with the agreement now that Wilko had died without signing it. I told him that, quite simply, it didn't exist and that it's conditions were unenforceable. He asked if that meant Susan Robertson would benefit from the conditions of the new deal. I told him that it wasn't my call. That was entirely down to Sean. He asked me, what, in the worst case scenario, this would mean Susan might inherit. I told him she would continue to receive Wilko's share as per Sean and Wilko's agreement; the one made when Wilko left the band. He then asked me whether I aware of any insurance policies Wilko and Susan might taken out on his life?'

'Yes we'd already checked that ourselves and discovered he hadn't,' Coles stated, as much for the record, Kennedy felt, as anything else.

'Correct, a fact I advised KP of.'

'Anything else?' Kennedy continued, as he took a swig of his tea. 'Yes. He asked me if Wilko had any pension plans or anything which matured upon his death. I told him, as I'm sure you've also discovered,' Russell began with a nod in Coles' direction, 'that there were absolutely none. They were a pet hate of Wilko's, a fact KP remembered when I brought it up. He'd always had other, more immediate, priorities for his money.'

'A very polite way of putting it, Leslie,' Kennedy smiled, 'Do you know if Wilko had anything put aside for Tracey McGee?'

'Another of KP's questions and the answer is no. I drew up the original papers, and I don't believe they've been changed, where absolutely everything goes to his widow, including the apartment. I don't believe he'd much else, apart from the property and his Circles' money.'

'How much was the property worth?' Kennedy asked.

'I'm not sure,' Russell replied.

'About one hundred and twenty thousand pounds,' Coles spoke up, referring to her notes.

'You see, Christy? As ever you chaps are ahead of me,' Russell replied, and sighed a sigh of feigned regret. 'I think that was pretty much the contents of the first telephone call.'

'Tell me, do you think that Sean would have made additional funds available for Tracey McGee? I mean outside the terms of the current contract?' Kennedy asked.

'I couldn't possibly comment on that, nor would I want to hazard a guess,' Russell replied.

'Okay,' Kennedy replied, and continued, 'What about the second call, the one late in the afternoon – what was that one about?'

'Well, that was more about Sean Green. He asked me several questions I couldn't, for professional reasons, give him answers to.'

'Such as?'

'How much was Sean worth? Had I ever seen Sean and Wilko argue? What were Sean's plans for the group now that Wilko was no longer around? What was KP's position now? Would the band continue with Robert Clarke back as lead singer? How long was Sean going to keep Edwards on as manager? He also asked me how close Sean and Colette were.'

'Interesting,' Kennedy cut in. 'We know, by the way, about Colette's affair. She told us about it herself.'

Russell shrugged his shoulders, saying nothing. After a moment's silence, he spoke.

'He also asked me did I know if Colette and Wilko had any communication these days.'

Kennedy was well aware that Russell was now in a very awkward position. Being involved in the band for such a long time, Leslie Russell knew all the dirty washing. He'd seen managers come and go. He'd seen egos come and grow. He'd seen fortunes come and be dealt with wisely by Sean and foolishly by Wilko. But through all of this Russell was professional, giving his advice only to matters that concerned him, and then only when asked. He kept his position by being discreet – as discreet as he was now being with two members of the Camden Town CID when he answered his own question.

'And I told him that to my knowledge, there was no communication between Wilko and Colette. He then asked me why Circles had played Dingwalls when they could, in KP's eyes, have played The Royal Albert Hall. I told him I knew Sean had been responsible for the decision. And that,' Russell concluded, 'was pretty much all we talked about.'

Discreet as ever, Kennedy thought. Even now Russell was leaving himself the slightest of openings in case anything else should crop up that he'd be called to task on. Kennedy couldn't feel bad about it, he knew Leslie Russell was doing his job as best he knew how. Which was, the detective had to admit, pretty darned good.

Forty

'Okay, let's head to the Green's of England's Lane,'

'That should be interesting,' Coles replied, as she engaged the engine of their unmarked car. 'Did we get much from the solicitor?'

'I'm not sure, to be truthful. What do you think?'

'Well, we confirmed a lot of things we already knew about Wilko,' Coles began.

'I don't mean that. I mean, additional info. What additional info do think we found out?' Kennedy pushed.

'Well, I wasn't one hundred per cent convinced on the Wilko and Colette not seeing each other line. I think there's more there than he telling us.'

'Good, yes, but you're still not thinking along the lines I am.'

'I'm lost then, Sir,' she admitted honestly.

'Well, the point of following the calls KP made yesterday is as much an attempt to try and pick up his trail. Try to see what he was chasing down, whatever angle he was working on was on the correct one, otherwise someone wouldn't have felt the need to get rid of him. Would anyone directly benefit financially from Wilko's death? He drew a blank there, as indeed we did. So he spreads his arc wider, to cover Robert Clarke, Tracey McGee, Susan Robertson and Edwards. He mustn't have been serious about Edwards because he didn't even make KP's list. That brings us back to Sean Green and his wife, Colette. Quite convenient,' Kennedy said as they pulled into England's Lane.

'I suppose you've come about KP?' Green asked as he opened the door. 'Who on earth would do such a thing?'

'Yes, Sean. We've come to ask you a few more questions. You'll be fed up with us by the time all of this is over,' Kennedy replied as he took off his overcoat.

'No chance, never. I really want to help you nail the person who killed Kevin,' was Green's reply. He then added, 'Oh, and Wilko of course. Do you think there's any chance the same person is responsible for both murders?'

'Well, I think that would be a fair assumption, wouldn't you? Tell me, is your wife in?'

'Why yes. Is it her you've come to see?'

Kennedy wasn't sure, but he thought he might have spotted a hint of panic in Green's eyes.

'No, actually we'd like to see both of you together, if you don't mind,' Kennedy answered.

'Perfectly fine with me. Show yourselves up to the study, you know where it is. I'll follow you up,' Green offered.

'Is Mrs Green down in the kitchen?' Kennedy asked, knowing the answer to his own question, 'Why don't we go down there? It'll be a lot quicker. We've got a lot to get through today, haven't we, WPC Coles?'

The detective didn't want Sean Green briefing his wife before they all had a chance to chat. Green reluctantly nodded and led the police down to the kitchen. A task not so easy for some, say those with platform soles.

Colette greeted them warmly, wiping her hands on her apron, and crossed the room to shake Kennedy's hand. Kennedy introduced WPC Coles.

'Oh, it's so sad about Kevin, it's it. He was such a dear, sweet man,' Colette began.

'We're trying to go though Kevin's last day to find what he discovered. I spoke with him several times yesterday and he seemed very sure he was on the trail of Wilko's murderer.'

'No! Really?' Sean uttered as he glanced at his wife.

'Oh, yes. He went through a lot of his information with me and in fact I was speaking to him on the phone just after six o'clock. He had to break off the call in a hurry. Apparently he was about to spring a trap on a certain person,' Kennedy said. He was picking his words very carefully. 'We see from the records that he rang here on three separate occasions yesterday.'

'No, sorry. That's not in fact correct. He only rang here twice yesterday,' Sean corrected the detective.

'Well, I have the official Orange log of KP's mobile calls for the day, and your telephone number showed up three times yesterday,' Kennedy replied.

'I'm sorry to contradict you, Inspector, but I took only two calls, one at noon and the other just after five. That was it,' Green insisted.

'Um, not quite, dear,' his wife corrected him. 'I took a call from Kevin just after three, so that would make Inspector Kennedy's notes correct.'

'You didn't tell me he ra...' Sean started to speak but apparently thought better of it.

'You were busy. He said he had a few questions for me, and we had a chat,' Colette replied.

Kennedy played a hunch. He decided to have Colette relay her recollection of the telephone conversation first.

'Well, first off,' Colette began, 'he told me he was trying to track down Wilko's murderer. He said initially he was excited but the further he dug into it the more depressed he was becoming.'

'Did he ask you specific questions?' Kennedy asked.

'Well...let's see,' she replied, 'He asked me when was the

last time I saw Wilko? If Sean and I had discussed Wilko coming back into Circles? What I felt about Wilko rejoining the group? If William knew that Wilko was his dad? If Tracey knew that Wilko was William's father? If Sean had given Wilko any money during his lean time? If I was aware of who may have given him money?' He asked this when I told him I thought Sean hadn't given Wilko additional money during the solo years. I asked KP why he thought I might know who would have given Wilko money if Sean hadn't. He also asked me if I had heard any of Wilko's solo songs? If I knew what Sean was now planning for the group? What I thought should happen with the group? And let me see now, what else? Oh yes, if I knew Sean was planning to look after Susan? And I think that was pretty much it to be honest.'

'And you replied?' Coles quizzed.

'I told him that the last time I'd seen Wilko was at a rehearsal about five days before the Dingwalls gig. I dropped Sean off at the rehearsal room; I think the place was called Joe Henry's or something. It's over Islington way.'

'John Henry's,' Sean corrected her.

'Yes, John Henry's, that was it. It would have been two Saturdays ago, I was out doing some shopping and Sean blagged a lift. When we got over there he said that I might as well come in and say hello to everyone. You're very good at all that, aren't you dear?' Colette said, turning to her husband. 'He's always keeping the flow going between the team. He likes everyone to feel a vital part of it. So coming into a rehearsal room with him when I'm looking absolutely dreadful shows everyone that he and I... were really one of them. It gives the team a bit of cement. That's what you think, isn't it dear?'

'I'm sure the detective didn't come to hear about that side of the group, love,' Sean replied, smiling.

'Did you actually talk to Wilko on that Saturday?' Coles continued.

'Well, yes, I did speak with Wilko that day.'

'What did you discuss?'

'He thanked me,' Colette began, and then hesitated.

'He thanked you?' Coles coaxed.

'Yes, and we discussed how the rehearsals were going.'

'Sorry, can we back up a bit?' Coles interrupted Colette. 'You said he thanked you, what was he thanking you for?'

The silence in the room seemed to last forever.

'I think what my wife meant was that Wilko was under the impression that Colette had been the one responsible for him being invited to rejoin the band,' Sean finally said.

'Was Wilko correct in his assumption?' Kennedy said, directing the question at Colette.

She looked like she was having a real struggle deciding which way to answer the question. Eventually she and her husband spoke simultaneously.

'No,' she said.

'Yes,' he said.

They both looked at each other in stage shock.

'Actually, both of us are correct, in a way,' Sean added. 'You see, I discuss all major decisions, in our life, with my wife. This was obviously a major decision and Colette was all for Wilko coming back into the band. Apart from anything else she...I mean *we*, felt it would be good, in the long term, for William. Wilko had somewhat botched his attempt at a solo career and I'm afraid the writing was on the wall and we knew that pretty soon he'd have blown all his money and wouldn't have any income.'

'Apart from his Circles' royalties,' Coles corrected.

'Apart from his Circles' royalties,' Green agreed, 'but he had a pretty expensive life style and I'm not sure the royalties would have been enough to keep him in the pink. Keeping two women must have been terribly expensive. I know how much it costs to keep one,' Green smiled at his wife without really looking at her.

'Two women, Sir?'

'Yes, I'm sure you know about Susan and Tracey,' Green replied giving his wife another little smile, still refusing eye contact.

'Oh yes, you told KP to tell us about that little situation, didn't you?' Kennedy said, sending out his own wild card. He was sure that Sean had mentioned Tracey's name for Colette's benefit.

'No Inspector,' Sean began, quite firmly. 'That's not 100% accurate. KP and I were discussing the case and we both agreed that it would probably be better for you to have that piece of information, in case it was relevant. We also assumed it was a piece of the band's history that Leslie Russell might not have passed on to you. He's much too discreet for that. So we agreed that whomever spoke to you next would be the one to impart the information to you.'

And KP's no longer here to deny that, is he, Kennedy thought to himself.

'Okay, Mrs Green,' Coles began again. 'Can we move back to the questions?' She checked her notes. 'He asked if you and Sean had discussed Wilko coming back into Circles. I suppose we've covered that?'

'Yes,' Colette stole a glance at her husband. 'I suppose we have.'

'And how did you feel about Wilko coming back?' Coles continued.

'Well, as Sean said, we both felt it was the best thing all around.'

Kennedy wanted to let that lie for now, so he said, 'Then KP asked you if William knew that Wilko was his dad?'

'No he didn't know. We planned to tell him when he was older,' Colette replied.

'Next was, "Did Tracey know that Wilko was William's dad?" Did she?' Coles' question this time.

'I told him I didn't know the answer to that one, but that I hoped she didn't,' Colette replied and then looked like she felt she must explain further, 'You see, the more people out there gossiping about William and his father, the more chance of someone mentioning it to him. That wouldn't have been pleasant would it? Did she know about William and Wilko?' Colette addressed her question to Sean.

Kennedy was surprised that she hadn't phrased the question, "Did she know about Wilko and me?" Probably nothing, he considered, just a turn of phrase. But at the same time was she suggesting that her husband was communicating with Tracey? Was this all going to get even stranger?

Did people only push and pull in their relationships because they could and because they wanted to see what it felt like to be doing something which was wrong. What did "wrong" mean? Why should Wilko not have slept with both his wife and her sister? Both were apparently willing bed partners. He assumed there was no force involved. Wilko couldn't have had something over Tracey to be blackmailing her with, blackmailing her into bed with? Could that something be that Sean and Tracey were also having a scene? God, Kennedy thought, all I would need then would be for Sean to be sleeping with Susan and that would tidy it up with them all playing happy families. But still he returned to his earlier niggle, why would it be wrong? If Wilko's wife was not giving him comfort any more why should he not seek it elsewhere? So what if the person he chose to comfort him was with his wife's sister? It had happened before where men had married their wife's sister, but you mostly hear of it when the wife died and the sister and husband were emotionally thrown together. Could someone have murdered Wilko because, with Wilko out of the way, the coast would have been clear for the murderer to have an affair with Wilko's lover? So that could mean, for instance, that KP murdered Wilko to be with Tracey and then either Tracey or Susan discovered this, and, in revenge, murdered KP. Tracey, Kennedy felt, was somewhere there in the thick of all of this trouble. He still was amazed that one so plain could rack such havoc.

'Did you hear any of Wilko's solo songs?' Coles asked.

'Yes, I did in fact. He sent me a tape of them,' Colette replied proudly.

'Did you know what Sean was planning for the group?' Kennedy asked, moving things right along.

'I think I've already answered that one for you, Detective Inspector,' Sean cut in. 'I told you that Colette and I discuss the major decisions in our lives before we make them.'

'Indeed you did, Sean, indeed you did. What about KP's final question to Mrs Green, did you know if Sean planned to look after Susan?' Kennedy said, leaning back in his chair.

'Well, I told KP that I thought Sean was still thinking about it, which I believed he was. But, at the same, time I told KP that I thought Sean should,' Colette started.

'You told him that? You had...' Sean obviously thought better and dropped the end of the sentence.

'We shouldn't really be discussing this in front of anyone, however,' Sean began again. 'And, listen, the band was dying when Wilko left. The reason the band's fortunes turned around was because of all the energy I put in.'

'Yes, Sean, I know,' Colette sighed, 'But *you'd* be annoyed if the band split up and someone at the record company found a way to sell your records and they were incredibly successful. How would you feel if they kept all the money except the little they'd agreed, to give you in a deal made thirty years ago? You'd be annoyed times ten. You'd think, "they're my songs and these so and so are making all this money out of my songs." That's my point.' Colette was obviously not going to politely let this drop, even with the police listening in.

'OK,' Sean smiled generously at his wife, 'we can leave this until later. We don't want to waste police time. I will say, however, and I want this to be the last word on this for now, that I turned this whole situation around. Wilko jumped ship, and I still made sure he was looked after. I will continue to ensure Susan does not run in to difficult times. We will make sure she is looked after. That's never been an issue. Now, Inspector, your next question?'

'Well, the next one is for you, and it's about your phone conversations with KP yesterday.'

'Ah good, if that means we're finished with Colette, perhaps we…'

'No, it's fine, we promise not to disrupt your wife's kitchen for too much longer,' Kennedy offered a smile to Colette.

'But I was thinking more of the stu…' Sean started hopefully.

'No, really, it's fine, I'm comfortable here,' Kennedy replied. 'So you spoke to KP at around noon and then again about five P.M.?'

'Yes, as I said, I'd a couple of chats with him yesterday. But that would be average for KP and me. We'd usually chat at least two or three times each and every day. Yesterday's chats weren't too long.'

'The first one was six minutes duration and the second one was seven,' Kennedy advised the pop star. He wanted Sean to known that they knew exactly how long he'd been on the phone to KP, so that he'd know "we had a brief chat and then he was off" wouldn't suffice.

'If you say so. You know what it's like rapping with friends, you don't notice the time go by. In the first one he was checking in with me to see what was happening, just a general chat you know. The first one, that was about noon, would have been early in the day for him. You know he was used to getting out of bed at the crack of noon.'

'Did he have any specific questions he asked you?' Kennedy asked.

'Let's see…'

'You see,' Kennedy began, 'Yesterday KP was a man on a mission, he was driven. Each and every person he spoke to had a list of questions thrown at them. So, I find it difficult to accept that he didn't have some for your good self as well.'

'Well, now that you mention it, he did want to know if Wilko had signed his new deal with the band. He hadn't. He wanted to know if Tracey had ever been on to myself or to Leslie Russell, asking business questions about the band.'

'A funny question.'

'I thought so too. I advised him that she hadn't. He asked me if Wilko had ever made any provisions for money to go direct to Tracey. I said he hadn't. He also asked me a couple of the same questions he'd asked my wife. My answers were the same as hers. That's pretty much about it, Inspector.'

'There were no other questions he asked you then?' Coles asked.

'Not that I remember,' Green replied.

'Well then,' Kennedy concluded, 'I think that's as long as we need to detain you. Thank you for your time.'

Forty-Two

'Why did you let him off the hook so easily at the end, sir? It was obvious he was lying,' Coles began, as they made their way in the unmarked car to the next interview.

'Well, I think I'd like to talk to a few more people before taking another step with Sean Green.'

'I see,' said Coles.

'Okay, next the McSisters,' Kennedy announced.

'This is going to be interesting, are we going to talk to them separate or together?' Coles asked her boss.

'Oh, you know what they say, WPC Coles, never break up a successful team, let's just carry on the way we are,' Kennedy replied. He couldn't help notice that she blushed slightly.

Susan appeared to have more difficulty coming to terms with the news of KP's death than Tracey.

'Anyway,' Kennedy continued, 'we're tracing KP's movements from just before he died. It appears that he rang this house three times.'

'Twice, Detective Inspector, and both times we were out and he left a message on the machine,' Tracey replied.

'Well, our information would lead us to believe that he left messages for you at 12.05 and again at 13.30. But at 15.45 he had a three minute conversation with somebody,' Coles advised them after consulting her notes.

'You must have got your wires crossed…'

'Well, Tracey, actually no,' sister Susan piped up timidly. 'I had a brief conversation with him sometime just before four. You'd nipped out to Marks and Sparks and, well, I felt sorry for him. Wilko liked him you know. I realise you and he had your difficulties, but I think that's because he genuinely cared for you.'

'Not a possibility,' Tracey cut in.

'Ah, don't Tracey. Don't be like that, it's not fair,' Susan replied.

'So what did you discuss?' Kennedy asked.

'He asked me a few questions about Wilko,' Susan replied.

'What type of questions?' Coles prodded.

'Augh, you know. Things like, had anyone ever come to the house looking for money from Wilko? They hadn't. Had Wilko bad feelings towards Sean? They weren't bad and they weren't good, I told Kevin. He certainly didn't love Sean Green. He saved his affection for another member of that family. Oh look, I'm sorry, that was a terrible thing to say and it was so long ago,' Susan said chastising herself.

'Oh, was it indeed?' Tracey cut in.

'What on earth are you on about, Woman? You know that was years ago,' Susan replied, more asking a question than stating a fact.

'Now here's a thing. When you have lots of money you can buy whatever you want. I know for a fact that Wilko was chasing someone at the time he died and, contrary to what Kevin Paul thought, it wasn't me,' Tracey announced. 'I'm not saying another word on the subject.'

This was more than Kennedy had hoped for. He was unsure about where to take it next.

'You see, Tracey, we've been checking into Kevin's story

and it seems you and Wilko shared a room at the Britannia Hotel the day he was murdered,' Kennedy said softly.

'Absolute crap! Yes, I was in the day room with him. But it was exactly that – a day room. You know detective, contrary to what you might think, you can do things in hotel rooms apart from bonk. I was hanging out with him, what else were we meant to do?'

'But you told us that you spent time with him at the Queens,' Kennedy said, persistently.

'Well of course I did – so? What do you expect, you guys have minds are like sewers. I'm not going to volunteer that I went to a hotel room with a bleeding pop star am I?'

'So, you've never had a relationship with Wilko?' Kennedy was nothing if not a tryer.

'Of course I had a relationship with Wilko, you stupid man, he was my bloody brother-in-law,' Tracey spat back.

'I didn't mean that kind of relationship, Miss McGee.'

'Look Inspector, a long time ago, when Wilko and Susan had split up, yes Wilko and I had a wee fling, sure we did, and our Susan knew about it. I mean, what do you take me for? But that was over, done and dusted a very long time ago,' Tracey said. Susan nodded to both members of the police force that she was aware of the relationship.

'So, are you telling us that there was absolutely nothing between you and Wilko at the time of his death?' Coles piped in.

'Not a dickey bird, Love. It was all over.'

'Are you further suggesting that Wilko's love interest, at the end of his life, might have been Colette Green?' Kennedy asked.

'I'd say the interest was more the other way around. But I've nothing further to say on that subject. And that's definite. Those that have eyes to see…' Tracey stopped.

'Mrs Robertson, by any chance did you refer to any of this in your conversation with Kevin Paul?' Kennedy inquired.

'I might have. I might have implied that our Tracey suspected Wilko and Colette were back up to their old tricks again. I didn't say I agreed with her though.'

'How did he, Kevin, react to that?' Kennedy asked.

'He said something weird actually,' Susan began as she cleared her throat, 'He said Sean felt he could live on through his music, Wilko obviously couldn't.'

'Kevin said that?' Tracey said quietly.

'Yes.'

'What did he mean?' Tracey continued in subdued confusion, 'Do you think?'

'Oh,' her sister replied, more up-beat, 'You know KP, a bit of an old hippie, probably didn't even know what he meant himself.'

Kennedy and Coles had reached the end of their questions. Well, Kennedy still had one and fortunately Tracey gave him the opportunity to ask it when she accompanied him, without Susan, to the front door.

'I have one final question for you,' Kennedy began very quietly, as they reached the door step. 'It's a very important question. Please think very carefully before you answer it and whatever you say I will promise to treat your answer in total confidence.'

Tracey McGee raised her eyebrows.

'Can you have children, Miss McGee?' Kennedy asked, hands deep in pockets, head slightly bowed but still managing to keep eye contact with Tracey. Tracey McGee's eyes filled slowly with tears.

'No inspector. I can't have children. Neither can Susan. That's why neither of us were able to hold on to Wilkenson.'

Then she shut the door in Kennedy's face, but gently.

Forty-Three

'We're beginning to make progress now, WPC Coles. I can feel it.' Kennedy slid into the Granada and fastened his seat belt.

'What? You know who murdered Wilko?' Coles asked, 'And KP?'

'No. Not yet. But at least now we are starting to accumulate some vital pieces of information. That's equally important. The more information we have the less chance that we are going to try and make the murder and motive fit the information. Pretty soon we'll have so much information that we'll have our culprit.'

'Or culprits, sir.'

'Or culprits, WPC Coles,' Kennedy agreed, 'Very good point.'

Kennedy and Coles had been joined in the DI's office by DS Irvine. Kennedy went over to his window and watched the traffic trudged through the melting snow heading towards Parkway. The office lights on the other side of the street were lit up and reflecting in the snow, but Kennedy's thoughts were elsewhere.

'So, you think Colette murdered Wilko?' Irvine asked.

'Well,' Kennedy began, picking up his cup of piping hot tea

and turning towards his notice board, 'That's a possibility, I suppose. But it could still be the McSisters. With our recent information, they may even have moved up our list. Then of course it could have been Colette. Or Sean…'

Irvine turned up his eyebrows at this.

'You don't think so then, James?'

'Sure, he's only knee high to a packet of Surf. He couldn't hurt a fly,' Irvine replied.

'Perhaps, but have you considered the fact that may be the reason the instrument of death is so small, needle like and very sharp, so that it is very easy for a weaker person to stab the victim? You just need to know where to put it and push. But then again, the security guard at Dingwalls swears Sean didn't go backstage on Thursday night.'

Kennedy got the call he was waiting for, through from the front desk. It was Sgt. Timothy Flynn, advising the DI that Rose Butler was waiting in reception for him.

'Okay, we'll get back to Wilko. In the meantime we have our other little adventure awaiting us.' Kennedy had previously briefed them both on the Dr. Ranjesus affair and he had enlisted their help on that night's wire tapping trip, all officially approved by Superintendent Thomas Castle.

Kennedy addressed Coles.

'Could you go and collect Rose and help her get fitted up with the wire?'

'Sure, I could do that,' Irvine joked.

'Not before you've had some counselling,' Kennedy replied, light-heartily. Coles laughed and left the room.

'Seriously, Irvine, you're sure you're okay working on this? This thing with Rose? I realise…'

'It's perfectly fine, Sir. Rose and I are okay with each other now. Maybe some day we'll even become great mates. I like her, I like her a lot. Don't worry, it won't be a problem for either of us. I just hope it's a major problem for that shit Ranjesus.'

The phone rang again. Kennedy picked it up.

'Oh, hi ann rea.'

Irvine mouthed the words, 'See you at the car.'

'Hey, Kennedy,' ann rea continued after the initial greeting, 'It's after seven. Are you coming out to play?'

'Not tonight,' Kennedy said with regret. 'I'm just on my way out on a surveillance job.'

'What time will you be doing that until?'

'Hard to say. Probably about nine,' he replied.

'Okay. Okay. Well how about this for an idea? I'll go pick up some food, something simple like pasta, and go around to your house. We'll be eating by, say, nine-thirty.'

'It's great for me, ann rea, but probably not your idea of fun.'

'Oh, you leave me to worry about the fun, but I wouldn't count on too much sleep tonight. You get the wine. See you at nine-ish,' ann rea said and Kennedy could hear she was wearing a grin.

Twenty minutes later, as arranged earlier in the day on the phone, Staff Nurse Rose Butler was knocking on the door of Dr Ranjee Shareef's grand house on Ulster Terrace. She'd told Kennedy that after she'd called Ranjesus earlier she went to the toilet and was physically sick.

During the call she had claimed to the doctor that she had proof, definite proof, as to what the doctor had done, or failed to do, with Sinead Sullivan. She further advised him that he had only one chance to do something about it before she went to the police and the hospital authorities. She was implying, but not suggesting, a bribe. A fact, Kennedy assessed, which could later be denied should Ranjesus and his lawyers claim entrapment. Rose could claim she just wanted to hear his side of the story before going to the police. However, should Dr Shareef offer Rose Butler a bribe then that would be a different matter entirely, wouldn't it?

'Okay, I'm just about to ring the door bell,' Rose Butler said nervously. She stole one final glance behind her, and Irvine flashed the car's headlights quickly to reassure Rose she'd been heard loud and clear.

As she rang the door-bell, Kennedy, Irvine and Coles could hear her whisper, 'Good Jesus, I can't believe I'm doing this,'

A beam of rich cream light spilled out of the hallway as the door opened and Kennedy immediately recognised the doctor. He could hear the doctor's clipped tones via Rose's microphone saying, 'Oh yes, Nurse Butler, I've been expecting you. Please come though to my study.'

'Who else is in the house?' Rose asked.

'No one but us, Nurse Butler. It's the staff's night off and my wife has taken the children to stay with her mother for a few days.'

The police could hear the creak of the front door as it closed, then footsteps.

'Please sit there, if you don't mind,' Ranjesus instructed Rose. 'Okay. Shall we get on with this? I have a limited amount of time I can give you.'

'I know what you did to poor Sinead Sullivan,' Rose began nervously.

'Fathered another Irish bastard, is that what you mean? I don't think we can be too sure about that, Nurse Butler. I've been hearing she was the hospital bike – and not a very good one at that.' The doctor laughed at his own crude joke.

'May God forgive you, Doctor. No, I don't mean that, Dr Shareef. If that were true I'd be happier. And please, do not speak disrespectfully of her. I knew her very well and I knew exactly what she was. A good, honest girl whose only flaw, as far as I can see, what that she fell for a prick like you.'

'Fifteen love, Rose to serve,' Irvine said proudly from the driver's seat in the police car, only about twenty yards away from where the nurse and the doctor were sitting.

'Charming tongues you Irish ladies have,' Shareef said.

'Better to have charming tongues than ten bellies. But look, let's not waste time sitting here insulting each other. Let's get back to Sinead. I know you got her pregnant. I know you helped her have an abortion. I know you got her pregnant again but this time you told her you would take care of her. I know you used hospital time and equipment to monitor her. I know you discovered that she was suffering from Placenta Praevia. I know you failed to give her treatment for this condition. I know that because you failed to treat her condition she haemorrhaged and bled to death.'

'Okay,' Kennedy whispered out in the car, 'this is it. Over to you, Doctor bloody Ranjesus.'

'And you know all of this for a fact, do you?'

'Yes, I do.'

'And how would you know this?'

'I know it!' Rose answered firmly.

'What? You were in bed with us when I supposedly shagged Sullivan? You were with her when she discovered she was pregnant? You were with us when I supposedly was monitoring her? You were there looking over my shoulder when I discovered she had Placenta Praevia? You were there in my mind when I, supposedly, made the decision not to treat her condition?'

'That's not what I'm saying,' Rose began to falter. She had nothing in reserve for the ace Shareef had just served.

'What exactly *are* you saying?' again Shareef, this time very aggressively.

'I'm saying you murdered Sinead and her little baby. I'm…'

'Oh come come Nurse, we've been through all of that. I'm asking you to give me one little bit of evidence. I'm asking you to give me one little fact which would prevent the police and the hospital authorities from throwing you out of their offices the way I'm going to throw you out of my house.'

By now the doctor was shouting at the nurse. Kennedy and Irvine knew that Rose Butler was not up to this. Shareef had just been playing with her to see exactly what she knew. Which was, sadly nothing more than a hunch.

'He won't harm her will he?' Coles asked from the back seat.

'Not physically, no. He wouldn't be so stupid. But he can hurt her mentally. Look, let's get her out of there. No more good can be served by this. James, he doesn't know you. Go and knock on he door, say you're a mini-cab for Butler or something. Quickly, man.'

'Your little Irish princess,' Continued the Doctor. 'Do you want me to tell you exactly what she got up to in bed? Shall I tell you exactly what she did to me, shall I tell you exactly what I did to her? Yes, that's probably going to be more interesting to you, isn't it? Let's see now, first I...'

The doorbell rang. Coles and Kennedy heard footsteps, a door opening, footsteps, another door opening and then the familiar voice of Irvine stating loudly, 'Minicab for Butler.'

The doctor said something too quietly for Coles and Kennedy to hear, but it must have been something along the lines of, "she'll be out in a minute." because they heard Irvine say, loudly again, 'Sorry mate, can't wait. She's got an important appointment I've been told to get her to, and I'm running a bit late.'

At this point, Rose, on hearing Irvine's reassuring tones, ran into the hallway. The closeness of her microphone to the doctor and Irvine put the conversation back on track for Kennedy and Coles.

'Ah, Miss Butler? Mini cab for The Royal Free.'

'Yes, yes. Thank you.'

'Why miss, you're crying. This chap hasn't been bothering you, has he?'

'Get out of my house, you...' the doctor stuttered trying to find a correct word to describe the best dressed mini cab driver he'd ever seen.

'Are you okay, miss? I must admit, he does look like a bit of a pervert,' Irvine said quickly.

'And what if she wasn't? What if she wasn't okay? What would you intend to do? Hit me? Surely you wouldn't hit a man with glasses.' The doctor laughed.

'No sir, I'd never hit a man with glasses, I'd use my fecking fist.'

'Get out of my house. Get out of my house now. Both of you. This is obviously some charade, some elaborate set-up. Dreamed up, I wouldn't be surprised, by Kennedy. Get out of here, both of you, before I call ...' Shareef stopped suddenly, he was about to say police.

Back in the car, Coles moved to the front seat and Irvine comforted Rose Butler in the back.

'It's no good. I let him get away. It's my fault. I messed up. You're never going to get him now. He's going to get off with it,' Rose blurted out and started weeping.

'I wouldn't concern yourself, Rose, about us getting Doctor Shareef. Someone as evil as himself will cross our paths again and next time we'll be ready for him,' Kennedy said. He'd always worked on the rule, Don't get mad, get even. And now, Kennedy was as mad as he could ever remember being.

Forty-Four

'Don't come, Christy!'

'What?'

'Don't come. I can tell from your heartbeat that you're about to come.'

ann rea and Kennedy were lying amongst each other in the early hours of the following morning.

'This is so gorgeous. I want it to last forever,' ann rea said breathlessly.

The only thing about coming, as Kennedy's Butterfly Technique advised him, was that you tended to be forever trying not to come at the wrong time, as opposed to coming; at the right time that is. But then, if you held on for her, gasping greedily for extra oxygen, for her sighing, for her moaning, for her groans of ecstacy, for her blissful climax – if you dared to tune into her earthy sounds for just a split second then you were lost – and if you managed to hold on for her and she fell on you breathing heavily, then you felt guilty about continuing when she had finished.

The Butterfly Technique had taught Kennedy that enjoyment should come from being together and prolonging that magic moment, slipping in and out of the build up, at the same time pushing it further and further away. Kennedy was relatively new to the technique and still had a lot to learn. He distracted himself from the inevitable by thinking about other things. This morning, for instance, other things like the death of KP. Oops, he thought, that'll do it for you. That'll lose it forever.

He decided to think about something more pleasant, like how beautiful ann rea was there rising and falling above him. Those beautifully shaped eyes closed so she could concentrate on her thoughts undistracted. Her hair was wet with the sweat of her endeavours. Sometimes she seemed to be having such a brilliant time he wondered who she was with. Where did she go to at these times?

Sure, she whispered words of encouragement and support, and always used his Christian name, but at those moments he knew she was lost, lost in her own world. In her enthusiasm for the euphoria she was experiencing she was more desirable than ever, more desirable than anyone Kennedy had ever known. Such thoughts were speeding up the process too much. He thought about Coles, she slipped quietly into his mind from nowhere and without invitation. No, that wasn't a good idea either. But before he'd had a chance to recover, ann rea sighed, sensually and loudly, and flopped on top of him, their sweat mixing. She convulsed gently in inner pulling waves. The waves were not so gentle that they did not cause enough movement to take Kennedy over the edge. He watched the butterfly float happily, and contentedly, away.

Perhaps ann rea was correct with her new approach to their relationship. Their love-making was so sweet, and getting better. Was there need for anything else? They were true to each other. They enjoyed each other's company. They gave each other the space required. No one was getting hurt. Was there anything else? Kennedy wondered, as he lay there in her arms.

Kennedy felt, considering the magic moment they had just shared together, that the feelings she had for him must be as deep as his feelings for her. But was that it? Was that what it was all about? To find someone who would not be bad to you and would allow you to share such exquisite intimate pleasures with them?

Was that what ann rea had discovered? Was that why she was in her new upbeat mood? Had she resolved this "being in love" thing? He couldn't believe that there could be more between two people than what they were experiencing together. Did they need to formalise it all? Move in together, officially become a couple? Did he need to marry this person, to convince himself or anyone else for that matter, that this was the best there could be? And, because of that, there was no need to go chasing anymore. No need at all to go chasing any more and risk losing what he had with this wonderful, special woman who someone had sent along to meet him.

'Thank you, thank you, thank you, whoever you are,' Christy Kennedy whispered as he fell into a deep and peaceful sleep.

Forty-Five

Kennedy started off the morning in his office updating his notice board. He focused on the scraps of paper found in KP's pockets. He was particularly tranfixed by the words written inside the heart.

McGee!
L
Wilko
L
?

Tracey McGee loved her brother-in-law. Wilko loved someone else. Why the exclamation mark? Who was the question mark? He turned the page and focused on the line

/OL>WILKO? C? COL? Colette?

'Very possible,' Kennedy said aloud to his notice board. Colette had already admitted that she wasn't in love with Sean. Could Wilko still be in love with Colette Green, the mother of his child? Tracey and Susan had already lost him.

Kennedy eyes returned to KP's note. Who was the Prat? And why was there a star beside the name? It was somewhere inside those scribbles, the answer to this. The answer that killed him.

'Come on, Christy...' he coaxed himself. 'It's in there, waiting for you.'

'I'm off to the canteen, Sir.' Coles entered Kennedy's office, followed by Irvine. 'Would you like some tea?'

'No, thanks,' Kennedy replied, a little distractedly. 'I was just about to make some here. You're welcome to join me.'

'No, thank you, Sir. I'm a little peckish as well, I need to get some food.' Coles turned to Irvine. 'And yourself?'

'Yes, please,' Irvine replied enthusiastically. 'I'd love a cup of tea. And a bacon buttie, well cooked. Bacon, no fat, brown bread. A Kit Kat and...'

'God, Irvine,' Coles cut in. 'What did your last servant die of?'

'Disobedience!' Irvine shot back, laughing.

After Coles left, Kennedy prepared his tea and turned to Irvine.

'How was Rose after you dropped me off?'

'Ah, upset, but she's a canny lass, sir. She won't let this get on top of her, believe me. She accepts that Shareef got away with it, but she said she's going to watch him like a hawk from here on.'

'Good,' Kennedy said. 'Good on her.'

'Actually, she wanted me to thank you for her. She was afraid she hadn't thanked you properly for trying. I told her you knew she appreciated the effort.'

'Ah, not at all,' Kennedy replied modestly.

Coles returned to the office, laden down with supplies. They drank their tea, ate their food, and went through the case one more time.

'OK, James,' Kennedy said, when the last of the food and tea was gone. 'We'll let you get on with your inquiries. WPC Coles and I are going to pay another visit to Colette Green.'

'What kind of fresh hell is this?' Kennedy was sure these were the words he heard being shouted as heavy footsteps neared the door he and Coles had just knocked.

'Ah, it's you again.' Sean Green stood in the doorway of his house. 'Come in, won't you. Sorry about all the shouting and all of that but I'm here on my own and I'm trying to get some writing done and if it's not the telephone it the door. Come on in'

'We're sorry to disturb you again, Mr. Green. We were actually hoping to have a few more words with your wife,' Kennedy said, unbuttoning his Crombie.

'Ah, well now, I'm afraid you're out of luck. She's out,' Green said, as he clambered awkwardly up the stairs. 'Come in, all the same. I'm sure Colette won't be too long.'

'We could come back,' Kennedy offered.

'No, no. It's fine, honestly.' Sean led the two police officers up the stairs to his studio, a bit awkwardly in his usual platform shoes. 'Although I thought we answered all your questions yesterday.'

'Oh, there're still a few bits and pieces we're trying to tidy up.'

Kennedy looked at Green. The tiny man wore a three-piece blue suit, without the jacket, a matching blue shirt, and a pair of platform shoes. The detective considered the shoes. Their platforms were half a foot high if they were an inch. For some reason, Green reminded him of Nick Lowe's song, 'Half a Boy and Half a Man'. It seemed absurdly appropriate to Sean Green. Take away the shoes and the afro-style hair, half the man in fact, and Sean Green was the size of a small boy.

'Actually,' the musician said, 'I'm glad of the opportunity to speak with you again after yesterday,' Green said, sitting behind his desk. 'I'd hate for you to think my wife and I were rowing or anything. She's been through a lot recently. She was really very fond of KP, you know. They were good pals. In the early days when she and I were getting to know each other she'd always hang out with KP around the gigs and television studios and such like. My wife's not really comfortable in all of that, you know. She's not really into the glamour of it all. She's more a people person. If she likes someone, she doesn't really care what they do, or what they are, or what they wear, she'll make a connection. She likes you you know, Detective. But, anyway, if you consider the fact that in the space of a couple of days she has lost KP and Wilko, the father of her first child. It's only natural that she'd be a little on edge right now and suffer from...well, I suppose mixed loyalties.'

'I don't follow, Sir,' Kennedy said, following quite well indeed.

'Well, all that stuff about looking after Susan. I mean, was that a classic case of insecurity or what? I mean, of course we're going to look after Susan. As I told you at one of our first interviews, one of the main reasons I want to continue as a band is to honour Wilko.'

'Pardon me if I'm wrong, Sir,' Coles said. 'But I thought your wife was more concerned about the *share* of money which was going to Wilko's dependants. My understanding was that she thought the three of you – yourself, Wilko, and KP – founded the band and should be earning equally.'

Well done, thought Kennedy. Couldn't have done better myself.

'No, but I can see how you might have been confused. It really is complicated. No, Colette was concerned that, following Wilko's death, Susan might be neglected. You know, there's more to the Circles organization than paying out money. We look after our people. We take care of details, look after things. It's one of our manager's principle tasks, organizing our people's lives for them. Our manager, Nick Edwards, that's what his office is good at. In the early days KP used to do it but now it's grown out of all recognition and it really takes a well tuned organization like his to take care of all the details, to look after our people,' Green smiled. 'You see, for instance, the case of Clarkey. Now he was in the band and then he was out of the band. But by that point he was one of our people and therefore he had the organisation behind him. The office looked after getting him into a studio, booking musicians, hiring an engineer for him, so he could demo some of his material. The office then started to advise him on how best to deal with his tapes. He feels a part of our organisation, he knows we'll look after him.'

'Once someone is in the group the organization looks after them?' Kennedy confirmed.

'Oh, yes.'

'Well, if you'll excuse me, why then didn't the organization look after Wilko?'

'Well, for one thing we didn't have Edwards' people working for us. But I think it's important to remember that Wilko dumped Circles in order to go solo. He was convinced we were over, and I don't think he really wanted any support or input from us. He was convinced that he could rise from the ashes of Circles. He wanted to be independent, and so we obliged him,' Green explained sadly. 'He was unlucky, and perhaps over-rated. I've heard the rough mixes, and there was something good in there. But he had no talent for finding it. With a bit of help on completing the songs, with a bit of vision, he could have had something special. I knew exactly what kind of record he should have made. If he'd had the balls to let me produce it, he could have had three hits, I promise you. Wilko could sing like nobody else, a natural front man, but he needed someone behind him to pull the strings. I could have helped him. I could also have helped him launch and promote the record.'

There was a pause in the room as, downstairs, the door opened.

'Aha. I believe that's my wife returning.' Green hurried to the doorway and called down.

'Colette, dear. I'm up here. Inspector Kennedy is here yet again, he'd like to talk to you. Shall I send him down to the kitchen?'

'Yes, of course,' Colette called back from down below. Green turned back to Kennedy and Coles. 'I'm afraid I'll be unable to join you. Now it's my turn to run a few errands. Can I assume we're done?'

'Yes. That's fine for now, Sir,' Kennedy said. 'Thanks for your time.'

Within minutes, the police officers were downstairs and Sean was out of the house.

Forty-Six

'I don't know about you two, but I fancy a cup of tea.' Colette was filling the kettle as they entered her kitchen. Kennedy broke into a warm smile.

'That would be perfect.'

Coles and Kennedy sat on the high stools by the counter.

'How was Sean?' Colette asked.

'Fine. We talked a bit more about Wilko. He went to great lengths to assure us that the two of you weren't arguing yesterday.'

'Ah,' sighed Colette. 'That's forever Sean. Always worried about appearances. I suppose it's his upbringing. You know, what the neighbours thought was always very important, and it certainly made him fight for what he got and I suppose it makes him want to protect it. I was different, I grew up never wanting and then I married Sean and he's been a great provider, so it's never really been a consideration of mine. Dump the lot I say, and then maybe we'll get down and be real and get a life.'

'Do you ever wonder how differently things would have been if you were with Wilko?' Kennedy asked gently.

'Now there's a question,' Colette said. 'It's difficult. I could see all his faults, I could see how they destroyed him. Yes, I suppose I wonder sometimes if I could have saved him. But I'm not sure I'd have had the patience. He had a lot of lessons to learn. He might, and I really mean this, have learned a few of them just before the end of his life.'

'Is that what KP and you were discussing the day he died?'

'Yes, as a matter of fact it was,' Colette replied, offering no further explanations. The tea was ready and she served them there at the counter.

'You see,' Kennedy chanced. 'I think KP thought Wilko was in love with you again.'

Colette looked at him for a moment.

'Yes, he mentioned that to me as well.'

Coles, Kennedy had noticed, was taking everything in but saying nothing.

"Tell me, Mrs Green, were you helping Wilko during his time away from the band?'

'Well, I couldn't, could I? I mean, I'm Sean's wife.'

'Actually, I meant more discreetly than that. You know, financially?'

Kennedy pushed gently. 'You see, the more we check into Wilko's life, the more we find that his expenses far exceeded his earnings. Several people have remarked on this, in fact, but no one could tell us how he managed it.'

'Maybe he was successful with his gambling, for once,' Colette suggested.

'We don't think so,' Kennedy continued. Colette offered him a blank stare. 'Mrs Green, I have to tell you that at this very moment Sgt Irvine is checking your bank statements. By the time I return to North Bridge House I'll have the information I'm looking for. Mrs Green, please.'

Colette turned away from the two, and crossed her arms.

'Well, you got me, Inspector. Of course I gave Wilko money. I had to, didn't I? He was William's father, after all.'

'And you still loved him?'

'I still loved him, still hated him. Who knows? What does love mean? I gave him everything, my body and my heart. We had a child and I thought he would change into the man I wanted him to be. He didn't, he still went around with other women, and I felt like a fool. But good old Sean, ever dependable, was paying me a lot of attention when I needed it. He offered me safety and I took it, yes. Of course I did. I took what was offered because I couldn't get what I wanted. But Wilko was always the one. He was the father of my first child.'

'Was Sean aware you were giving money to Wilko?' Kennedy asked.

'I don't think so, but KP thought he was.'

'Did KP say why he thought that?'

'He just said that it was something in the way Sean was acting.'

Kennedy decided to go for broke.

'Do you think Sean knew you and Wilko had feelings for each other again?'

'Well, he knew I'd always be fond of William's father,' Came Colette's cautious reply.

'I didn't mean those kinds of feelings, Mrs Green. I meant deeper feelings,' Kennedy pushed a little further.

'We had to stop,' Colette replied, in a hushed tone.

'Excuse me?' Kennedy asked carefully.

'When Wilko contacted me a couple of years ago I thought he was just after money. I was prepared to help him because he was, as I say, William's father. His life was a mess, and I did think that Sean wasn't exactly treating him fairly. I always felt that Wilko and KP were entitled to more that they were given. Maybe Sean did deserve the lion's share, but what he was taking just wasn't fair. So I thought helping Wilko out was justified. Circles generated money, Sean took the money and gave me some of it, and I gave some of it back to Wilko. It was his own money, really. A bit of poetic justice.'

'You say you thought he was just after money. Could you explain that?'

'He wanted more. He wanted me. I had started giving him money. We'd have a drink every once in a while. I began to realize that he wanted to see me as much as get the checks. That got me thinking, and I realized that I felt the same way. I still had feelings for Wilko. Pretty soon we were seeing each other once a week for dinner. One week I intentionally didn't give him a check and he didn't mention it. He wasn't there for the money, he was there to win me over. Pretty soon, he did.

'At first it was exciting. We were like kids stealing off to the Britannia Hotel for a few hours. It was great. But Wilko wanted too much, he wanted all of me. He wanted me to leave Sean. I couldn't, not with the kids. I didn't want to make a mess of their lives because of us. Sean was starting to get suspicious. Do you know what he resorted to? He dressed up as a woman and followed me around town. He followed me up to the Britannia. He was waiting, in his disguise, in the lobby when we came down from the room together. I recognized him immediately, but Wilko hadn't a clue. Sean was good enough not to cause a scene right there, but back at home...I'd never seen him so mad. I think if he had been bigger he would have beaten me. But physical force was never his strong suit.'

'He didn't hit you?' Kennedy asked.

'No, he never laid a finger on me. He disappeared for three days, just stormed off but he had calmed down when he returned. He told me very calmly that I was to stop seeing Wilko immediately. If I didn't, he divorce me and he would take the children. I would never see them again. I told him I'd only started seeing Wilko again initially because he wasn't being treated fairly. Sean and I struck what you might call a deal. I would stop seeing Wilko if Sean took him back into the group. He agreed, and that was that. That was that until somebody murdered Wilko.'

'What did Sean say to you when that happened?' Kennedy asked. 'How did he explain it?'

'He said he heard Wilko had been running up a few debts, gotten himself in too deep, and was topped by a couple of thugs. I didn't think twice about it until KP called.' Colette stopped in her tracks, taking something from the look on Kennedy's face. 'God, you don't for one moment think that Sean could have murdered Wilko?'

Kennedy considered the question.

'You do, don't you?' Mrs Green said. 'But he couldn't possibly. Wilko could blow him away without batting an eyelid. No, Inspector. Believe me, Sean is not a murderer.'

Forty-Seven

Kennedy wanted to get back to his office and examine his notice board once more. Four minutes later on that Wednesday morning he was doing exactly that. Sean Green was now the number one suspect. However, Kennedy still wasn't prepared to rule out Tracey McGee. She had a very strong motive.

Part of the thing which was troubling Kennedy was the whole rigmarole of the locked door. What did that have to do with anything? Maybe, for some other reason, KP had worked out who had committed the murder of Wilko Robertson, but had he worked out how it was done?

Kennedy stared at KP's scraps of paper once more. Again, the first thing which caught his attention was the word PRAT, written at an angle across the top of the page at an angle with a star drawn beside it. It looked like he had written the word in last, squeezing the letters into the available space, barely getting it in. The T spilled over the side of the page.

'Who was your PRAT, Kevin?' Kennedy asked his notice board. 'Who was the Prat who murdered you?'

Then the penny dropped.

It came to Kennedy in a flash – how could he have missed it until now? He could have kicked himself for being so dumb.

'The PRAT who murdered Wilko is PRATLEY!' Kennedy exclaimed in absolute glee.

Kevin Paul knew Sean Green when he was called Sean Pratley and he'd obviously still thought of him as Pratley. Kennedy couldn't believe he missed something as obvious as that. He wondered what else was staring at him from KP's pieces of paper.

Now, in light of Colette's disclosures and KP's message from beyond the grave, Kennedy was convinced Sean Green was the murderer. He had the man, he had the motive, but what was the method? He needed that to prove his case.

Now Kennedy had Green in his mind's eye at the scene in the Roundhouse. The security guard had told him the woman who came to see KP that night had a walking stick and had trouble getting down the stairs. The same kind of trouble Green had going down the stairs in his own house while wearing his platform shoes. A walking stick would have helped him and hadn't Colette just told him that Sean had dressed up as a woman to follow her and Wilko to the Britannia Hotel?

Was that when he decided to murder Wilko? The day he saw his colleague step out of a hotel lift having just shared some intimate moments with his wife. Had he decided there and then to get rid of him? Was that why he'd spent the three days away from his wife? Had Sean spent the cooling down period deciding not to get mad but to get even?

This tact of Kennedy's worked. The trick of collecting all the information until all the pieces fit together.

Forty-Eight

Sgt. Timothy Flynn, his nine-year-old son Timmy Jr., WPC Anne Coles, DS James Irvine, DI Christy Kennedy and Sean Green stood together in the makeshift dressing-room at Dingwalls Dancehall. Kennedy had a few books with him, tucked under his arm.

'OK,' Kennedy announced, 'Could you please stand over here, Sean. Just beside Timmy here.'

Green shrugged and did as he was told.

'Could you please stand back-to-back?'

Again, Green complied. Kennedy carefully placed the books, one on top of the other, on the ground. He asked Timmy to stand on the pile of books.

'This is just to show,' Kennedy said, 'that if we take away Mr Green's platform shoes and afro hairstyle, he is approximately the same height as Timmy here. If anything, perhaps Timmy is a shade taller.'

'Very funny, I don't think,' Green muttered, as he quickly took a couple of steps away from Timmy.

'No, there's more. There's more,' Kennedy said. 'Ok, Sgt. Flynn, could you please take young Timmy off now. You know what to do.'

Sgt. Flynn smiled a knowing smile and left the room with his arm around his son's shoulders.

'Now all we have to do is wait.'

Kennedy found a seat, and invited the remainder of the party to do the same. He wasn't sure, but Kennedy could swear that Green was getting a wee bit twitchy. He was definitely the only one of the four staring at the dumb waiter hole in the corner, near the stacks of soft drinks cases. Including the several stacks of Lucozade cases, which Kennedy had guessed was the LUZOA from KP's valuable scraps of paper.

They sat in silence.

The silence was broken when the motor from the lift sprang into action. They could all now hear the lift section of the dumb waiter make its way down from the floor above. Two painfully long minutes later, the dumb waiter appeared in its shaft and out sprang Timmy Flynn. He didn't appear too uncomfortable at having had to squeeze into the little lift.

Sean Green dropped his shoulders and sank into his seat.

'OK,' Kennedy announced. 'I am hereby charging you, Mr. Sean Green Pratley, with the murder of both Mr. Wilkensen Robertson and Mr. Kevin Paul. Take him back to the station, read him his rights and book him.'

Forty-Nine

'You see,' Kennedy began, as he and ann rea sat down to dinner upstairs at The Queens. 'If he hadn't tried to be too clever with the locked room, he would have been fine. But by doing it the way he did, with the lift and whatnot, it either had to be him or someone equally small.'

'But how did you know it was him?' ann rea, glowing as ever, gasped.

'Well, I must admit that up until quite recently I still thought there was a possibility that it could have been Tracey McGee. She fell for Wilko, committed the ultimate sin of betraying her sister and, even after all that, Wilko still shunned her. That's a powerful motive. But it was Wilko's failure as a solo artist that was his downfall. Had he succeeded, none of this would have happened.'

'Yes?' ann rea inquired, mid-bite.

'When Wilko left Circles, Circles had a new lease of life and became very successful again. Wilko, meanwhile, bombed. Correct?' Kennedy placed his knife and fork back on the table and folded his hands. This was going to be a long explanation.

'OK, I'm with you so far.'

'He started to think of his own mortality. What would he leave behind? Artistically he had already judged himself a failure. He wasn't going to have a family with Susan.'

'What about William Green? He was Wilko's son, wasn't he?'

'As far as William was concerned, Sean Green was his father. That's where his ties lay, and probably always would. So Wilko gets itchy feet and hits on the closest woman to him, his wife's sister. She falls for him hook, line, and sinker. Within days, they are involved, they're doing the wild thing right under Susan's nose. They're trying to have a child, no less. Can you imagine his disappointment when he discovers she's barren?' Kennedy paused for a drink of his crisp dry wine. All this talking was making him thirsty. He savoured the aftertaste for a few seconds before continuing.

'When he first contacts Colette, it's out of necessity. His overheads are exceeding his income.'

'He and the majority of the nation,' ann rea interrupts.

'Perhaps, but at least he's got a fairy godmother to go to. He enjoys his excuses to see her, and she surprises him by responding to his flirting. There's still some love there, it turns out, and soon *they're* sleeping together.'

'Good Heavens, Kennedy. If they ever make this into a movie it will have to be X Certificate.'

'I think you mean an 18 Cert,' Kennedy corrected ann rea before proceeding. 'Wilko thinks "Well, I've already had one child with this woman, so I can do it again." He probably openly declares his intentions. She's unsure of her feelings. Don't forget he is the father of her child so there will always be some kind of bond between them. A bond that no human could ever break. She most probably was considering it. In the meantime they've thrown caution to the wind and are enjoying themselves. But they're a wee bit careless, and eventually Sean Green discovers the two love birds coming out of the Britannia Hotel.'

Kennedy and ann took a moment to eat. Another drink of wine.

'Sean has proven over the years to be an exceptional

strategist and so he bides his time. He agrees to Colette's demand that Wilko must let Wilko into the band. That means he's in close contact with him and he can choose his moment. He knows that if he's patient the right opportunity will present itself, and it does. Circles is due to play a London gig. Everyone's surprised when they play a venue as small as Dingwalls, but Sean has done his homework. He's been there to see the new groups and he's been invited back to the dressing-room. He's seen the dumb waiter, and he's hatched his plan. Fast forward to the night of the gig. Sean and Wilko take their break. Sean's supposedly is wandering around the audience while Wilko goes down to the dressing-room. He locks the door to change out of his sweaty clothes.'

'He's so sweaty he has to change mid-show?' ann asks, so engrossed in the conversation she'd forgotten her food.

'Believe me, you've never seen anyone sweat like this,' Kennedy continued. 'Anyway, Wilko has changed. He's sitting down, enjoying a fag, and the dumbwaiter behind him springs into action. With all the noise of a live band in a packed club, he doesn't notice a thing. Sean creeps out of the dumbwaiter, sneaks up behind him, and stabs Wilko in the heart. The door Wilko locked to give him some privacy also gave Sean the security he needed to carry out the murder. It also throws up a bit of a smokescreen which is probably why he used a variation of it when he murdered KP. Anyway, he hides the long thin needle in Wilko's suit bag and escapes back up through the dumbwaiter. One floor up, he puts back on his platform shoes, and wanders back towards the stage. He runs into KP, asks him where the feck Wilko is, and goes back out onstage with the band.'

'Kennedy, you have to admit it was a clever way to murder someone,' ann rea said as she finished off her wine. They both looked at the empty bottle in mock surprise and Kennedy ordered a second one.

'Yes, but he had a lot of time to plan it. KP's murder, on the other hand, shows just how clever he was. He hadn't planned this one, it was all done on the hoof...'

'I think you mean "on the platform", don't you?'

'Funny, yes. Hilarious? I'm not sure. Anyway, he speaks to KP on Monday and discovers that KP has got him sussed. KP thought he was being clever, trapping Sean in the room under the Roundhouse. When I spoke to him he was waiting for someone to arrive. The reception wasn't great, so he was obviously in the white room on his phone. He was discussing springing a trap on someone. That someone he was waiting for was the murderer. KP had some trick up his sleeve to catch Sean out. Enter Sean Green, disguised as a woman with a bad leg, so bad a leg she needed a stick to help her walk. In fact, Sean needed the stick to help him negotiate the steep steps at the Roundhouse in his platforms. This *woman* walks in, surprises KP, and stabs KP in the heart. Exactly the same MO as Wilko's killer. She, really Sean, locks the door behind him with the fishing line. He pulls the bolt into place, then tugs on the fishing line hoping to leave little or none of the line as evidence. Yes, I admit, he was clever.'

'But not as clever as you,' ann rea raised her glass in salute.

Fifty

Two hours later, following one more bottle of wine, their main course, and dessert, ann rea and Christy Kennedy stood atop Primrose Hill. It was a cold November night, but they were both glowing from the wine. The snow had all but disappeared – leaving only some little white blotches scattered around them. The sky was clear, the moon was new, and they held each other's hand.

'This is good,' ann rea said.

'Yes, it's beautiful,' Kennedy replied. He looked at the busy city lights. A city getting ready for Christmas.

'No,' ann rea whispered quietly, the steam barely leaving her mouth. 'I mean us.'

'Yes, ann rea. You're right. This is good.'

'Did I hear a "But" lurking around there somewhere in your sentence?'

'No. No buts. I was just thinking about KP. He probably would have been a good chap to get to know. In fact, he definitely would have been a good chap to get to know. And Sinead Sullivan. She'll be missed. You know, catching Sean Green doesn't make up for KP being dead. At one point I was convinced that if only we caught Dr Ranjesus it would have in some way made up for the death of Sinead Sullivan. You know? I felt it would have made it right for Rose Butler. But it doesn't work that way, does it? Locking up Sean Green doesn't make up for the loss of Wilko Robertson or KP, and locking up Dr Shareef wouldn't make up for the loss of Sinead Sullivan.'

'I know, Christy. I know,' ann rea said. She turned to him and took him in her arms. 'But that won't stop you from trying to catch him, will it?'

The Do-Not Press
Fiercely Independent Publishing

Keep in touch with what's happening at the cutting edge of independent British publishing.

Simply send your name and address to:
The Do-Not Press (Dept. BSW)
PO Box 4215,
London SE23 2QD
or email us: thedonotpress@zoo.co.uk

There is no obligation to purchase
(although we'd certainly like you to!)
and no salesman will call.

Visit our regularly-updated web site:
http://www.thedonotpress.co.uk

Mail Order

All our titles are available from good bookshops, or (in case of difficulty) direct from The Do-Not Press at the address above. There is no charge for post and packing.
(NB: A postman may call.)